The Bronze Key and the Red Door

by Teresa E Lavergne

ISBN: 978-0-9966237-7-3

If you have ever lost important keys, you know how valuable they are. Keys are vital things; they turn engines on so you can go places, and they unlock doors and give us access to entrances.

Scripture tells us that the fear, or reverence, for the Lord is the key to a great treasure of salvation, wisdom, and knowledge. Jesus gives us keys that will open Heaven's storehouse of His grace, to us. These are the most valuable of keys.

They are the keys we cannot afford to lose. They are not physical keys, so finding them or losing them is not something we experience in the natural. It is rather like a parable; and so is the story in this book.

I hope that in reading this book, you will discover some keys for yourself that lead you to Heavenly treasures. If you have not gone through The Door, which is Christ, I hope you will.

Other books by Teresa Lavergne:

The Angel in the Garden

The Antique Mirror and the Ancient Secret

In the Garden of His Grace

In the Garden of His Grace volume 2

Treasures in Words:
Poems, Prayers, and Personal Stories

Books by Guy and Teresa Lavergne:

Act Upon a Story: 60 Bible Skits for Ministry

Act Upon a Story: A Series of Skits about Joseph

Act Upon a Story: A Collection of Christmas Plays

Chapter 1

The little girl held tightly to her father's hand as they walked through the beautiful blooming garden surrounded by poplar trees swaying in the breeze.

The sunshine was crisp and the wind was cool. The flowers sparkled like jewels in the brilliant sunshine that accented their colors.

"Daddy," said the little girl, "If the Prince is good, why did he let my mother die?"

"Your mother isn't dead," said her father. "It was only her body that died. She is with the Prince in his beautiful home. Where he lives, the flowers are even more beautiful than this."

"Let's go there right now," said his daughter.

"It isn't our time to go yet," said the father gently. "We will have our turn eventually."

"But Daddy, I'm lonely. I miss her," said the little girl.

"I know," said the man with the red curly hair. "I miss her too---very much."

The young man looked as if he would cry but he made the effort to smile instead. He picked up his little girl and held her close to him.

"We still have each other," he said. Then he gently set her down, took her hand, and they walked around the garden until they reached the gate.

There was a stone angel near the gate, and it seemed to smile graciously at the two as they walked out of the garden.

There were many such walks in the days that followed. This prayer garden, as it was called, was a place of solace and healing for Rusty and his little daughter April Rose.

The jewel of his life, Rusty's lovely wife Pearl, had been laid to rest in a similar garden. He and his young daughter now lived in a different Southern state, not as arid and dry as the little town in central Texas had been.

It was spring and everything around them was lush and green and bursting with life. Rusty's heart ached from the desire to enjoy this beauty with his best friend and lover, who was absent from him now.

He spoke often to the Prince about this pain; he knew the Prince would understand the loss and separation better than anyone else.

The Prince had helped Rusty to find a childhood

acquaintance of him and Pearl---a girl named Cornelia who had come to the Kingdom of Grace when they were all children.

This prayer garden belonged to Cornelia; she had established it for just such a need as Rusty now had. Rusty knew that the Prince had provided this for him and others who also had pain that could not be eased any other way, and he was grateful.

April Rose was growing like the flowers. She was going to be taller than her mother, and her hair was red like her father's, but her brown eyes were almond shaped like her mother's.

She was a rare beauty, and she could sing like a nightingale. Sometimes she and her father would sing together; she sang the soprano part, and he sang the tenor part.

When Rusty was a young boy, he had often painted the birds that lived in his childhood home. But now he painted pictures of April Rose. He wanted to remember every stage of her childhood, so every year he painted a portrait for her birthday.

He also painted pictures of the nature around them, and sold these in his little antique shop to supplement their meager income. It was a quaint and pleasant shop, with many curious historical antiques, and Rusty was well read in history. He could explain the use of the various items to curious customers.

I think I should tell you that Rusty had also lived in another time period, when many of these artifacts were a part of his daily life. His childhood had been spent in another era, in another time, in another place---the Kingdom of Grace.

April Rose had never been there, nor could she go, unless she was especially granted that gift. But her father talked so often about this place, that she felt that someday she would go. As his daughter, she felt that she *should* go.

But as she grew older, that feeling became more dim and distant. I'm afraid that she began to think of it as one of the fairy tales that she had enjoyed reading. The present world was so much more compelling---and demanding.

She was trying desperately to grow up without a mother's help, and there were many things that her father did not seem to comprehend. He did not seem to grasp the cruelty of her classmates, or the sarcasm of her teachers. Her father seemed to be unaware of the pressure of her competition among her peers, or the backlash from her actions that were considered odd.

She drew her heart within herself, and in her guilt,

she would not speak of this daily struggle. Yet her father was more aware than she realized, and it pained him that she drew away from him just when she needed his counsel the most. He continued to paint her portrait every year, but it seemed to him that her countenance became sadder and sadder in each painting.

There were times when April Rose was away, engaged in some activity, and her father went to his room and wept. He poured his heart out in tears and gave vent to his grief. Then he would ask for discernment and courage to be a better father. April Rose would return home in a brisk hurry to attend to some details in her schedule, and she never noticed his eyes were red. She never noticed that his heart was breaking. But someone else always did.

Cornelia had a keen heart, and she could always recognize a breaking heart through a person's eyes. Cornelia's gift was healing, and she learned to minister this faithfully through prayer. She and her husband prayed often in the prayer garden for those with broken hearts. Rusty was among those who received this attention from them.

And there were letters from Audrey, with much affection and encouragement, though she could not come and visit. Traveling was difficult now for

Audrey, with her trio of small children. But she expressed so much love and hope that Rusty looked forward to her letters.

It was Audrey who had gone with Cornelia to the Kingdom of Grace when they were children, and there was a close bond between these four: Rusty, Audrey, Cornelia, and Pearl.

There was another who Rusty was very fond of, but he had not heard from Roger or his sister Sundae in quite some time. This troubled him, but he had not given up hope. Rusty and Pearl had become the benefactors of Roger and Sundae, when they lived in the same little Texas town.

Oh, they did not monetarily support these children, but they had enabled Roger and Sundae to have their own experience in the Kingdom of Grace. As a result, Roger and Sundae's lives were much changed and transformed by the love they had experienced in that wonderful place.

If it would not have been for April Rose, I am sure that Rusty would have begged to go back to his childhood home in the Kingdom of Grace. But he knew that there was more to the Prince's plan; it was not complete yet. He knew he must wait for the next step in the plan.

So he dusted and rearranged the items in the

antique shop, carefully maintaining the artifacts, especially one small black birdcage. This item was not for sale, and you will find out why somewhere along the way through this book.

The years went by as Rusty watched his daughter grow into a young woman. She was very attractive in a haunting melancholy way, and her dark eyes always had a far-away look.

She did well in her studies at school, although she did not look entirely happy even with those earned academic achievements. Her discontent resulted in daily frustrations and discouragement.

Rusty loved his child and wanted so badly for her to enjoy their lives, but he could not find a way to give her this aspiration.

He planted a garden, hoping she would find some delight in helping with this. He taught her to cook, and Cornelia taught her to bake.

Nothing helped; his daughter was yearning for something he could not give her. At the realization of this, he felt his loss more grievously than ever. He yearned for Pearl's attention and her intuition, which he had to live without.

Rusty so desperately wanted to go back to the Kingdom of Grace, but even more so, he wished that there might be some way that April Rose could go there and be healed.

He often looked into the antique mirror that once held a way for two troubled children to find this place, but he never saw what he was looking for….at least, not yet.

But perhaps that was not what the Prince intended at all. Rusty knew that the Prince did not always do things the same way. In fact, he usually did things that were very surprising.

So Rusty reasoned that it might happen when he least expected it, or in a way that he never would have imagined.

However, as the years went by, he wondered if he had been mistaken in hoping for this at all.

Chapter 2

April Rose was becoming impatient. She was in her final year of secondary education in the local high school, and she was considering pursuing a degree at a university. There was a school nearby, but she was looking at one in another city. She felt confined in this small town.

She and her father had many discussions which always ended dismally, he felt. She thought he was holding her back out of the fear of loneliness, and he could not convince her otherwise.

Worse yet, he felt he was losing her totally to the grip of this world on her mind. Her conversation made it appear so, and it vexed him.

"Daddy," she said, "I've got to get out of this town and see what else is out there in this world. I can't see myself running an antique store all my life. That's *your* life, not mine."

If he even attempted to mention the Prince or the Kingdom of Grace, she cut him off quickly.

"Daddy, I've outgrown those fairy tales," she said with an air of superior haughtiness. "I have to live in *this* world, and find my place in it."

Rusty tried to attest to the reality of the unseen world, but she resisted this. "If there ever was such a person, I am not acquainted with him. I don't even think he exists. I'm just trying to deal with the world I can see, much less one that I can't see," she said emphatically.

So in the fall of that year, she packed her things and left her childhood behind. Rusty drove her to the school of her choice, and she entered into university life. She waved goodbye, and went inside the tall metal doors of the building, which closed heavily behind her.

Rusty drove home in silence, barely noticing the scenery he passed. Back in his own town, he couldn't stand the thought of seeing her empty room, or the memories she disdainfully left there. So he drove immediately to the prayer garden.

He was relieved that no one else was there, and he broke down in sobs that shook his chest. In a little while, he heard the hinge of the gate creak a little, and he knew that someone had entered the garden. He didn't lift his head to see who it was, but he heard footsteps coming closer.

It was Cornelia. "I had a feeling you would be here," she said.

Rusty lifted his tear streaked face. "She's gone,

Cornelia," he said. "And I don't know if she will ever come back home." Then more sobs made his chest heave.

Cornelia said that she was going to pray, so she walked away to another area of the garden to give Rusty the privacy that he needed. Rusty's head ached and throbbed, and he felt so weary. He went to the center of the garden, where there was one large stately oak tree, and he sat down to lean against the tree trunk.

Cornelia found him a little later, and said she had good news. "Someone special will be coming to see you soon," she said confidently.

"Oh, Cornelia," Rusty said with some dismay. "I don't want another wife. I want Pearl." Again his sobs shook his chest.

Cornelia sat down beside him and listened.

"Why, Cornelia? Why did she have to leave me so early?" Rusty implored, and Cornelia sighed. "I don't know," she answered. "I had to watch her die," said Rusty, looking at the sky. "I watched her take her last breath."

"Rusty," said Cornelia. "Don't forget that Audrey, Pearl, and I watched *you* die when we were only children. We had never seen death before, and you were our friend. There was nothing we could do to help you; the poison in your system was too strong."

"Why did the Prince send me back, if it would only end like this!" exclaimed Rusty. "He said he was sending me back because there was someone who would need me in the future. But now, Pearl is gone---she was the one who needed me."

"He sent you back, so there would be an April Rose," replied Cornelia. "Her story isn't over. It's just beginning, and you don't know the end of it."

Cornelia stood to go, and then she said, "Why don't you come have supper with us tonight? The children would love to see you, and you know that Vance and I would enjoy your company. Don't go home to that empty house," she encouraged Rusty, and he willingly complied.

It was only a few days later, when Rusty was home in the early evening, that there was a knock at the door. Rusty opened it and stood there, amazed. "Roger?" he asked the tall young man standing there.

"Yes, it's me," said Roger and then he hesitantly asked, "May I come in?" "Of course," said Rusty, as he recovered from his momentary shock that had frozen his reactions. "Come in," he said again and his face relaxed into a huge smile as he led the way into the living room. Then he turned abruptly saying, "No, let's go in the kitchen and have some of Pearl's cranberry vanilla tea, like old times."

Rusty began filling the old tea kettle with water and set it on the stove to heat. Then he sat down at the kitchen table across from Roger. "I'm in shock," Rusty said. "I can't believe you're here!" Roger smiled back as he said, "Well, it took a while to find you since you had moved."

Rusty looked troubled, then he quietly asked, "You know about Pearl?" Roger nodded. "As I was searching, I saw the obituary. I'm so sorry---and so sad that I didn't get to see her again."

Rusty looked down for a minute, then he said, "I wish you could meet our daughter, but she's away at college." "Have you got a picture?" Roger asked. "I'd love to see what she's like."

Rusty went to his room and got a framed picture from his dresser and returned with it to show Roger. "Wow," exclaimed Roger. "She's just beautiful." Then he laughed with joy and said, "She's got Pearl's eyes, and your hair!"

"Except a little less curly," said Rusty, smiling. It felt good to smile again, he thought to himself.

"Now, tell me about yourself, Roger," he said. "And Sundae---how is she?"

Now Roger's smile grew. "Sundae would have loved to see you again---but she is on tour. Sundae is part of a ballet company---a very good one. Part of the proceeds they earn goes to help impoverished children. They provide scholarships for these children in the arts."

Rusty smiled with delight at the thought. He could envision Sundae on pointe in his mind. "Do you have any pictures?" he asked.

Roger immediately took out his phone and began scrolling through photos until he found the one he wanted to show Rusty.

"This one is my favorite," Roger said as he held the phone up for Rusty to view. There was Sundae in an elegant shimmery dance dress, on pointe, with a radiant smile and sparkling eyes. Her arms were curved in a graceful ballet stance, and her face had a glow. Her hair was swept up to the top of her head in a traditional ballet style, and she wore a delicate tiara to hold it in place.

"When she performs," said Roger, "it brings the audience to tears. She has such a gift. And the fact that she didn't start lessons until she was ten makes her skill even more amazing."

Rusty grinned. "I remember those ballet slippers the Prince sent to our shop," he said. "And the spurs he gave you---whatever happened with that?"

"Well," said Roger. "Let me back up and tell you about my father." Rusty leaned in closer to hear about this very important subject.

When Roger and Sundae had appeared at the little antique store so many years ago, they were frightened of their father, who had been pursuing them. Their mother had custody of them because of the father's mental state, but the father felt denied his rights and he stalked them. The two children and their mother were never sure of what he might do in his unpredictable fits of rage, so they stayed out of reach and tried to hide their location from the father.

"After my last letter to you, my father eventually had a break-down and had to be admitted to a recovery facility. That was the best thing that could have happened to him. This recovery program was run by people like you, Rusty. They believed in the promises of the Prince. My father was healed---truly healed," Roger told Rusty. "And your mother?" inquired Rusty eagerly.

"It took a while for my mother to trust in this," continued Roger, "but after several years, they were reunited. While my father was in the recovery program, we as a family were finally able to settle down and concentrate on schoolwork. And then Sundae was able to enroll in ballet classes for the first time in her life, through a special scholarship fund."

"What are you doing now?" asked Rusty. "Let me explain," said Roger. "It's another miracle in itself. While Dad was in that facility, we could make limited contact with him, so I did. I felt so much compassion for him, after my experience in the Kingdom of Grace. I forgave him."

"Good, good!" exclaimed Rusty.

"I became friends with the directors of the recovery group, and I decided that after high school, I would like to work with troubled kids like myself. Those directors put me in touch with some other groups who specialized in that, so for several summers I was a volunteer at those facilities. During the fall and spring, I went to college and worked toward a degree in counseling and social work."

"I am so proud of you," said Rusty. "So did you finish college?"

"Yes," answered Roger. "I did, and then I worked as a school counselor for several years. When my only grandfather passed away, he left me a gift.

He gave me a sizable inheritance, and I bought a ranch. I had a dream of making a recovery ranch for boys---and of course, there would be horses."

"Now the puzzle pieces fit!" said Rusty. "The spur was a sign."

'Yes," said Roger. "It all happened. We now have a ranch house, stables, and a staff."

"What about a wife?" asked Rusty, with a twinkle in his eye and a hint of a teasing smile.

"That's why I'm here," said Roger. "One of those staff members is soon going to become my main partner for life, and I just had to find you to invite you to the wedding. And your daughter."

"I don't know if I can get April Rose to come with me, but I will definitely be there. Just give me all the details," Rusty assured him.

"There is one more thing I want to ask you," Roger said quietly. "I have been thinking about this ever since I found out about Pearl."

"Yes?" Rusty answered inquisitively.

"I wondered if you might like to come and stay awhile at the ranch and teach the boys about horses," Roger explained. "I remembered all the things that I had heard about your horsemanship."

Rusty was very surprised at this request. "You know, I haven't been around horses in quite some time," he said. "But I'm sure you have not lost that gift," Roger assured him. "And I could sure use your expertise."

Cornelia and Vance agreed to take care of the antique shop during Rusty's absence, and so it was settled. Rusty began to get excited at the thought of being around horses again, and he caught himself singing as he packed his clothes.

His only regret was not being able to see April Rose before he left. He had called her numerous times, and left messages, but she never returned his calls. He wrote one last note to her, and left it in a special place.

Chapter 3

April Rose was exhilarated. Here she stood at the junction of intersecting paths leading up to and winding around the various brick buildings of the university. She felt she was just on the verge of discovery---of new freedoms and a new life. She could leave her old uncomfortable life behind her. She had quite outgrown it, and she was ready for this one to begin.

She found her classes to be fascinating and her professors intriguing. No one knew her past here, and she did not have to live up to any of those old expectations. A new identity was cause for some celebration! When acquaintances invited her to go to a party, she accepted with no hesitation.

She also felt no qualms about accepting the drinks that were offered to her. This made her feel readily accepted into the group, so she drank all that she wanted.

When it was time to leave, she was embarrassed that she could barely walk. Someone had to help her because she was dizzy and she staggered so much. She barely made it back to the dorm before she began throwing up. After hanging over the toilet most of the night, and then spending the next day in bed with a horrible headache, she changed her mind about this aspect of university life. The party lifestyle simply was not worth all the trouble that it brought.

Though that experience was disappointing, there were others that compensated. She met a guy named Arlo in one of her classes, and he was very talkative and amusing. She was much impressed and excited when he asked her to eat lunch with him at the university cafeteria and dining room. They found a quiet place to sit and talk, and Arlo seemed genuinely interested in April Rose.

Every day after that, they ate lunch together, and took long walks together around the campus when they had a break between classes. April Rose enjoyed his company and his animated engaging personality. She looked forward to the time they had together each day.

The next week, Arlo asked April Rose to come to his room. He said no one would be there, and April Rose felt some apprehension. In her thoughts, she began to question Arlo's intentions and to distrust his affectionate mannerisms.

With each passing day, Arlo became increasingly insistent, and April Rose disliked the pressure she was beginning to feel. She continued to decline the invitation and it seemed Arlo became more agitated and annoyed. Finally he spoke candidly about the subject.

"You won't know what it's like if you don't try it, April," he said. "I know you will like it. You're free here to do whatever you want to with your body. And if there is any problem, you can just take a pill and fix the problem right away."

April just stood there and stared at him. Could he really be serious, she asked herself. Did he really believe that she would just casually give away her most private sacred part of herself to someone she had only known for a few weeks?

"No," she said and she saw his countenance change to anger. "Fine!" he said. "If that is how you are going to be, I'm done."

April Rose watched him walk away without any other comment. Suddenly she felt very tired and went to sit down on one of the metal benches placed along the sidewalks.

It was extremely disappointing to realize that she was considered only as something to satisfy a physical desire, and nothing more.

She had a flashback moment just then in her mind. She saw herself again in her backyard along with her mother and father. She smiled to herself as she remembered how Rusty chased Pearl with a lizard just to hear her scream---but Pearl wasn't really terrified because she was laughing, too. Then Rusty caught up with Pearl and he tossed aside the lizard and kissed Pearl. Then they hugged each other.

"No, I don't want some cheap experience in a dorm room," thought April Rose to herself and she sighed. She tried to remember---what was it that her dad used to tell her? Oh, yes, that was it.

"Don't throw your pearls to pigs," he had told her. "The pigs will trample your pearls in the mud and then turn around and hurt you."

She had not understood that before, but she did now. Sadly, she got up and walked back to her dorm room. She had a paper to write and that would take her mind off this disturbing incident. So when she got there, she did her best to fully concentrate on this paper.

In the following days, she tried to keep her focus on her schoolwork and not on Arlo. He seemed to have no problem forgetting April Rose; he never looked her way again. In a few days, she saw him with another girl and they were laughing together.

April Rose turned and went a different way to avoid walking past them.

She was beginning to have a different sort of problem. Her roommate Deidra was involved in a social group that believed in the blend of genders. Now that April Rose was not with Arlo, Deidra began to try to coerce April Rose into becoming involved with this group. "You can be whatever you want to be---you're not forced into being what people say you are. You are free to choose the gender you want to be," said her roommate.

From her observation, it seemed to April Rose that the pressure from Deidra did not come from any sense of freedom, but rather a need to convince other people in order to support her own fickle decisions. It was as if Deidra thought that if more people believed as she did, it would be more certainly true. Wasn't that what the professors taught---that there was no longer any absolute truth, so truth was whatever people believed the most in the moment?

April Rose began to doubt the sincerity of this notion as well. She instinctively began to suspect the shallow motives behind this declaration of no absolute truth. She wondered if it was merely another way to shirk responsibilities that are the foundation of society.

She found herself in mental conflict with her professors at this point, and some of the heady excitement she previously felt was wearing away.

She also found herself thinking about her mother and father very often now. She remembered how they took turns pushing April Rose in the swing at the park, and helping her go down the slides which had looked so huge at the time.

She remembered how they took her to the zoo and how they laughed at the monkeys with the red behinds. "I think they are showing off their behinds to us on purpose," her mother said, and then her mother and father laughed and laughed at that.

She thought of how they pulled her in her little red wagon all around the neighborhood. They never had much money, but they managed to enjoy their lives together, and found ways to do kind things for their neighbors, too. Everyone they knew was sad when Pearl died.

That part she did not want to remember, so she tried to focus on thoughts of her dad. He had always been so kind and loving; why had she pushed him away? She began to be concerned when she realized that now she had been out of contact with him for over a week.

She had lost her phone, and had to buy a new one. She lost all of the phone numbers stored in the old phone, including Cornelia's number.

April Rose sat down and pressed the key for her dad's phone number. He didn't answer that call, nor the next one or the next.

She realized that she could not even contact Cornelia because she had not memorized that phone number and it was lost with her old phone.

She began to be disturbed after the fifth attempt to reach her dad was not successful. She decided that immediately after classes ended on Friday, she would take the bus home.

On Friday, she packed her suitcase and left a note for her roommate that said: "I'm going home for the weekend." The bus station was conveniently within walking distance of the campus, so April Rose bought her ticket and boarded the next bus headed back to her hometown.

April Rose was so worried and anxious about her dad that she was beginning to feel sick on the way home. There was a man who boarded the bus she was on at one of the stops, and she looked up at him as he walked down the aisle of the bus and sat across from her. The man had no suitcase or briefcase or anything at all in his hands.

April Rose took her textbook out of her book bag and tried to start reading the next assignment. She couldn't keep her attention fixed on the page at all.

When she looked up, the man sitting across from her looked directly at her and asked her how her classes were going. Somewhat startled, she warily replied rather evasively. He smiled kindly and said that he hoped things would improve for her. Then suddenly he stood to get off at the very next stop.

Before he walked back up the aisle, he turned to April Rose and said, "Do not worry about your father. He is all right." Then the man walked away to exit the bus, leaving April Rose in wonder.

Did she really hear him say that? Who was he, and how could he possibly know who she was or what was going on in her life? She was absolutely stunned and could not figure this out.

She was grateful for the hope it gave her, at least, for when the taxi brought her from the bus station to her house, she was dismayed to see that the house was completely dark.

Chapter 4

I wish that you could have seen Rusty when he first got back on a horse. The look on his face was the kind that you only see when a man has just experienced a great victory. It was pure joy. He leaned over and spoke softly into the horse's ear, pressed the mare's sides with his legs, and then loosened the reins.

The mare began a lope, and then broke into a run. She carried Rusty away in the golden sunlight, flying through the fields on the ranch. The sky was bright blue above them with feathery white clouds. Rusty wore an outback hat, and a grin as wide as it could be.

Roger and Cammie stood on the veranda of the ranch house watching this scene as it developed. Roger had a faraway look in his eyes, and he was smiling. Cammie looked up at Roger, enjoying what she saw in his face. Then she looked back at the man on the horse.

"How did you know he would be like that?" she asked Roger. For as long as Roger had known Rusty, he had never actually seen Rusty on a horse. This was the first time Roger saw him ride, and it was a memorable event.

"It was Cedric who told me," Roger said. "Rusty was like a brother to Cedric in the Kingdom of Grace, and helped train Cedric to ride horses. I met Cedric while I was there."

Cammie watched again as Rusty rode further away toward the low mountain range on the side of the ranch.

"Cedric told me stories about Rusty that amazed me," said Roger. "I hope Rusty won't mind telling us about some of those adventures while he is here at the ranch."

"I hope he finds some healing from his grief while he is here," said Cammie thoughtfully, and Roger put his arm around her. He appreciated how very much she cared about people. This was one of the reasons he asked her to marry him; she was the kind of person he wanted to spend his whole life with. He trusted her discernment and her faithful nature, too. He decided he couldn't live without her, so he asked her to marry him.

Rusty liked Cammie immediately when he met her. Cammie lived in the small town nearby, but she came to work at the ranch very early in the morning to make breakfast. Rusty raved over her homemade biscuits, saying they were the best he had ever eaten, and that made Cammie smile.

Her skin was brown, her hair was dark, and just now she had a big smudge of flour on her cheek.

When Rusty rode back and dismounted, he saw that smudge of flour and he felt so at home. He remembered two little girls so long ago, who were learning to bake and had tried so hard to impress Rusty. Audrey and Cornelia were also like Rusty's sisters in the Kingdom of Grace. He thought about how he had sampled a lot of pastries back in those days, and he grinned.

Rusty felt at home here in so many ways. He began teaching a few of the boys at a time.

They would learn first how to "bond" with the horses, then to care for them and the equipment for riding, and last, how to ride them.

There was an archery range at the ranch, and if you remember Rusty's past in the Kingdom of Grace, you will know that this was another one of his skills. So in the afternoon, Rusty introduced the boys at the ranch to archery.

Rusty also set up an obstacle course at the ranch to help the boys develop more muscle control and endurance. Many of the boys had never before participated in anything like this, but Rusty was patient with them. When they resisted, he was firm but kind, and gradually they began to appreciate the discipline that he was teaching them.

In the evenings, everyone met together after supper in the large council room for devotions, prayer and testimonies. This was, as well, an opportunity for Roger to observe carefully and notice which boys needed extra attention and individual counselling. Rusty also made his own observations even as he told stories that thrilled and captivated the boys.

Rusty was staying in a guest room of the ranch house, a small rustic room paneled with tongue-in-groove cedar planks. There was a bed with a brass headboard, a nightstand, a dark oak chest of drawers, and a rag rug on the wood floor.

Each night when Rusty went to bed, he was so satisfied with the day's activities that he had no problem going to sleep. It was so gratifying to be with horses again, and to practice archery, that he almost forgot any other life for a little while.

This night, however, he remembered to check his phone. He had been out of contact with April Rose for several weeks now, and the reception here for cell phones was not very efficient. Again he wondered why she had not returned any of his calls, and he was concerned that she might have tried to reach him here.

He finally fell asleep, but it was not a deep sleep. He began to dream a few hours after midnight, and in his dream, he saw April Rose at a bus station. He saw her board the bus, but he did not know where she was going. Then he saw a man standing by April Rose, and the man said, "Do not worry about your father. He is all right."

The dream ended and Rusty woke up, wondering what this meant. Did this signify that April Rose was possibly concerned for him? But he was concerned for her and the lack of communication was distressing. Finally he fell asleep again.

The next morning, Cammie arrived with a small letter in her hand. The ranch had a post office box in the small town, and Cammie usually checked it before she came to the ranch. This letter was for Rusty, and he was glad to see that it was from Cornelia. Rusty had given Cornelia the address to the ranch before he left.

Cornelia had received a gift that was similar to the one that Authentica had. Authentica had the rare ability of receiving messages from the Prince and delivering them to the right person.

Authentica had been the mentor and assistant for Rusty, Audrey, and Cornelia when the Prince sent them on a rescue mission into the domain of the evil Prince. Now it was evident that her gifting had passed to Cornelia.

Rusty knew this, so he eagerly opened his letter and read these words: Dear Rusty, all is going well with the antique shop, and I truly hope that you are busy and happy there! I know that you have been concerned about April Rose, but the Prince told me to tell you that he is working everything out for her good, and to trust him. He has special plans for her. Love, Cornelia.

Timely, thought Rusty to himself: very timely. So wherever April Rose was going on that bus, it will work out for good, Rusty mused silently. He only wished he could know what the special plans were for April Rose, but that was not always his granted privilege with the Prince. Trusting often involved the not knowing aspect of the future.

The hardest part of trusting, for him, came with Pearl's death, and the not knowing the answers he was looking for---for the question of why. He just couldn't make any sense of the pain, so trusting was very difficult. His motivation to help April Rose had helped him to seal away some of the pain so that he could focus on her needs.

As she closed off her heart to him, his own heart agony began to throb painfully again.

She picked up little objects that had meant so much to her before and looked at them intently. They were little items of memorabilia that used to represent big and little milestones in her memory. She used to treasure them. Now she felt like an entirely different person who was looking at the memories from someone else's life.

It was far too late to go to Cornelia's house, or even call, so she brushed her teeth and put on her pajamas. Then she just sat on her bed, thinking. She really wasn't sleepy yet, so she wandered around the house, looking at everything. Not much had changed since she left.

She wasn't sure why, but she was glad. She looked in the pantry to see what she could eat in the morning. There wasn't much; she found only a few granola bars. There was no milk or juice in the refrigerator, so she would just have to drink water. Then she remembered that they always had cranberry vanilla tea bags in the cabinet by the stove. She opened that cabinet door, and yes, there they were. And the tea kettle was still on the stove.

She went into her father's room and sat on the bed. Rusty had taken the pictures of April Rose and Pearl that he usually had on his nightstand, so it looked bare and empty and lonely. She looked in his closet to see what clothes he had taken with him. Most of his jeans were gone---he usually only wore jeans and casual shirts, but she noticed he had taken his suit with him. That seemed strange; why would he need a dress suit at a boys' ranch?

She lay down in the middle of her parent's bed, remembering how she used to climb in bed with them when she was very small. She was always surprised when she woke up in her own bed in the morning; as soon as she fell asleep, Rusty would carry her to her bed and tuck her in. Even when she got a little older, she still got in bed with them to hear a bedtime story, before she went to her own bed. Her mom and dad called it snuggle time.

Finally, April Rose got up and went to her room, pulled the bedcovers down, and got in between the sheets. It was still unsettling to be here alone, but sleep eventually came.

Morning light woke her up and she got out of bed and went to the bathroom, glancing in the mirror. She always thought she looked rather odd, with eyes that turned down at the corners, and a mass of thick red wavy hair. She didn't always enjoy what she saw in the mirror.

Breakfast was a granola bar and a warm cup of cranberry vanilla tea with a teaspoon of sugar in it. Normally, she liked hers with a little bit of milk, but this would have to do. She brushed her teeth and put on jeans and a pullover shirt, and then went out to the carport. She intended to go right over to Cornelia's house and get the address of the ranch. Then---well she wasn't sure what she would do after that.

She put the key in the ignition of her dad's car, pressed the gas pedal slightly, and the engine started up. The gas gauge registered almost full; that was helpful. So she slowly backed out down the driveway, checked the traffic and pulled out. The car was still driving smoothly; her dad always took care of it and changed the oil faithfully. Her old neighborhood stretched on either side of her as she moved down its streets until she reached the main thoroughfare.

Cornelia's house was about a twenty minute drive away from her own house, but the prayer garden was a little closer and she would pass it first. On a sudden whim, she turned off onto the side street that meandered down to a more isolated area where the prayer garden was located.

She pulled into the parking area between the plant nursery and the garden and stopped the car. She actually had no idea why she had stopped; it was as if a giant magnet pulled her towards the turn. But since she was here, she decided to get out and look around. Stuffing her purse under the seat, she locked the car, and shoved the key into her pocket.

No one was here this morning, so it was very quiet. Usually there was beautiful peaceful music playing through some hidden speakers, but no one had come yet to turn it on. She enjoyed the quiet solitude and the sunshine on the sidewalks which made a large wide circle around the large oak tree in the center. The wind was gently moving the tall poplar trees which formed the outer border of the garden. They stood like sentries close to the rock walls completely surrounding the garden.

April Rose always felt it was like a castle courtyard garden—very stately, spacious, and also private because of the height of the rock walls. She felt hidden away and safe….yet sometimes she felt as if someone was watching her---someone unseen.

It always seemed to her that the stone angel not far from the gate had such a knowing expression as if the angel knew many secrets she would not reveal. Today April Rose looked at the solemn silent smiling angel and wished the angel could talk. April Rose had a sudden urge to touch the tip of the wings---but she refrained.

She didn't *really* believe that story that Cornelia told about the time Audrey and she went to the

Kingdom of Grace by touching the tips of the angel wings. April Rose felt silly that she even for a few minutes wanted to touch the wings.

But the angel had that same placid knowing look--- that smile that never changed. Suddenly on the edge of her vision, April Rose saw something odd glinting and shiny in the grass. There was an old-fashioned bronze key hidden in the grass in front of the angel.

April Rose picked it up, and turned it over in her hand. There was no inscription on it; she could not see any identifying marks on the key. Behind the angel, farther away in a corner of the garden, she saw that there was a garden shed. She had not really paid much attention to it before; she had hardly noticed it was there.

Now she walked straight over to it; the door was ajar, so she peeked in. It looked rather dark and musty inside the shed. The key obviously did not fit this door, as there was no appropriate keyhole in it for this type of key. It was a very antique sort of key. She would have to show it to Cornelia and see if she might know who it belonged to.

Just then, the light shifted, and a ray of light came through a small window in the back, and April Rose noticed another door, further inside the shed. And this one did have an old round metal doorknob, and a keyhole beneath it. Why would there be a door with a keyhole in the back of this shed? She couldn't help herself; she had to try this key in that keyhole to see if it fit. So, stepping over clay pots and squeezing between ladders and garden rakes, she got to the door and stooping down so she could see a little better, she slid the key into the hole.

She held her breath and turned the key----there was a click, and the door was unlocked. She slipped the key into her other pocket, and turned the doorknob. She expected to see the poplar trees and the stone wall when she opened the door---but that is not at all what she saw in this doorway. Now the harder decision had come; should she go through this door? There was a moment of hesitation and then her feet moved forward; she had done it.

Chapter 6

April Rose stepped out into another garden—an even larger garden. This garden had no walls and had many paths circling around groups of brilliant colored flowers. Here and there grew tall trees; yet there was some sort of pattern in their placement. The bark on these trees was not dark brown or gray; it was hues of dark blues and reds. She stared in fascination.

The leaves on the trees were orange and green as if someone had painted them to look much like an Impressionistic painting. There was some gold lacy stuff that draped on the tree limbs similar to the way moss hangs on the great old oak trees in the southern states. She wanted to touch it and see if it felt like spider webs, but the tree limbs were too high.

She saw that there were white cloth and wood chairs on the walkways of the circled areas, and then she saw a well---an old fashioned well made of gray stones.

The walls were thick, and she went to look into the water. There was a dipper on the top of the stone walls, and as the water was not that far from the top of the well, she dipped out some of the water.

She was looking at it and considering whether to taste it, when the sound of a voice startled her. Looking up, she saw a woman wearing a long light blue shimmering dress, which matched the color of her eyes. "You are welcome to taste the water here," said the woman and her voice sounded melodic like water swiftly flowing in a brook.

So April Rose did, and to her surprise, the water had a sweet taste---but not too sweet. It had no chemical or metallic aftertaste, as the water did at home. She took another sip…and another. "This is so good!" she exclaimed and the woman in blue smiled graciously. "Drink all you want," she said. "This well is always full."

April Rose drew out another dipperful and drank it all. She set the dipper down where she had first found it, and thanked the lady with the sparkling blue eyes. Suddenly April Rose saw the largest butterfly she had ever seen, floating up from a group of flowers near the well. She stared in rapt wonder, and forgot all about the fact that she didn't even know where she was, or the identity of this person who had spoken to her.

The butterfly floated away to another group of flowers and then went further and further away, until April Rose could see it no longer. Then the thought startled her again; where was she?

The smiling woman answered as if she heard April Rose's thoughts. "You are in the Kingdom of Grace," she said pleasantly. "I am Saphire."

These words jolted something in April Rose's memory. She was really here, after all these years! "How? How did the other garden lead into this one?" she wanted to know. "I've never heard of anyone coming into the Kingdom of Grace this way," she said in a bewildered tone.

"There are many surprises here," said the melodic voice of the woman in the blue dress.

April Rose noticed that the woman's skin was brown, which made her blue eyes exceptionally bright. "Saphire," she thought to herself, trying to remember where she had heard that name.

"So...do you know my parents?" asked April Rose guardedly.

"Yes," answered Saphire, smiling even more. "I know Rusty and Pearl very well."

"You do know that Pearl is deceased, right?" April Rose prodded cautiously.

"Yes," Saphire answered somberly. "I know what happened in your world. But she is very alive in another world."

"Is she here?" asked April Rose excitedly, yet trying not to succumb to uncertain hope.

"No," said Saphire gently. "For your sake, I am sorry that she is not, but she is in a much better world than even this."

"Oh," said April Rose glumly. "Why am I here?"

"The Prince would like you to meet him," answered Saphire.

A feeling that she had suppressed rose up in April Rose at that moment, and she answered bitterly, "I'm sorry to disappoint you, but I do not want to meet him."

"If you change your mind," said Saphire, "The palace of the Prince is in that direction," and she pointed out the way for April Rose to go.

"No thank you," said April Rose in a resolute self-determined way. "I think I'll just explore for a while and then go home."

"Be careful," warned Saphire. "There are predators at night. You will be safer at the castle or in the village. I can make arrangements for you."

"How do I get home?" asked April Rose, beginning to be concerned. This adventure was not sounding so good at this point.

Saphire paused before answering. "The way back to your home has not reappeared yet," she told April Rose. "It is not yet time for you to go back."

"What?" asked April Rose in disbelief and dismay. "Are you saying that I am stuck here? That I am being held here against my will?"

"It is a great privilege for you to come here," said Saphire. "Not many get this privilege, and there is a very good purpose for it. The Prince has planned special things for you."

"The Prince?" asked April Rose and her voice rose in anger. "He allowed my mother to die, and my dad is heart-broken, and you bring me here like a prisoner with no way to get home? You think that is special? Well, I don't."

After she said these words, April Rose walked away from Saphire. She began looking for the way out of this garden—anywhere except the direction of the palace. She headed toward the path that looked as if it led to the mountain.

Despite her extreme displeasure with the situation as it appeared to be, she could not help but relax her tension somewhat in these extraordinarily beautiful surroundings. She came out of the large garden into a clearing that was a lush meadow of shorter grass, green and bright with sunlight.

The sky was a candy blue with puffs of white clouds softening its color, and there seemed to be no end to the beauty surrounding her. Like a dome over her, the blue sky was everywhere that she looked---except for one secluded gray area which seemed very distant.

In front of her beyond the clearing, there was a little foot bridge with low stone walls, which arched over a brook. She could hear the sound of the water rushing and tumbling over stones in its bed.

As she got closer, she heard something else— something musical, almost like a flute. She stood on the little bridge leaning over and looking down at the water, and realized that the sound was loudest here. The brook itself was musical!

That realization triggered a few more memories--- of Cornelia telling her how the animals did strange things in the Kingdom of Grace---like dancing to music. She stood still on the bridge, hoping for a glimpse of something like that.

She was not disappointed in this at least, for in a moment or so, several creatures came into the clearing and began to dance to the music of the flute. A white deer was among these animals, and April Rose was intrigued at the sight of it. When the animals had finished their dance, they silently slipped back into the woods.

April Rose was cheered by this presentation; at least she had seen one thing that was as unique as the stories she had heard.

She continued crossing over the little bridge, and found herself in a field of yellow grain like wheat stalks. But she realized that she was getting further from the mountain where she intended to go, so she crossed back over the brook and walked under the trees alongside the brook.

There was a sound of wind chimes here; and it seemed to come from the trees themselves, as if the leaves made the sound. She saw pink fruit here on some of the trees; it looked like a small banana. She peeled it and tried the fruit inside; it tasted like strawberry mixed with banana.

She laid the peeling on top of a rock that was on the path and continued on. When she looked back, the peeling was gone.

She came out of the woods into a large meadow. The grass was sparser here, and there were very large flat rocks dispersed over the area.

In the distance, there was a stone cottage of some sort at the base of the mountain which loomed over this meadow. She thought she recognized the shape of woolly sheep grazing up on the mountainside.

She decided to see how far she could climb this mountain. It didn't look extremely steep, although it did have some large crevices and gullies.

She looked down at her tennis shoes, hoping they were not too slippery. Well, they would have to do; after all, she couldn't even leave this place yet.

At least, she could try one thing that she had never done before, while she was here. She continued on undeterred towards the mountain.

Chapter 7

She was alone in this paradise, or so it seemed, and the panorama of beauty stretched everywhere she looked all the way down to the horizon line---except in that one gray area.

That part, she decided she would just ignore, and she continued on the trail that was leading to the mountain. Now that she was closer, she could tell that the shapes she saw up there were indeed sheep. They moved very slowly, she observed.

Sheep would be accompanied by a shepherd, she surmised, so she avoided that direction and she headed for a different part of the mountain.

She was still upset and did not want to talk with any of the inhabitants of this land, who most likely were enamored with the Prince.

It took several hours to reach the base of the mountain at the place she wanted to climb, and she looked at her watch. This still showed that it was 8:00 in the morning! So evidently time was different here. She would have to learn how to recognize the time by the placement of the sun.

According to that, it looked as if it might be the middle of the afternoon or later.

In all her determination to climb, she had not thought much about food or water, but now her stomach was beginning to remind her about the lack. Well, after she climbed, she would just have to go back and eat some more of that pink fruit and go back to the well for water. Maybe by then, she would find the way home. Surely that shed door had to be somewhere in the large garden she first came into.

If she got high enough on this mountain, maybe she could see better into the garden! That thought encouraged her and spurred her on, so she gladly proceeded to begin the climb.

There were rocks and clumps of dirt and grass she could grab hold of and help pull herself up, but she was a little afraid of snakes that might be hiding, so she refrained from that as much as possible. Sometimes she was forced to grab on or else risk sliding and falling.

She had never been that much of an outdoors person, so this was more of a challenge than she expected, but she did not want to give up that easily. She went slowly and laboriously up, trying to avoid the deep fissures and gullies. The gusts of wind were stronger here, and she could actually feel the change in altitude. There were wildflowers growing here and there, and she admired the lilac, periwinkle, and saffron colors. The wind waved the flower heads back and forth in the sunshine.

She reached a slightly level spot and stood there, shielding her eyes with her hand, and looked back over the landscape where she had come from. She discovered she would not be able to see into the garden; the trees in the woods around it were too tall. She decided to try to go a little higher and see if it made any difference.

So she turned around and began to climb again, stepping carefully over crevices in the dirt.

Where rocks jutted out enough, she could use them like stepping stones, as long as they were not too far apart. So she clambered up slowly, trying her best to use the terrain to her advantage and not her detriment. She was beginning to feel more confident, and just as she stretched to put her foot above the next protruding rock to step up, she realized the stretch was too far. She lost her grip and began sliding…she was sliding down the steep slope and couldn't stop herself. When she tried to halt her rapid plunge down the mountain, her foot got twisted and then she fell into a gully.

Thankfully, the gully was not too deep, but she had injured her foot. It was probably a sprain, she thought to herself, as she examined her ankle. She tried to get up and climb out of the gully, but she discovered it was extremely painful to stand up on her foot. In dismay, she wondered how she would limp her way down this mountain.

She managed to pull herself up and out of this ravine, but she couldn't go any further. She was afraid of falling and of suffering a worse injury. She sat there looking around and trying to figure out what she should do.

It was late afternoon by now, and she shivered in the wind which felt much colder now that the sun was making its descent on the horizon. She didn't seem to be making wise decisions, as it appeared now, and she was disgruntled over today's rash decision particularly. Why had she even unlocked that door! She began to be very annoyed with herself.

And now there was really no way to remedy her situation. She was not only stuck in this place, but she was stuck on the side of a mountain with a sprained ankle and it would be nighttime soon. And she had no food or water. This was not going to be any kind of pleasant adventure at all.

She looked to the side where she had earlier seen the sheep, hoping now to get a glimpse of another person, but the sheep were gone. There would be no chance of alerting any shepherd now. What should she do? She tried to think of a solution, but nothing came to her.

She began to cry, but quickly tried to stop that. She had no tissues with her, and would have to wipe her nose on her shirt. That was disgusting, so she tried hard to hold back her tears.

She watched as the sun began to go down, and made the shadows grow larger and larger on the mountainside. What an idiot she had been, she accused herself. And she was so, so thirsty now that it felt unbearable. Her throat was parched.

Then she heard a terrible, frightful sound that sent chills down her back. It was a scream that almost sounded human, but she could tell it wasn't. A mountain lion was somewhere around! No, no, no, she pled silently with whoever could possibly help her---whoever might really be there. She did not want to go out of life this way---her dad would not be able to stand it. She felt worse for him than for her---he had already lost the love of his life. And this was her own doing; yes, she chose this, she thought with anger at herself.

Suddenly, she heard another sound that was almost too good to be true! It was a person's voice, and he was calling to her. "Are you lost?" the voice was saying.

And here is the irony: as much as she wanted to be found, she did not want to admit that she was lost. So it took a few moments before April Rose said yes.

"I am coming to find you," said the voice, and the wind carried the words up to her ears.

She waited in her spot on the mountainside, straining to see who it was that was coming to find her. When he came into view, she saw a man with shoulder length brown wavy hair. He was wearing faded blue trousers, and brown boots that came to the middle of the calves of his legs. He wore a long loose white shirt with billowy sleeves, and a brown belt. He had a brown leather satchel slung over his back, and he carried a wooden staff.

"This must be the shepherd," she thought to herself. And as he came closer, he had a warm friendly smile, so she wasn't afraid. He looks very used to walking up mountainsides, she observed to herself as she watched him approach, and this gave her some comfort.

"This is a not a safe place at night by yourself," he said to her as he came closer. "Give me your hand," he said, and she willingly obeyed. There was something about him that made her feel that you could not argue with him, even though his eyes were very kind.

Those eyes….she had never seen anyone with such blue eyes. They were the color of deep blue water. Suddenly she realized she was staring, and she looked away.

He didn't seem embarrassed or disturbed at all, but merely concentrated on pulling her up. This seemed very easy on his part. He must of course be very strong, April Rose thought to herself. He helped her to her feet, and asked her to try and stand on her injured foot. She yelped at the pain, and then he supported her weight on his arm.

"Don't be afraid," he said. "I will steady you, and I won't let you fall."

"Okay," she answered timidly. She held onto him, and he very slowly began the descent, carefully choosing where to step, while she hobbled down, holding her injured foot up as much as she could.

Of course, it was impossible to not use her foot at all, and it was quite painful whenever she did, but the shepherd was extremely patient and conscious of her pain.

The descent seemed to take forever, and it was dark by then, and the stars were brilliant and white in the midnight blue sky. She had never before seen the stars like this---they were so visible and their light was crisp and not blurry. She could see the night sky in sharp detail.

When they finally reached the base of the mountain, the shepherd said to her, "I shall have to carry you from here." And in one swoop, he had picked her up in his arms and began walking.

"Where are we going?" she asked him. His steps were so sure and not faltering at all. He supported her back with one arm, and his other arm held her under her knees, but she felt secure.

"I am taking you to my cottage, where I can take care of your ankle," he said. She leaned her head back against his chest as he walked. His strength was so comforting to her.

The cottage, it turned out, was the stone cottage she had seen at the base of the mountain.

Chapter 8

When they arrived at the door of the cottage, the shepherd turned his back to the door and pushed it open. Then he turned to the side so that April's foot would not bang against the door as they went in. He walked over to the bed covered with a woven blanket and gently laid April Rose down on the bed.

The shepherd stepped out of the cottage again and was gone for a few minutes. April looked around the room. It was simple and quaint; there was only a bed and a small wardrobe on this side, and on the other side, there was a cupboard and a table and a few chairs. All the furniture was rough and rather primitive, as if it was made by hand.

The shepherd returned from wherever he had gone, and he had something in his hand that looked like a plant. He went to the cupboard and took out a wooden mortar and pestle. He put the plants into this, poured something else into the bowl and began to crush and grind the plants and mix this together.

Then he went to the wardrobe and took some cloth out of the bottom of this. He began to tear the cloth into long strips.

He brought these and the wooden bowl over to the bed and set them down on it. He helped April Rose into a sitting position and then knelt by her feet and began slathering her injured ankle with the stuff in the bowl. "What is that?" she asked, and he told her that it was an herbal paste remedy for sprains. Then he took the cloth strips and wound them around her ankle to make a bandage, tying the ends so that it would not come undone.

"What is your name?" she asked the shepherd, and he said that it was Ro'eh.

"I need to get back home," she told him, "but I don't know how."

"I think you will be staying here awhile," he said. "Your ankle has to heal before you can do much walking." Then he stood up, as the bandaging was completed, and removed the bowl.

"Where will I stay?" she asked, beginning to be perturbed again.

"Here," he answered. "I will take care of you. You can sleep here, and I will sleep in the loft."

"But I don't know you," she protested.

He looked at her with those deep blue eyes and said firmly: "You are safe with me."

Again, she felt that he was a person who could not be argued with, so she said nothing. She hoped that she would not be an inconvenience to this shepherd or get in his way. The whole thing was very embarrassing and she wished she could undo all that she had done.

"You are not in my way; you are my guest," the shepherd said suddenly and April Rose looked up, startled at his words. Did he read my mind? She wondered to herself.

She watched as he took out a flask of some kind and poured an orange liquid into a cup. Then he took a loaf of brown bread and a large slab of cheese out of the cabinet. He placed these on a wooden board, cut slices of cheese and bread, and then put them on a plate. He brought this to April Rose on a wooden tray.

"You haven't eaten anything since early this morning," he said. "You must eat."

April Rose looked at him in amazement. She was so baffled that she was speechless. She took a sip of the orange drink, and it was so good that she drank it all. Then she began to eat the bread and the cheese.

"This is so good!" she exclaimed, and the shepherd smiled. He filled her cup again.

"Now rest," he said. "I will help you in whatever you need. Just call me."

"Wait," she said. "How did you know that about me? Do you even know my name?"

"Yes," he answered. "I know who you are, April Rose, and where you came from. I know that you left your home early this morning, and then you came here."

"What else do you know about me?" she felt emboldened to ask.

He smiled then and it seemed to April Rose, that it was a little bit teasing. "That will be for later, when you trust us a little more."

The most humiliating thing occurred not long after this; she had to ask his assistance to go to the privy, which was in an outhouse behind the stone cottage. He hung the lantern in the outhouse and waited for her a few yards away. She hobbled back to the cottage, leaning on his arm. He did not carry her, since he needed to bring the lantern back and forth.

"Tomorrow I will make a crutch for you," he said.

Just then she heard that sound again---the scream of a mountain cougar. It can sound like a woman screaming. Those chills went down her spine again, as she realized how very dangerous her situation had been.

"Thank you so much for coming to find me," she told the shepherd. "How did you know I was up there?"

"Another one of my secrets," he said.

"Well, I am very grateful, however you knew." she told him.

Once they were back inside the cottage, she realized how extremely tired she was, and she was grateful for a place to sleep. The shepherd blew out the lantern and went up to the loft.

April Rose still did not know what to think about all that had happened, or of explanations for what the shepherd said, but she was too tired to think much anyway, and she fell asleep.

The next morning when she woke up, the pain was already lessened in her ankle. She saw that the shepherd had indeed kept his promise, for there, leaning against the wall across from the bed, was a wooden crutch.

It was made from a tree limb with a fork on one end, like a wide-spread "y" shape, and this end had been wrapped well with strips of cloth, and then covered with sheep's wool as a cushion.

She was delighted to try this, and managed her own way out to the privy in back. After that errand, she looked around at the enclosure encircling the cottage. There was a well, and a washing area right next to this. Close by, there was a fire pit with a black grate over it and a black hanging rack over that. Near this, there was a rounded brick oven built over another fire pit. April Rose guessed that this is where the shepherd baked bread, for there was no stove inside.

One area had a rough wooden fence around it, and as the fence was not too tall, she could see inside it. It was a garden of some kind, and though she was unfamiliar with any of the plants, she assumed that this is where the shepherd got the herbs he used for her treatment.

Next, she looked around hopefully for a place to take a shower. Just behind the cottage, there was a wooden stall with a wooden barrel on top of a cross beam which went over the top of the stall. April Rose was glad to note that the sides of the stall were tall enough to give privacy.

There was a ladder nearby, and she supposed that this was to stand on and fill the barrel with enough water for a shower. At least this primitive experience would make her grateful for modern conveniences, she thought to herself.

She hobbled back inside, using the crutch, and saw that the shepherd had left food on the table for her. He was nowhere to be seen; perhaps he had taken the sheep up to graze, she thought.

She went to the table and sat down, resting the crutch on the side of the table. There was some sweetbread, some of the pink banana type fruit, and some of the orange juice in a cup for her.

She ate all of this, savoring the taste and smelling the honeysuckle flower scents which wafted in from outside. She would have liked to wash her dishes, but she couldn't carry them and use the crutch at the same time.

She sat there, wondering what to do next. Just then, she heard a girl's voice singing. This girl arrived at the door of the cottage, tapped lightly on the door, and then opened it gradually.

"Hello?" she said, and peeked around the door. "Oh good, you're up," she said, as she stepped in and laid something on the bed. "I didn't want to disturb you. I'm Lillian---you can call me Lily."

April Rose was so surprised that she didn't answer right away. She had not expected any visitors.

"You're April Rose, aren't you?" said the girl, who looked to be in her late teens and close to April

Rose's age. "Yes, I am," said April Rose, trying not to stare at the girl's clothing.

"I'm from the village," said Lillian. "The shepherd asked me to come and help you, since you hurt your foot. I'll just take these dishes and wash them for you. You could come outside and keep me company, if you'd like to," said the girl.

So April Rose followed her outside, hobbling on her crutch. She was actually quite grateful for the company, since it was obvious that she could not go anywhere.

Maybe she could find out some clue about the hidden door. Maybe this girl could tell her the shepherd's secrets.

Chapter 9

There was much excitement at the boys' ranch as preparations began for Roger and Cammie's wedding. The wedding itself was to be held at an open-air pavilion in the center of the small town nearby. There was an area for chairs to be set out by this pavilion, and Roger and Cammie had reserved all of this for the wedding.

The reception would be held at the ranch house, and all of the staff was involved in getting the place ready. The boys too were excited to be included in the event and they were eager to help. Everything was cleaned and polished, swept and dusted to the satisfaction of Miss Reba, the staff housekeeper.

Jolene, who was the main cook, and her assistant Anika, had been working for days preparing dainty sandwiches, tiny sausages, and meatballs for the reception. They also made several kinds of fancy cookies, dips to go with crackers and chips, and concocted a delicious pineapple punch. One of Cammie's friends was making and delivering the wedding cakes.

Another friend made Cammie's dress; she wanted something so unique that she could not find it in any store or online catalog. She wanted a cream muslin dress in a vintage style, with cream lace accents. So she and a friend designed it together. Roger decided that he and the groomsmen would wear vintage Old West style outfits.

Rusty had brought the only dress suit that he owned, but Roger found a vintage outfit for him, as well, and that suited Rusty perfectly. He had never felt very comfortable in a modern suit.

The rest of the staff members were also dressing in vintage Western, and even the boys were dressing like vintage waiters, as they wanted to help in some way. They would be helping to serve the food. Jolene had experience with a catering service, so she was giving them tips and training them in restaurant service.

Roger was so grateful for the staff he had at the ranch; besides the cook and housekeeper, he had several teachers on staff, who could give the boys individualized tutoring so that they had an ongoing education. Each of these teachers also possessed practical skills they could use to enhance the boys' activities at the ranch. Bart was experienced in 4H projects, and helped the boys start a garden, and he was knowledgeable in horsemanship. Maddox knew about woodworking and leatherworking, camping and canoeing. Winston taught music and drama and was an avid rock climber and skilled spelunker.

Cammie had been hired for accounting, but her greater purpose soon became apparent as Roger saw her passion for people. She had the idea for the boys to market the vegetables they grew, at the local Farmer's Market.

The boys would share the profits between them, and learn fiscal responsibility through the project. They would have to determine how much to use to invest back into the garden, and so forth. Roger was very impressed with her plans. He asked her to supervise the project and teach some business accounting to the boys.

It was also Cammie's suggestion that the boys participate in some community projects that would benefit the elderly, the handicapped, and the homeless. She felt it would teach the boys about civic responsibility, and help them to think about other people instead of always focusing on their own needs and problems.

Roger's admiration for Cammie grew into love. She later admitted that when she first came to work at the ranch, she was attracted to Roger right away, but she kept this to herself. Rusty teased her that her biscuits were the bait, and that Roger was marrying her for her biscuits. Both Roger and Cammie laughed and said, "Maybe."

So Roger had talked to his friend, who was the pastor at the "cowboy church" in the area and he had agreed to do the ceremony. This is the church where they brought the boys on Sunday, and to some of the special events which took place there.

One of the boys had the idea that Roger and Cammie should come back to the ranch on horseback after the ceremony, and both Roger and Cammie liked his idea immediately. However, it would take too long on horseback to go the whole eight miles from the town to the ranch, so it was decided that Rusty would drive the truck and horse trailer to the wedding and afterward, take Roger and Cammie about seven miles in the truck. They would unload the horses there so they could ride back for the last mile. It would be the perfect ending, and would also give everyone more time to have things completely ready at the ranch.

The day finally came; Roger and Cammie's friends had decorated the outdoor pavilion with garlands of chiffon and tulle and silk flowers. The ranch staff hung lanterns and lights all around the ranch house and yard. They had used old wooden doors laid over barrels and sawhorses to make outdoor tables, and it gave the décor a rustic look. The rented white wooden folding chairs would be brought over from the pavilion to have more seating at the ranch.

Cammie's two sisters were her bridesmaids, and they wore vintage flowered dresses of plum, rose, and forest green. Roger's two best friends from his college days were his groomsmen. Sundae had come with Roger's parents, and Rusty was delighted to finally meet their parents.

Later in the evening, Roger's parents took Rusty aside and Roger's father told Rusty how grateful they were to him for helping Roger and Sundae. Roger's dad almost looked as if he would cry, and then on an impulse, he hugged Rusty. And then Roger's mother also said thank you very softly and she hugged Rusty as well.

Rusty's face was beaming with joy, and he assured these parents that he was very glad to know Roger and Sundae, and that he was so proud of them and what they had achieved. It was a special moment that Rusty had long imagined, but never thought would happen.

And he rejoiced to see Sundae—she was a beautiful, tall, slim graceful girl. She was so excited to see Rusty, that she stayed by him during at least half of the reception. He showed her pictures of April Rose, and they exchanged addresses and phone numbers.

After the wedding ceremony at the pavilion, everyone got to the ranch before Roger and Cammie did. Rusty drove the truck and trailer back and parked, and joined the waiting group.

They wanted to see Roger and Cammie as they first came down the road to the ranch, and they had colorful flags and streamers to wave as they rode up. It reminded Rusty of his days at the Prince's castle, as they would often celebrate events in this way.

He started getting a little misty-eyed, thinking of this and of Pearl, but he reminded himself to focus on Roger and Cammie, for this was their day. He was glad to see that they had hired a videographer for the occasion, as well as a photographer, and they were in place to capture the moment when Roger and Cammie arrived on horseback at the ranch. Cammie rode sidesaddle in her dress, and they made the perfect picture.

After they dismounted while the boys cheered and shouted, Bart took the reins of the horses and led them to the stables. Rusty insisted that Roger had to carry Cammie "over the threshold" of the ranch entrance, and then everyone joined in and also encouraged Roger.

Roger didn't need much cajoling; he picked Cammie up and to the delight of everyone, he carried her into the ranch house, turned around and came back out, still holding her. There was laughter and clapping and stomping.

Roger had picked a fast bluegrass waltz for the traditional bride and groom dance, and they executed this now while the onlookers clapped and tapped their feet with the beat of the music. Then it was time for the food, and the boys had their opportunity to demonstrate their training as waiters. All of the guests were so complimentary of the boys' manners, and found them endearing. This was an exhilarating feeling for these boys, who had grown up without any loving attention, much less tributes or compliments. They grinned with pleasure at all the appreciative comments they were receiving.

When everyone had eaten as much as they wanted, the food was brought in and placed on an inside table, and the makeshift outdoor tables were dismantled and set aside. More bluegrass music played and Sundae led the boys---and whoever else wanted to join in---in an impromptu line dance. Rusty joined in; he still remembered the Celtic style steps that fit this kind of bluegrass instrumental music. This bluegrass was closer to Celtic than country music.

"Look at Mr. Rusty clogging!" said one of the boys, and they all stopped to watch him. "You have got to teach me how to do that," said another boy. They were entranced watching him. Rusty wasn't shy and kept on dancing, and Sundae started dancing next to him, imitating his steps. Finally they were out of breath and had to stop, and Roger and Cammie applauded.

On the next song, all the boys jumped in and tried to clog with Rusty and Sundae, laughing when they messed up. After that, everyone joined hands and did a circle type folk dance. And then it was time to end. Sundae and her parents were going to bring Roger and Cammie to the train station.

For their honeymoon, they thought it would be nostalgic to ride a train farther west and see the Grand Canyon. They would be gone a week, but arrangements for the ranch had all been made. The whole group escorted them to the car for their departure, and they got in and rolled the windows down so they could wave goodbye as they left.

"Wait! You can't go," said Rusty, teasing. "How will we live without Cammie's biscuits?"

Chapter 10

April Rose sat down carefully on the cut stump of a tree that looked as if it was meant to be a seat. She watched as the girl named Lillian filled the two water buckets from the well, and began to wash the dishes in one of these buckets and rinse them in the other one.

"Here," she said, handing a towel and the wet plate to April Rose. "You can dry them."

April Rose complied and then set it on a small rough wood table close to the washing area. Lily finished washing the cup and handed it over to April Rose to dry it. April Rose dried this and set it on the table by the plate. She watched as Lily emptied the washing buckets on the ground behind the enclosed garden and came back to stand by April Rose.

"I brought you a change of clothes so I can wash those for you," she said to April Rose, indicating April's dirty jeans and top. "You look like you went for a slide on the mountain," she said cheerily. "I'm glad your ankle is only sprained and not broken."

"It's already feeling better," said April. "What is that stuff the shepherd put on it?"

"Oh," said Lily. "He knows all about the herbs and which ones to use. He probably used arnica, witch hazel, and lavender for your sprain."

"Is that his herb garden?" April Rose asked and pointed to the enclosure.

"Yes, that's it." said Lily. "When your foot is better, I can show you which plant is which."

"I have another question," said April Rose. "It was night time and no one saw me go up there on the mountain. No one knew where I was. How did the shepherd know to find me there? And sometimes I think something---but I don't say it---and then he answers me as if he heard my thoughts. How does he do it?"

"I can't tell you that," said Lily solemnly. "I know he would not want me to tell you that."

"But why?" persisted April Rose. "Why can't I know that?"

"Because," said Lily. "Those are his secrets, and he will explain to you when he wants to."

April Rose sighed. This was going nowhere, and she could not think of any way to convince Lily that she should tell her these secrets.

Well, she would try one more time.

"Look," she said to Lily, "I'm not from here, and I don't understand the ways here. Couldn't you just explain a little bit to me so I could understand better?"

"No," said Lily. "The shepherd would not trust me if I did that, knowing he wants to explain things to you himself."

"So what he wants is very important to you," said April Rose.

"Yes, it is," said Lily. "When you know him better, you will understand why."

"Hmmm," thought April to herself. The shepherd knew she was going to ask these questions, and he sent a person who would not be persuaded to tell her his secrets. "Very clever of you, shepherd," she thought in her mind.

"Would you like me to wash your clothes for you?" Lily asked again.

"I would really like to take a shower," said April Rose. "But how would I do that, since I can't stand up very long?"

"I can put a stool in the shower stall," said Lily. "You can sit on the stool. There's a hose with a nozzle on it to rinse yourself. I think that we have everything that you will need."

"Oh, wow, that's good," said April, who was surprised to hear this. "How does this work?"

"I'll fill the barrel on top with water—I'll have to heat some over the fire, so the water will be warmer. There's a spigot on the barrel to open or shut off the flow of water. Then the water goes into some copper tubing and there's a nozzle on the end of that with small holes in it," explained Lily.

"It sounds great. Thank you so much for helping me with all of this," said April gratefully.

"I'll hand you your towel when you're finished rinsing off and your clothes when you're dry enough to put them on. I brought some of my clothes and shoes for you to wear; I think they will fit you," said Lily.

"Oh," said April Rose, very surprised. "That's so kind of you."

Secretly, April Rose was not looking forward to wearing a muslin dress and a cotton tabard overdress like Lily was wearing. She wouldn't mind the short boots, though, that Lily wore.

Lily put some cut logs in the fire pit under the hanging rack, and then used flint and steel to create a spark that ignited a small pile of wood shavings she had placed on top of the logs. When the fire was blazing enough, she hung a black kettle filled with water over the fire.

Lily went back and forth from the well with buckets of water to fill the barrel on top of the shower stall, and last, she added the hot water. She had to climb on the ladder each time, to reach the barrel.

When April Rose saw all the trouble Lily went to for this shower, April Rose decided that she would not take a shower every day in this place. She couldn't ask Lily to do that every day.

April hobbled into the shower stall, and leaning against the stool, she removed her clothes and handed them to Lily over the wall of the shower stall. There was a little shelf with soap, in the stall, and Lily handed her a cloth for washing.

The nozzle worked well, she thought; it looked like the end of a metal watering can. April Rose tried to save most of the water for rinsing off, since she didn't know how long the barrel of water would last. Lily handed her the towel when she was finished, and April managed to dry herself, using the stool for support.

Then Lily handed the clothes to April, over the wall. There were cotton drawers for underwear that had a drawstring, and a cotton camisole that closed with hooks. April Rose pulled on the muslin dress and then the over dress. Inside this shower stall, there was a wooden plank floor, but it was wet so she had to dry her feet again on the towel before putting on the shoes Lily brought for her. Everything fit well, so that was a relief. The boot did not seem too tight on her sprained ankle, but she couldn't bend over very well to tie the laces.

She opened the door of the stall, and Lily handed her the crutch. April hobbled out and went to sit on the stump by the wash area. Now April could tie the laces of the boots for herself. That was less humiliating than to ask for more help.

Lily had already begun washing April Rose's clothing in a washtub. April Rose watched as Lily rubbed a bar of soap on all the dirt stains on her jeans and shirt and then rubbed them vigorously. April's underclothes were already washed and hanging on a rope clothesline stretched between two short trees in the enclosure. Lily used wooden clothespins that had no metal spring in them; they slipped over the clothing.

April Rose then decided on another thing, after observing how Lily had to wash the clothes. She would wear the same thing several days in a row. It was too much trouble to wash clothes here, she determined. Anyway, she didn't intend to be here very long; as soon as her own clothes were dry, she would put them back on and look for the way home. Surely there was another door somewhere.

Lily stayed with April Rose all that day. She baked bread in the brick oven outside, so April got to see how she did that. When April tasted that warm bread cooked over a fire, she was amazed at how good it was. She thought it was probably the best bread she had ever eaten.

Lily and April Rose talked about their families, although Lily had much more to say since she had such a large family. April Rose was intrigued. "Maybe you can come spend the day with me in the village when your foot is better," Lily said hopefully. April Rose almost consented, but then she reminded herself about her immediate goal of leaving. "I really need to go home," she told Lily and then felt very badly about it because she saw the disappointment on Lily's face.

It was late afternoon by then, and Lily had to go back to the village before dark, so she told April goodbye and began walking back. April Rose sat there feeling suddenly lonely in that place by the mountain. There were no other people around; there was only the mountain looming behind her.

So when she saw the shepherd coming, she was overjoyed. "April Rose," he said when he was within speaking distance, "You look happy. Did you have a nice day with Lily?"

"Yes, but after she left, I was so lonesome. I'm glad you are back," April Rose admitted. The shepherd came to sit by her near the fire pit. He took a stick and poked at the embers of the fire. With a little stirring, he was able to get a flame going again. This time he toasted some cheese over the fire, and they ate this with the bread that Lily made, for their supper.

"This is so good," she exclaimed eagerly, and the shepherd smiled. When they had finished eating, they sat there by the fire a little longer, and the shepherd said, "Tell me about your father."

April Rose tried to speak, but suddenly she burst into tears. "I haven't treated him right," she said. "And I don't know why I am telling you this."

She kept on sobbing, and the shepherd went and got a handkerchief from inside and gave it to her. "I know you need this," he said. "I know that you don't like to use your sleeve."

April Rose looked up at him, surprised again. "Thank you," she said in a teary voice.

"April Rose, why didn't you treat your father right?" the shepherd asked.

"I don't know," she answered. "I don't know why I gave him pain after he already suffered the loss of my mother. Something is wrong with me." The tears kept streaming down her face.

"You are right. Something is wrong---on the inside of you," said the shepherd. "It is something that you cannot fix."

"What should I do about it?" she asked.

"You will know in a few days," said the shepherd. "But tonight let us go in and I shall make another paste for your ankle and wrap it again."

The shepherd made more of the herbal remedy and doctored her ankle with this paste, and then he wrapped it again with the bandages that Lily had washed and hung up to dry.

He stepped out of the cottage so that April could change into the nightgown that Lily had brought for her. She got under the covers, and then shortly after, the shepherd came back in. He blew out the lantern and was about to go up to the loft when she asked him something.

"Ro'eh, why are you so kind to me?" she asked.

"It is who I am," said the shepherd. "Now get some rest." So she did, and it was a very peaceful sleep.

Chapter 11

For the next few days, Lily came every morning and helped April Rose with whatever needed to be done. April Rose's ankle was improving quickly, and she hobbled into the shepherd's garden with Lily to receive her lesson on herbal plants.

The shepherd's garden was full of interesting herbs and smells. He had the arnica plant, which looks something like a sunflower, the calendula which is an orange flower, and a witch hazel shrub tree. He had an Echinacea plant which makes a cone flower, as well as parsley, peppermint, lemongrass and turmeric. There was a gray bushy plant with purple flowers and a very nice smell; that was the lavender plant.

On one occasion, April Rose tried to start the fire with a flint rock and a piece of steel, under Lily's supervision, and discovered it takes determination and patience. Lily showed April Rose many things she had never tried before such as kneading bread and baking it in an outdoor oven, and cooking a bean stew in a kettle over the fire pit.

And so the days passed with Lily's help, and April Rose was comfortable with her company. But the thing she really began to enjoy was the time when the shepherd came home. Lily would leave in the afternoon, and then April Rose would wait to see the shepherd come walking down the path.

She would watch and see when he brought the sheep down into their pen, and then he would turn to come to the cottage. April Rose would wave to him, and he waved back and smiled. They would have supper together and then sit by the fire.

Every evening he would check her ankle and he was pleased at how it was healing so soon. April Rose felt so secure and safe when she was around him, and she liked the way he smelled. It reminded her of the seashore and a rose garden somehow, and it was very reassuring although she didn't understand why.

One evening she asked if she could come with him to tend the sheep on the mountain. He looked pleased that she had asked, but he did not give permission. "April Rose," he said, "There is no privy up there and I don't want to have you sliding and falling again if you try to come down by yourself. But if you would like to come just before we head back, we will not be so high up and you can see the flock."

April Rose was delighted with this concession, and so she made plans to do this the next day. She could hardly wait until the time came for her to go and see the sheep. Lily was not convinced that April Rose should climb yet, but April Rose was confident that her foot was well enough. She had abandoned the use of the crutch.

The time came, and April Rose started up the slope to reach the shepherd and his flock. She was so happy when she saw him, and he showed her the lambs running about and playing.

She sat down on the ground and the shepherd brought one of the smaller lambs so she could hold it in her lap. Its fuzzy head was so wonderful to touch, and its nose was soft. Then it was time to go, so she gently helped the lamb to stand. It was still a little wobbly.

The shepherd insisted on helping April Rose on the way down, as he did not want to ruin her good recovery. The sheep stayed close to him and followed him all the way down, bleating as they moved together in a group. After all the sheep were in their pen, and the gate securely shut, April Rose and the shepherd went to the cottage. They had their supper together and sat by the fire as usual. April Rose was quiet; she was thinking about a song she had heard Lily singing earlier in the day. Lily had said it was the shepherd's lullaby.

April Rose had a great longing that night, and after she was in bed and the shepherd had blown out the lantern and was about to go to the loft, April Rose called out to him.

"Ro'eh," she said.

"Yes, April Rose," he answered her out of the stillness of the night.

"I miss my mother," she said. "I haven't seen her since I was six years old." She hesitated for a moment, then timidly asked, "Would you sing a lullaby for me?"

The answer was a song. The Shepherd began to sing this song for April Rose:

"Wherever you go I am with you; I will never forsake my love. Even in the darkest night, even on the coldest day, I will be your light. If you stumble I will catch you; I will never let you fall. If you're lost I am coming to find you; if you call out my name I will hear you. If the path is steep I will steady you; if you cannot walk I will carry you.

Don't let go of my hand; never let go of my hand. When you run from me, I will follow you; you will never be out of my sight. I pledged my love with my blood; for your sake I lay down my life. Though your heart is hard, I will rescue you. You are my child, I have claimed you. Come back to me with all your heart."

April Rose said, "Thank you, Ro'eh" very softly, and then she fell asleep.

The next morning, the shepherd sent the sheep up on the mountain with another shepherd from the village, and he stayed with April Rose. This day, they had breakfast together.

"April Rose, do you enjoy the time you spend with me?" the shepherd asked.

"Yes," she said, "I do." She was wondering what this conversation could mean.

"April Rose, do you trust me?" the shepherd asked her, looking intently at her face.

"Yes," she answered, though she was very puzzled now.

"Do you trust me enough to do something for me?" the shepherd questioned.

"What is it?" April Rose asked.

"I would very much like to introduce you to the Prince," said the shepherd.

Suddenly the old bitterness that was still buried there in April's heart rose up in her. "So that is why you have been so nice to me?" she asked angrily. "You were trying to trick me into going there?"

"I don't trick anyone," said the shepherd. "I am asking you to go because you need to. Do you remember when you asked me what was wrong with you, and how it could be fixed, and I said you would find out in a few days?"

"I can't go there---I hate the Prince!" April Rose said bitterly. "He let my mother die."

"April Rose, I need to tell you a story," answered the Shepherd gently. "Will you listen?"

"Okay," she said, but resentfully.

"Once there was a good King who had only one son, who he loved very much. The people of his kingdom were in danger, however, because they had an evil sickness inside them," said the Shepherd. "This good King asked his only son to go and rescue the people of the kingdom."

"But the people of the Kingdom did not trust the good King's son, and the evil prince stirred them up to violence and they killed the king's son."

"But this actually fulfilled the King's plan because through this sacrifice, the blood of the King's son became the only thing that could heal the people."

"The good King made his son alive again and his blood has the antidote for the evil sickness."

"What does this have to do with me?" said April Rose vehemently. "I don't have anything to do with that man's death."

"Oh, but you do," said the shepherd earnestly. "You have that same sickness."

"I don't know what you are talking about," said April Rose. "I'm going home."

After that statement, she grabbed her own clothes and went to change in the shower stall. Then she laid Lily's clothes on the bed. For a moment, she regretted what she was doing, but she did not ever want to meet the prince. She wanted nothing to do with him---ever.

The shepherd looked at her sadly as she began to walk away, but he said nothing. She didn't know what she expected him to do at that point, but now she would have to follow through with what she said. Somehow she would have to find the way home by herself.

She started walking away, down the trail alongside the mountain, but not the one that led to the village or the palace. This was a lonely trail and she felt the loneliness intensely. She could see the sheep and other shepherds up on the mountain, but she didn't look that way very long. It might make her miss the shepherd, and she could not let that sentiment get in the way of going home. So she kept walking on the trail.

After a while, there was a turn and it led to a place where the ground was rockier and there was less vegetation and trees. She continued on her way, though she had no idea of where she was going. Surely she would meet some more people eventually, she thought to herself.

And suddenly she did---there was a young man coming from the opposite direction. "Hello," he said in a friendly voice.

As he came closer, she saw that his hair was golden and his face was like burnished bronze. His features were very handsome, and April Rose thought he looked like an angel.

"You look like you might need a guide," he said to April Rose. "May I be of assistance?"

"Well, I do need some direction," said April Rose.

"Where do you need to go?" asked the golden haired man.

"I need to go home," said April Rose. "But I don't know how to get there from here."

"Where are you from?" asked the young man politely, and he seemed sincerely concerned.

"I don't know how to explain it," said April Rose. "It seems I went through some kind of door from my world into this one."

"Oh, yes, I see what you mean," said the young man. "Well I can take you to my very wise friend who knows about such things."

"Really? That would be great," said April Rose in relief. "No one would help me back there."

"They're very disagreeable people," said the golden haired man. "The prince of that kingdom practically makes slaves out of the villagers."

"They wouldn't let me go home," said April Rose.

"That's a shame. Well, my friend will know how to help you," said the man. "It's this way." And he began walking on the trail with April Rose.

April Rose began to feel a little cold as she noticed that the atmosphere here was more gray and dreary and the wind was beginning to howl with a melancholy sound. But the young man continued talking so cheerily about his friend and the village where he lived, so she tried not to pay attention to the change in the surroundings.

They went through a dreadful woods---it was terrifying. The trees seemed to mutter curses against her with low rumbling voices, and there were screeches and eyes that peered at her out of the dark places in the woods and scuttling sounds in the dead foliage on the ground.

"Come on now," said the golden haired man. "It's not so bad; we'll be out of here soon." And he persuaded her to go on.

When she stepped out of the woods, she really wished she hadn't---the terrain was the bleakest and most dismal thing she had ever seen.

April Rose began to wonder if she was making a terrible mistake---but then, how would she know if she did not thoroughly investigate?

Chapter 12

This place was gray everywhere she looked. The wind was howling fiercely, and kept busy swirling the dust around frantically as if it had nothing else to do. The one lonely tree was barren and crooked and stood out starkly against the monotone sky.

"What is this place?" she asked in dismay.

"Oh, don't worry, it will get much better than this!" the golden haired man assured her. "We just have to get through this part."

Getting through that part was much more of an ordeal than he pretended, and it took many hours of trudging in the dusty dry ground, pushing back against the fierce gales of wind. Her mouth had grit in it, and she was longing for water, but there was none.

When the man went behind some large rocks to relieve himself, April Rose began to suspect that he had a supply of water and secretly drank from it, but he did not offer any to her.

The terrain stretched out before her like a barren plain, but they were coming closer to a dark gray mountain. She thought she could make out the shape of buildings somewhere in the distance, but it was hard to determine with all the swirling dust and grayness.

Then without warning, a black carriage pulled by a black horse appeared in front of them; the driver pulled on the reins roughly to stop the poor fretful horse, and the horse stopped with a jerking motion on the carriage. The horse had wild nervous eyes, and moved its head as if the bit was hurting.

The golden haired man spoke to the driver, but April Rose could not hear what they were saying. Then he turned to April Rose and told her to get in the carriage.

"We're almost there," he said, "And there will be food and water."

That was enough to persuade April Rose. She didn't know how much longer she could go without any water. So she climbed into the carriage and sat down on the seat. The odor inside bothered her immensely; it smelled like urine and sweat and cigar smoke.

The golden haired man did not seem to notice. He signaled the driver and the carriage began to move. It swayed as the horse trotted and April Rose felt nauseated. The wheels of the carriage ran over rocks and there was a sudden bump each time that jolted her.

They came to the village she thought she had seen in the distance, but it was not anything she would have hoped to see. The buildings were shabby and drab and unkempt; they were dreary gray, too. Everything looked hopeless and sad, including the few faces that she saw.

The carriage did not stop in the village and then she saw where it was headed.

A monstrous dark castle was now coming into view; it was leaning against the backdrop of the dark mountain. There was nothing about it that would give anyone the slightest feeling of hope.

"Is that where your friend lives?" she asked incredulously.

"Yes," said the man gleefully. "The inside is nothing like the outside. It's very cheery."

The horse now pulled the carriage up to the gate which led to a bridge over a moat. The moat water was greenish black and smelled foul as if dead things were in it.

The man with the golden hair now opened the carriage door and told April Rose to get out and to come with him, so she did. She cautiously stepped down onto the ground and reluctantly followed the man through the gate and over the bridge.

They came to the portcullis of the castle, and there were two guards standing there. They obviously knew the man she was with and let them both go through without any hesitation.

"Follow me," said the golden haired man and he walked through part of the castle and on into a courtyard. There was nothing pleasing about the part they walked through; it was damp and dark and the only light came from a few smoky torches attached to the walls.

They walked through the courtyard and April Rose had a slim hope that maybe in the next part of the castle things would be different. But when another man came and met them as they approached this wing of the castle, all hope disappeared.

"April Rose," this man said in a smooth but cynical voice and it made April shudder. She looked at him and saw that his skin tone was greenish and his eyes were yellow. His head was bald and he had bony protrusions on the back of his head and down his neck.

She made a startled gasp, and the golden haired man took her arm roughly and pulled her with him, as he followed the other man through a dark door.

She looked at the golden haired man and then she screamed. His hair was no longer golden; his hair was black and his face was pasty white and he had black broken teeth in his sneering mouth. His expression was hideous and revolting.

April Rose tried to pull away from him. "You lied to me!" she yelled.

"Of course I did," said the man smugly. "In this kingdom everyone lies. In fact, the better we are at deceiving, the more rewards we will get."

The man with the yellow eyes walked into another room and she was pulled into this room by the horrid man who had once looked so handsome.

"Welcome to my castle," said the evil prince with the yellow eyes and the bony spurs down his neck. "This will be your home now, so you might as well get used to it." The evil prince spoke in a menacing voice, and then he began to slowly walk around April Rose, eyeing her.

"I'm told you sing like a nightingale," he said in his smooth sinister voice. "Why don't you sing for me? If you please me, you could be my pampered pet. You would have many privileges."

Every time he made an s sound in a word, it made a hissing sound. It sounded like a reptile to April Rose. She looked at him in horror and then turned away. This nightmare is so awful, she thought to herself; when will I wake up? Please wake up! She pleaded silently to herself.

"I won't be ignored," said the evil prince to April Rose. Then he turned to the other man and said, "Put her in chains and see if she changes her mind. A little persuasion may help."

"If she won't sing, then she's worthless," said the one with black hair. "Can I burn her up?"

"You know nothing," said the evil prince, looking contemptuously at the other man. "She's valuable for leverage. I prefer to torment her with her own failures and her fears. I feed off of it."

The one with black hair pulled her roughly down a short flight of stairs into a dungeon room. She kicked her way free and tried to run back up the stairs but he grabbed her, pulled her back, and snapped a metal band around her wrist. There was a chain attached to this band, and now she was chained to the wall.

She kept kicking so that he couldn't reach her ankles, but he grabbed her other arm and twisted it behind her back as he snapped another band around her other wrist. When she tried to kick him again, he laughed and stayed out of reach. "You won't be going anywhere," he said mockingly and left the room.

He came back shortly with a bowl of water. "Here, little dog," he said tauntingly and held it just out of reach. Then he splashed it in her face, and threw the bowl down. Just as he was leaving, the evil prince walked by and saw this scenario.

He ordered the black haired man to pick up the bowl and get her some water. "That's not very persuasive, Hanson," the evil prince said. "We want her to adjust to her surroundings."

The evil prince watched as Hanson grudgingly brought her the bowl of water. She drank it all, though the taste was bitter. She hoped they had not drugged her.

"Now, Hanson, go get some food for her. She may be more agreeable if we feed her," the evil prince suggested. Hanson went away and came back with some stale bread that he handed to April Rose. "Now, get her some more water, Hanson. We need to make her feel at home," said the evil prince mockingly as he walked over to April Rose.

He looked at April closely and ran his greenish finger down the cheekbone of her face. "I really would like a nightingale to sing to me," he said.

April Rose jerked her head away from his touch. "You will have to get used to me," the evil prince said in a threatening voice to the girl in chains.

The evil prince and his cohort Hanson left the room and shut the heavy door behind them.

April slid down to sit on the filthy floor and slowly took bites of the stale bread, chewing it a long time to make it easier to swallow. She took tiny sips from the bowl of water, trying to make it last.

She discovered that the most difficult task was trying to relieve herself in a bucket while chained to the wall. This is so nasty, she thought to herself as she carefully pushed the bucket away so that she wouldn't knock it over and spill it.

Whoever thought castles are romantic is crazy, she said to herself. She surveyed the room, trying to see if there might be any way she would be able to escape this hell hole.

The only exit she could see was the door. There was only one tiny hole for a window, and it was much too high to reach. Most of this dungeon was underground, and though the window was high, it was still barely above ground level.

Thankfully there was a torch on the wall, or it would be totally black in this room at night.

She couldn't believe she had been so gullible. Why had she listened to that man? She was angry with herself that his phony good looks had made her trust him. She remembered the words of the shepherd; maybe he was right. There must be something wrong with her. She was cruel to those who loved her, and she was no judge of character.

The shepherd had been so kind to her; why did she run away? She sighed as she thought of it, and put her head down on her knees.

There definitely was something wrong with her. She did this to herself; she was a captive because of her own choices.

There was no way out of this that she could see.

Chapter 13

April Rose didn't know how much time had passed because her sense of time now was distorted by despair and the darkness of this room she was held in. She had cried out all her tears until she couldn't cry anymore. Her jeans were wet from her tears, and her eyes burned. Her heart felt numb.

Then the door opened again, and the evil prince came in with a woman. This woman had black hair also, and April Rose saw tattoos of many writhing snakes on her neck. As she stared, the snakes seemed to pulsate as if they were alive. April didn't know if it was because her eyes were so blurry.

The evil prince coldly asked April Rose if she had reconsidered. April just stared blankly at this evil personage and didn't answer. The evil prince began to pace back and forth impatiently as he became more and more enraged.

"All I ask is that you sing to me," he demanded. "I want to be worshiped!" His voice rose in volume as he became more vehement, and his evil face contorted in anger, as he looked at April Rose.

"And you refuse---you are silent!" He was furious with her lack of compliance to his demands.

"Since you resist what I want, you will suffer the consequences. If you won't sing for me, you will sing for no one---ever," said the evil prince in his rage. "You will be silent forever." Then he turned to the woman and said, "Get the serum ready."

The woman had a bottle of potion and a syringe which she inserted into the bottle and drew the potion into the canister of the syringe. She set down the bottle and went to April Rose.

April Rose tried to get up and away from this woman, but her distance was only as far as the chains would allow. She screamed as the woman injected the substance into her neck.

April felt a burning and then numbness. Her voice choked on the scream, and then it was gone. Her voice was gone. She instinctively put her hands on her throat, but it was too late.

The evil prince gloated over his captive and his revenge for her rebellion against him. The vile woman's eyes glowed with an evil fire and the snakes in her tattoos writhed and squirmed.

"You will remember this day for the rest of your life," the revengeful evil prince told April Rose.

The evil prince turned and left triumphantly, along with the snake tattooed woman.

April Rose was in torment; she was mute! She could not utter a word or call out for help; she could not even make a whimper or any sound of distress. Of all the things they could have taken from her, she could not think of anything worse--- unless it would have been her sight.

What if they thought of that? She had to get out of here before they came back again!

All pride was gone; she no longer cared about any of that. She had to escape----and now.

Then a thought came to her; Ro'eh could read her mind---he could hear her thoughts. Would he even want to come and find her after she ran away from him and treated him so ungratefully?

The only thing that she could do was to try.

"Ro'eh," she called fervently in her mind. "Ro'eh, if you can hear me, please help me."

Wonder of all wonders, she heard his voice in her mind. "Are you lost?" he said to her in her mind.

"Yes," she answered back.

"I am coming to find you," he said. Then in her mind, she heard him say the words that shocked her to the core of her being. "I am your prince, and I am coming to find you."

"The Prince?" she said in her confused state. "I called Ro'eh----and you sound just like him."

Then he answered her with the most bewildering statement: "That is because we are the same person. I am the Prince."

April Rose was horrified; this is the one of whom she declared that she hated! How could she dare to ask for his help now?

Now was his opportunity to take vengeance on her for the things she had said about him. She would not be able to blame him if he refused to help her.

If there was any hope at all, she would have to give up her pride, and ask for his mercy. It was not an easy thing for her to do. For twelve long years, she had built up that hatred, and carried a grudge against the Prince. It was hard now to let it go.

Finally, in desperation, she made herself ask him.

"Will you still help me, even though I said those things about you?" said April Rose in her mind, and her body was trembling with her remorse and the shame of her predicament.

"Yes," was the answer that came into her mind. "I have always known how you felt about me," said the voice. "I still want to help you."

"What do I do? I cannot speak. They took my voice!" said April Rose to this unseen person.

"I will tell you what to do. Listen carefully." said the voice of the Prince. "Do you trust me, April Rose---and will you do exactly as I say?"

"Yes," she said humbly---and it was the first time she had ever felt that willingness.

"Good," said the voice. "Now your chains will fall off."

And instantly the bands around her wrists opened and fell to the floor. She rubbed her wrists and looked at the bands on the floor in amazement.

"April Rose, do you remember the story I told you? About the antidote in my blood?" the Prince asked her.

"Yes….although I don't quite understand it…" she affirmed.

"You will. For now, all you need to know is that my blood is the way to be free. Now look at the rock wall in the back of the dungeon," the voice of the Prince told her.

"But it's so dark, I can't see back there," she told him plaintively. "There is only one torch in this dungeon and the light doesn't reach that far."

Suddenly a light glowed there against that wall.

"Can you see it now?" the Prince asked her.

"Yes! There is a light!" she exclaimed.

"That is my light," said the Prince. "Now look more carefully…you will see a red door there in the rock wall."

April Rose stared hard at the rock wall, and then suddenly, the image of the door began to appear in the wall. There was a red wooden door in the rock wall; it had an old round metal doorknob and a keyhole below the knob.

"I see it!" she told him in her mind.

"You have the key to that door in your pocket," said the Prince. "You have had the key all along. I am the door to freedom and the key is faith. Now use the key and unlock the door."

"Then what do I do?" she asked.

"There will be a tunnel in the mountain. You will go straight, and then the tunnel will curve upwards and you must go up for a short while. After that, the tunnel will become level again, and you will see an opening. I will be waiting for you there."

"Will you talk to me in the tunnel?" she asked him.

She had always been afraid of tight spaces.

"Yes," the voice said. "If you are frightened, call my name."

"What shall I call you?" asked April Rose.

"You may call me Ro'eh," said the voice. "I am both your shepherd and your Prince."

"I don't have a light," she said. "Will the tunnel be dark?"

"I will be your light," the Prince said. "Don't be afraid, I am with you."

So April Rose took the key from her pocket, and went to the red door. The voice of the Prince spoke to her again just then.

"Think of this red door as my blood," he told her. "You must go through me to find life and healing. Put the key in the keyhole and unlock it."

So she did, and then she cautiously opened the door. A draft of cold wind came into the dungeon, and she shivered. She removed the key carefully out of the keyhole and put it safely back into her pocket. She looked into the dark tunnel, and for a moment she didn't think she could make herself step into it. Then she saw the light hovering a few yards away, and she stepped towards the light.

No matter how many steps she took, the light remained a few yards ahead of her. She made it through the first part of the tunnel, and now she was on an incline and walking upwards.

"Ro'eh," she said. "Yes," he answered. "I just wanted to hear your voice," she said. "I'm here with you," the voice said.

Now she was walking through the third part, which seemed as if it was the longest part. The light remained there a few yards ahead of her, until the light was in front of an opening—she could see a little bit of the outside world. It was night time, and the stars were out, shining brilliantly against a dark midnight blue sky. She walked steadily towards that opening.

She had to bend over to come out of the opening, and then when she stood up, there he was.

Chapter 14

"Take my hand," the Prince said, and April Rose did. "We have to go down the mountain to the place where I have hidden my horse," he told her.

She looked up at him. He was dressed as the shepherd, and looked just the same as he had before—but there was something different in how she saw him. The change was in her, she realized.

She saw a Prince now, dressed in shepherd clothing.

He guided her carefully down the mountain so that she didn't slip and fall. They were on the side of the mountain where the castle guards would not see them in their descent. April thought ironically that she didn't have to worry about being quiet.

She couldn't make a sound.

Finally they reached the ground and there was a beautiful white horse waiting behind a darkened rock formation at the base of the mountain. The Prince mounted his horse, and reached down for April Rose. He took her hand and arm and swung her up behind him on the horse as if this feat was nothing. She marveled at his strength.

The horse picked her way through the rocky terrain until she came to more level ground. They skirted the village in a wide berth, for although it was dark, there were always the drunken revelers who roamed its streets. Now they were in the clear beyond the village and out in the vast gray bleak wilderness April Rose had come through.

The Prince gave the horse her lead, and she moved from a lope into a gallop. "Hold on tightly," he told April Rose, and she clung to his back.

After a bit, he slowed the horse down to a trot to rest her legs from her strenuous task. Then he let the horse slow down to a walk.

"Are you thirsty?" he asked April Rose. "Yes," she answered in her mind. "I'm very thirsty."

The Prince kindly instructed April Rose in how to dismount, and then he dismounted and drew out a water canteen from the saddle bag. He handed it to April Rose and she eagerly drank.

"We need to go on now," he said and he mounted and pulled April Rose up behind him on the horse.

"What is her name?" April Rose asked him through her mind. "Magnificent," the Prince answered.

"Oh, it suits her perfectly," April replied to him in her mind.

The rest of the journey through this wilderness, Magnificent went at a canter. April Rose saw that one lonely stark tree---and then she saw the terrible woods in the distance beyond the tree.

"I know you don't want to go through there," said the Prince. "But we have to."

April Rose clung more tightly to him during this segment of their trip than any other part.

She hated the woods with its sinister mumbling and the weird shrieks and rustling noises. It was slimy and dark and there were creatures in the tops of the trees spying on them.

She couldn't see them, but she could sense they were there, and she could feel their movement. Even the trees seemed as if they were cruel.

The Prince was not disturbed by these things, though he knew that April Rose was. So he began to sing the lullaby song:

"Wherever you go I am with you; I will never forsake my love. Even in the darkest night, even on the coldest day, I will be your light. If you stumble I will catch you; I will never let you fall. If you're lost I am coming to find you; if you call out my name I will hear you. If the path is steep I will steady you; if you cannot walk I will carry you.

Don't let go of my hand; never let go of my hand. When you run from me, I will follow you; you will never be out of my sight. I pledged my love with my blood; for your sake I lay down my life. Though your heart is hard, I will rescue you. You are my child, I have claimed you. Come back to me with all your heart."

April Rose laid her head against his back, and listened to the words of the song.

"I'm sorry," she said with her mind, to the Prince. "I'm sorry that I didn't want to know you, yet you didn't give up on me."

"No," said the Prince. "I have loved you with an eternal love."

"But if that is so, where were you all my life?" said April Rose with her mind.

"I have always been there," he said. "You were not willing to let me get close to you. But I have been protecting you. It was I who kept you back from giving your body to Arlo. It was I who kept you safe from the perversion that your roommate is involved with."

"Where were you when my mother died?" April Rose finally asked. "How could you let that happen to a six year old?"

"April Rose, I gave you a loving father who has so much compassion for you---more than you ever realized. Your world is only temporary; people have only a limited lifetime there. For some it will be shorter than others. But the real world is truly permanent---it is forever. And that is where your mother is; she has passed beyond what is only temporary to what is forever," the Prince told her.

"Your world is temporary because of the sin-sickness. Everyone is born with it. That is why I became the sacrifice so that my blood would have the antidote for everyone who would receive this healing," said the Prince.

"How do I receive this?" asked April Rose.

"You must surrender your life to me," said the Prince. "That is the only way."

April Rose didn't say anything for a while. She was contemplating the meaning of all that the prince had just told her. Now she realized that there definitely was something wrong with her. It was the sin-sickness, as the Prince said. Could she believe in his cure?

"What will happen when I do?" she asked him.

"A transformation," he said, "As when a caterpillar is changed into a butterfly. The old person dies, and there is an inner change into a new person."

"That's drastic," she said.

"Yes, it is," said the Prince. "My sacrifice was very drastic, as well."

"What happened?" April asked.

They had just emerged from the woods; the Prince's horse Magnificent could only walk through there, as the forest floor was soggy and the trees grew closely together. She seemed relieved to be out of it, shaking her mane and stepping briskly.

There was still a considerable distance before they would reach the shepherd's cottage. The Prince said to April Rose: "I will allow you to see a vision of what happened."

Suddenly April Rose was eerily transported to somewhere else, and there was a mist swirling around a terrible scene. In the mist of this ghastly vision, she saw the Prince crudely dressed in a ragged burlap prisoner garment. He was dragging something very heavy—heavier than a man could carry. It was a very large bag of rocks. There was a group of men following him, but they were more like animals and they were snarling at the Prince. They had sticks and they were driving him and beating him. Finally they came to a wall and she saw spikes protruding from the wall. The men took the Prince and impaled him on the spikes. There were seven spikes and they pierced his body and the blood ran down on the ground. Then the men opened the bag and took out the rocks and they threw these at the Prince. They used the stones and crushed his bones and his skull, and then they took him off of the spikes and threw his body over the wall. The horror of what she saw in the vision made her nauseated and weak.

The vision ended and April Rose was back on the horse, seated behind the Prince. She couldn't bear the thought of what she had seen. Now her tears began to wet his clothing.

"How did you come alive again?" April Rose asked with her mind, as her tears spilled out.

"My father gave my life back to me," the Prince told her. "And now I can give life forever to all those who surrender themselves to me."

"Do you still have the same body?" she wanted to know.

"Yes....it has been restored, although I will carry the scars always," said the Prince. "But I do not regret that---they are the proof of my love."

April Rose could say no more; she held on more

tightly to the one she had not wanted to meet.

Now she didn't want to let him go….ever.

"April Rose, do you understand what I have done for you?" asked the Prince.

"Yes," she spoke to him through her mind. "I didn't deserve it….I don't deserve your help now. But I will surrender to you. Please let me stay with you."

"You are my child. I will not let go of you," affirmed the Prince. "Now hold on….I am going to allow Magnificent to go faster---I think she has become tired of walking."

Magnificent began to trot and then moved into a canter effortlessly. Her strong muscles moved in rhythm; the horse and her people seemed to glide over the fields under the moonlight. They were now getting closer to home.

Indeed, the cottage now seemed like home to April Rose. She was becoming very weary after her terrifying ordeal, and now she desperately wanted to see that familiar cottage.

They passed through a much nicer woods---it was rich with color, and the moonlight glistened on a lagoon in the center of these woods. There was a small waterfall, and its ribbons of water streaming down looked like strings of diamonds.

"Oh…it's beautiful," April Rose said with her mind to the Prince.

"Your mother liked it very much," he told her. "She was rescued as you were, from the dungeon of the evil prince. When she first came here, she had never seen butterflies before or flowers like this."

"Who rescued her?" April Rose asked.

"You have forgotten many things, April Rose," said the Prince. "It was your father…and Audrey and Cornelia."

Then the cottage was in sight---oh wonderful sight! April Rose sighed with relief. The Prince rode Magnificent right up to the door, and April Rose slid off the horse's back. She almost collapsed but the Prince picked her up and carried her in and then gently laid her on the bed.

"I will be back quickly," he said, and he left the cottage. In a few minutes he returned with plants from the herb garden. He ground these up and made something liquid that he put into a cup.

April Rose was barely awake, but he had her sit up to drink the medicine he had made. She was teetering between sleep and mental confusion. Then she fell into a deep sleep, and did not wake up for many hours.

Chapter 15

April Rose finally woke up. The sunlight was freely streaming in through the windows and it was bold and bright. April Rose had lost all sense of time, but it was afternoon by then.

The Prince stepped in and came to sit on the end of the bed. He looked at April Rose with such deep compassion in his eyes, that it almost made April cry. "Thank you," she said in her mind.

"You are welcome," the Prince said kindly. "I have more medicine for you to drink." He went to the cupboard and retrieved the cup in which he had placed more of the medicine.

"Will this make me sleepy?" she asked him with her thoughts.

"Not this time," he answered her. "It will help to remove the toxins from the evil prince's poison. What he injected into you paralyzed your vocal chords. It also affected the part of your brain that controls speech."

"How long before it works?" she asked with her mind. "The rest of your healing must come from the antidote in my blood," the Prince replied. "We are going to the palace. Are you ready, April Rose?" he asked.

She turned and put her feet on the floor to stand. She still felt a little wobbly, and the Prince took her hand and helped her up. He led her to the chair at the table.

"I don't think you should try to go without eating something," he told her, and he gave her a serving of the sweet nutty bread along with a thick slice of the pungent cheese. He poured out some of the orange drink into another cup and set it before her on the table.

"I will be gone only for a few minutes---I am going to put the saddle and bridle on Magnificent while you eat. She stayed here in the stable which is not far away," he said and then he went out.

April made herself eat slowly because she was so hungry that she was shaking. Her clothes were filthy and her hair was disheveled, but somehow she didn't care about anything except staying with the Prince.

As soon as he came in the door, she was ready to go. The Prince mounted Magnificent and pulled April Rose up behind him, and they began the journey to the palace. This time, April Rose was at peace with where she was going with the Prince.

Magnificent walked and April Rose was able to appreciate the beauty around her this time. They went through the rocky meadow, and then came to the woods with the leaves that chimed. They crossed over the little bridge that arched across the musical brook, and then they were in a field of golden grain that looked like wheat.

Here they parted company with the brook and went on to a different path. This led to a clearing covered with wild flowers of pink and blue colors, waving in the wind.

Beyond that, April Rose saw glimpses of a white glistening castle. Before they reached it, they went through a border of tall evergreen trees and then entered an area containing small farms and a quaint rustic village.

"Is that where Lily lives?" April asked with her thoughts.

"Yes," said the Prince. "She does."

Now just in front of them, there was another meadow filled with vibrant purple, scarlet, and gold flowers. These too were waving in the wind like giant ripples of color, moving back and forth.

And there was the white palace before them, glistening in the sunlight, like an opalescent pearl of great dimension. Its turrets and walls were rounded; there was no moat, but the palace was built up on a hill. There in front of the castle, was a colorful stone sidewalk which led up to brick steps. April Rose saw that one must go up these steps to a gate which opened onto a corridor high above the ground, and this corridor led to the great door of the castle.

They were coming close to this stone sidewalk, made of large colorful square stones, laid in a diamond pattern.

"April Rose," said the Prince. "You must go alone from here, up to the door."

"Why?" pleaded April Rose with her mind. "I can't go in alone."

"You will see me again soon," said the Prince. "But this must be your choice. I chose you; now you too must choose me. Choose me over every lie you have ever believed. Choose me over every desire you have ever had. Choose me as your way of life, forever. If you do, I will cause you to see things you could never see before."

"Like the red door?" April asked silently with her mind.

"Yes, like the red door," answered the Prince.

April dismounted carefully, and took a step onto the colorful sidewalk. She looked back at the Prince and he nodded in affirmation. She took another step and another, and another and kept going until the end of the sidewalk. Now she began her ascent up the brick steps, taking each step with deliberation and determination. She was almost at the gate, and she turned and looked back---but the Prince and the horse Magnificent were already out of sight.

She sighed and faced the gate. She had forgotten to ask how it would open. Then she remembered that she still had the key in her pocket; could it open this as well? There was no doorknob on the black metal gate, but it did have a keyhole, and she inserted her key into this and turned the key. There was a gratifying click, and the gate opened. She went in, stepping out onto the long corridor which led to the door. The walls of this corridor were made of stone.

It seemed very long, but finally she approached the great doors of the castle. These were tall arched and carved doors made of a thick wood. Then she saw the words above the door.

These words had been carved above the doors and painted with something that made the letters glow like fire. She read these words and her heart began to sink with despair when she realized their meaning: NOTHING IMPURE MAY DWELL HERE.

She was so alarmed at the sight of this that she almost wanted to turn around and run all the way back. But then she would not receive what she needed most of all: to be changed and healed. Suddenly, she noticed that the doors were a dark red! The blood of the Prince---she thought within herself. I can enter these doors because of the antidote in his blood.

She remembered what the Prince had said when she was in the dungeon: "I am the door. You must go through me to find life and healing."

There was no keyhole here; so she decided that she would knock and see what would happen. As soon as she did, the door was opened and there was a woman standing there in a long lavender dress, and April Rose noticed the strangest thing about this woman: her eyes were a clear shade of purple. This woman smiled kindly at April Rose.

"Welcome," said the woman. "We have been expecting you, April Rose, and we are very glad you have arrived. My name is Mercy."

April couldn't answer, of course, but she smiled gratefully, and as the woman held the door open wide, she stepped inside. Now this is the kind of castle she had dreamed of, she thought to herself, as she saw the splendor in this large hallway.

The woman escorted April Rose down the hall to a small but elegant round waiting room. "Wait here," she told April Rose. "I will bring you some of our refreshments, and I will tell the Prince that you have arrived."

April Rose nodded and went into this room. There were beautiful velvet covered chairs, but she was reluctant to sit on these in her dirty clothing. So she stood and waited.

The woman came back soon with a full plate of delectable pastries and a cup of mint tea. When she saw that April Rose was still standing, she quickly realized why April Rose had been hesitant to sit on the furniture.

"Please make yourself comfortable. These chairs are meant for you, no matter what condition you find yourself in, and they are easily maintained," said the woman in a very assuring voice.

So April Rose was convinced and she sat down gratefully and began to eat one of the pastries. Even the sunlight coming into the room felt inviting to April Rose. The woman excused herself and set out on her errand to speak with the Prince.

In the meantime, April Rose enjoyed the delicacies and the tea and began to look around the room. There was a table which had picture books laid out on it, and a pedestal table in one area of the room which had a large golden book laid on it in an open position. This book seemed to have its own luminance. April eyed it curiously, but she did not investigate, because something else caught her eye at that moment.

She saw a book on the table with a picture of a boy with red curly hair. "This looks just like my father," she thought to herself. And then she saw the name of the boy. "It IS my father!" she thought excitedly, and she began to read the narrative.

It was all about how the Prince had found Rusty when he was an orphan living on the streets, and he had adopted him. Rusty lived in the palace and was raised by the Prince.

April Rose was rather in awe; it's not every day that you walk into an opulent palace and discover a book written about your very own father! She looked through some other books, and there she saw a book about a petite girl with a very light complexion, straight black hair, and brown almond shaped eyes. It was Pearl; it was her mother. April Rose was enraptured to read about her mother's story, as well.

As soon as she had finished it, the woman came back and said that the Prince would like to see April Rose now. So April got up and followed the woman down a long hall that had twinkling lights all over the ceiling. On either side of her on the walls of this corridor, there were life-like and life-size paintings of animals in a forest. They all seemed to look at her as she passed by.

There was something familiar about the birds painted in these murals, but she couldn't decipher what it was.

Her attention was fixed on the reason for being here; it was so amazing for her to realize that she was actually in the palace of the Prince she had fought in her heart for so long.

She thought of other things he had told her as they returned to his home. He had said, "I understand you better than you could possibly know. But I couldn't explain myself to you---you shut your heart to me. I can't reveal myself if you don't trust me. If you open your heart to me, we can have fellowship together. I will give you the life I have been longing to give you."

"Will I die? Will I even know myself?" she had asked him. "April Rose," he answered, "You are already dead and you don't know it. The real you is not alive yet. But if you give yourself to me, I will raise you up to life…a life you never knew you could have."

April Rose was troubled then. "I don't know if I can be what you want," she told him.

And then he told her: "All I want is for you to love me. I am not asking you to change yourself to please me. I will do that when you let me. If you give yourself to me, I can give you the antidote in my blood that will allow you to live with me forever. Your world is only temporary. Nothing in it is ever permanent and nothing will last. But my love lasts forever. April Rose, do you know why you never fit in anywhere? Your uniqueness is my doing—you were made for my kingdom, not for your world.

Your real life is in me. You will never know who you really are without me."

Now---now April Rose was ready.

Chapter 16

Mercy went before her, as April Rose came to the doors of the throne room. She didn't know what to expect, but her heart trusted the Prince now, so she wasn't afraid or reluctant. Then Mercy opened the doors and April Rose stepped in.

She stood there in a frozen state at the sight of this room. The ceilings were incredibly high and frescoed with golden patterns and designs. There were huge arched windows along two walls with white filmy curtains tied back with golden cords. There were tall white columns with ornate carvings on the capitals, and the floor was tiled in designs of red, blue, and gold.

Then her eyes riveted to the throne, and to the person sitting on this throne. He still looked like her shepherd Ro'eh in his features, but there was light emanating from his regal face. When he turned his face and looked at her, it was as if beams of light flowed over her with a warm glow.

He was wearing a woven cream tunic with billowy sleeves, dark plum trousers, brown suede boots with gold trim, and a gold sash. There was a gold circlet crown on his wavy brown hair. She stared at him in wonder. His presence was captivating.

Then the light of his face drew her closer and he spoke her name. "April Rose, come close to me," he said. "Do not be afraid to draw near to me, and receive your help."

She approached his throne and knelt down at the base of the throne.

"April Rose," he said to the kneeling girl, and she lifted her head to look at him. His face was brilliant with light now and she had to lower her eyes.

Then he spoke again in that voice she had come to love. "In just a short while," the Prince said, "We will have your adoption ceremony in this room. I wanted you to see me first, so that you would not be afraid. I am still your shepherd as well as your Prince."

She could not answer him, but she nodded in reply.

"Mercy will bring you to the bathing rooms, and give you clothing made for this day," the Prince told her. "I will see you again very soon." He smiled at her, and light flowed over her like a warm embrace.

Mercy beckoned to April Rose, and she followed Mercy out of the room. She had questions she so wanted to ask someone, but she had no voice whatsoever. This distressed her, but she had already seen the miraculous and she had hope in the Prince's healing.

Mercy led her to a luxurious room with marble bathtubs, velvety towels and curtained enclosures for privacy. There were fresh roses in pink vases everywhere in this room, and the soap smelled like roses. Clear glass chandeliers were suspended from the ornate ceiling.

On one side, there was a tall walnut wardrobe with mirrors and Mercy took a dress and underclothes and shoes from this closet and laid them over a velvet covered chair within one of the bathing areas enclosed by thick brocade curtains.

April Rose was delighted to see that there was a spigot and heated running water here. She filled the bathtub to a reasonable level and climbed in with great satisfaction. It was so pleasurable to be clean again. She washed her hair with some rose scented liquid soap.

The dress Mercy gave her was perfectly her size and so were the shoes. The dress was a soft white finely woven fabric with lace sleeves and pearl buttons. There was a filmy overdress with a faint image of roses imprinted on it. The shoes were white leather slippers with a strap and button closure.

When she was dressed, she asked permission to walk outside and let the wind dry her hair and Mercy showed her the way to the Prince's garden.

April Rose walked about this garden and admired the circular seating area surrounding a water fountain in a circular pool. She was enchanted with the bushes sculptured into shapes of animals, and the many different colors of roses. There were trellises of vining flowers and huge amphora jars profusely filled with varieties of brilliant colored flowers.

She heard someone walking towards her and turned to see Mercy smiling at her. "Come, April Rose, it is time," she said. April Rose followed her down the garden paths and back up into the palace. She felt as if she were going to a royal coronation or something of that sort. There was such an excitement in the atmosphere.

Mercy led her through the hall again, and then they came to the doors of the throne room. Here April Rose realized that once she went through those doors, this time, she would not be the same person when she came out.

She hesitated for just a second, realizing the finality of her decision---and then she thought of her Prince who loved her and she went in. Her fear could not keep her from him this time.

This elegant room looked even more beautiful than when she had just seen it! There were many ladies of the kingdom dressed in beautiful long dresses, and they all looked happy to see April Rose come in; and there were men of the kingdom dressed in regal clothing similar to the Prince's. There were warriors dressed in armor standing at attention on the large white marble platform where the throne was centered.

Then she saw the people from the village, and there was Lily smiling happily at her. There were young children from the village, who were waiting expectantly.

It was quite overwhelming to see the room filled with people to celebrate with her. But after she saw the Prince, her gaze went nowhere else. Her eyes were fixed on him. He was resplendent in his royal attire, but it was the love in his eyes that drew her like a magnet.

"Come, April Rose," he said to the waiting girl.

She was so mesmerized that she hardly felt her feet moving, but somehow she went to him.

Then the Prince stood up, and all the people in the throne room bowed in deference to him. He then stepped down to the bottom step of the throne platform and gazed lovingly at April Rose.

"I have waited nineteen years for this day," he said. "I have waited for the day when this young lady would become my daughter, and one of my royal heirs."

April Rose looked at him with a little bit of puzzled confusion, but he smiled at her and explained. "She is eighteen years and a few months old, but you see, I knew her before she was born," he said with a radiant smile. "And I have always loved her. But as you know, our enemy lies and deceives people into believing that I have caused them pain, when it is his doing all along."

"It is my joy to heal people and give them life," said the Prince, "And now April Rose is here for that reason. She has expressed to me her faith in my antidote and has pledged to surrender her life to me, so that I can give her my life."

April Rose saw that the Prince had a golden scepter in his hand; she knew that this scepter represented his authority over the sin-sickness within her. This authority had been granted to him by his father, because he had given his blood as the remedy.

The Prince spoke softly to April Rose. "Come; all that you need to do now is to touch my scepter and my light will go into you and destroy the sin-sickness. You will be made new."

April Rose stepped closer to the throne until she was just below it. The Prince stepped down off of the platform and came to April Rose. He took her by the hand and had her step onto the platform so that all could see and witness her pledge to the prince.

"April Rose," the Prince said, "Do you consent to be my daughter, and my royal heir?" April Rose nodded her head. "Do you willingly agree to surrender your life to me?" he asked and again, she nodded her head. Tears were running down her face, but she was smiling with joy.

"Then let it be done," he said, and he held out the scepter to April Rose. She reached out with her hand and as her fingers touched the tip of his scepter, his life and light began to flow into her. She closed her eyes, because a deep change was happening inside of her. She felt a new sensation; she was light-weight, as if a heavy burden had been lifted off her shoulders---as if even gravity could not keep her down! And suddenly, her voice returned, and her heart spoke with tangible words: "I love you," she said to the Prince. "I love you."

The Prince was crying with joy, and he held out his arms to her. That was the first time she had ever embraced her Prince, but it would not be the last. As he held her, she knew she had found peace.

When he released her, she saw that his face was full of light. She didn't realize that her own face was glowing from the effect of his light that was now within her too. All that she knew was how wonderful it felt to be free from the evil sickness that had kept her from seeing him as he truly is--- and how wonderful it felt to belong to him. Forever.

The ceremony was not over; now April Rose saw one of the attending ladies bring in a large ornately decorated book and April watched as she laid it on a pedestal. She opened it to a certain page, and the Prince wrote April Rose's name in this book.

Then another attendant brought in a small box wrapped with a satin ribbon. The Prince handed this to April Rose, and she carefully untied the ribbon and opened the box. There was a ring inside; it was a small sculptured rose of pure gold. April took it out of the box with trembling hands and handed the box to the attendant. Then she slipped it onto her finger, and it fit perfectly.

"Read the inscription on the inside of the band," the Prince urged her, and she slipped it off again to look at this. There were the words "To my April Rose from the Prince" engraved upon the band.

April Rose looked gratefully at the Prince and said, "Thank you, it's beautiful."

Chapter 17

It was evening by now, and this night was a clear, cloudless night. The Prince led the procession of people out to the palace lawn, with April Rose by his side and her hand in his. She gasped in great surprise when she saw what awaited them on the lawn. It was a lawn party of grand proportions.

There were lanterns hung on poles all around the perimeter of the lawn, and the moonlight was very bright on the grass. The moon itself looked larger and closer and its light seemed magnified. It lit up the lawn that was filled with round tables covered in white cloths and trays of food. One long table was set upon a raised dais; this was for the Prince and his guests of honor for the night.

April Rose had a place next to the Prince, but there was an empty seat next to her. She looked up at the Prince with a question in her eyes, and he said that he thought she might like to have a friend sit by her. Immediately she thought of Lily and went to find her.

When she found her, she hugged her. "Lily," she said. "I know I hurt your feelings that day when you invited me to your home. Please forgive me. I do want to come and visit with you. Would you honor me with your company at the Prince's table?"

Lily was overjoyed to see her friend again, and was delighted to be included at the Prince's table. "I'm so glad you are back," she told April Rose. "I was so concerned when you ran away."

April Rose had a question for Lily. "When you washed my clothes," said April Rose, "Did you see the keys in my pockets?"

"Oh, yes," answered Lily. "But the Prince had already instructed me to be sure and put them back in the pockets once the clothes were dry."

"He thought of every detail," mused April Rose.

"He always does," remarked Lily. "Now do you see why he made me promise not to tell you why he had those powers?"

April Rose remembered how frustrated she had been, but now it seemed so long ago. Then she realized what made that memory so far away; she was now a different person from the girl who had begged Lily for answers.

"Yes," she told Lily. "I see now. That knowledge had to wait until my heart was surrendered to him as the prince---only then would I truly understand. Before, the sin sickness would have prevented it."

Lily smiled with satisfaction. "I'm so glad. It was a burden to me not to answer you."

April Rose thanked Lily for being obedient to the Prince. "I see now how important it is that we obey what he says---someone else's life may depend on it," said April Rose.

Lily's face registered even more joy with that wise statement, and April Rose realized what a genuine friend she had in Lily---a friend who was faithful to the Prince was a genuine person.

The rest of the evening was filled with music, and special songs, and introductions to many people who were acquainted with April Rose's parents, Pearl and Rusty. April Rose had never before felt so accepted; there was no ulterior agenda here. There was no agenda at all other than the Prince's desire to help people.

Towards the end of the reception dinner, a man approached April Rose and said, "I have been eagerly waiting to meet you, but I thought I would wait until last. I was very close to your father; he was like a brother to me. My name is Cedric."

Suddenly some locked-up memories were jarred loose in April Rose's mind, and she remembered the stories about Cedric and the bird in the cage, and how Rusty bought the bird to set it free. She remembered Cedric's broken leg, and how Rusty taught him how to ride horses.

"Oh....my father told me stories about you!" April Rose exclaimed. "He was so fond of you."

Cedric grinned, and then he replied, "I'm not so sure that all those stories were good ones, but hopefully you remember the ones that are."

"Oh, but they all were---and now I can truly say that I appreciate them," April Rose said earnestly. "I ran away too because I didn't trust the Prince."

"Well, my dear, my heart goes out to you because I totally understand what causes people to do that. And I'm thankful you are here now," Cedric told her. "I look forward to speaking with you again. Let me introduce you to my family."

He walked to a nearby table and escorted a lady and two children back to the Prince's table. "This is my wife, Channah, and my children Talia and Gilead."

April Rose saw a woman with dark wavy hair and very dark eyes, and a girl and boy.

Their eyes were very dark like their mother's but the boy's hair was like his father's. "I am so glad to meet you," said April Rose. The girl was seven years old and the boy was ten, for Cedric had married later in life than his friend Rusty. (And he was several years younger than Rusty.)

"My father will be so excited when I tell him that I met you and your family," said April Rose.

"We will have you come to dinner while you are here," said Channah, and April Rose thanked her and Cedric, and shook the children's hands. And then there was an announcement about special fireworks, and everyone began to move over to the area where they could see these better. April Rose said goodbyes to Cedric and his family and went to find Lily again.

She and Lily took their chairs to the viewing area and sat by each other to watch. The dazzling elaborate fireworks displays spread out in many colors and there were some that exhibited special designs. The last one was a golden rose. That one drew the most applause, and April Rose knew it had been designed just for her, for this occasion.

At the conclusion of this special evening's events, the Prince sang to April Rose in his vibrant voice, and this is what he sang:

"I rejoice over you with singing; I love you with all of my heart. Now you belong to me; we will never, no never part. From this day on, you are my treasure. From this day on, you are my child."

April Rose stood close to the Prince as he sang, looking at his face, and she was enthralled. When he was finished, he held out his arms to her again, and she was enfolded in his loving embrace.

"Come with me," he said then, "I want to show you my river. You can come too, Lily."

So Lily accompanied April Rose and the Prince as they walked into the castle and through its great hallway until they reached the other side and went out through other doors.

And there April Rose saw a great river flowing with water so pure that its color was a deep blue-green; and along its shores there was clean white sand though the water was not salty.

"Go and try it out," said the Prince to April Rose and Lily. "In my dress?" asked April Rose. "Yes," said the Prince smiling. "Watch what happens."

So April Rose and Lily took off their shoes and waded in. The cool water was so refreshing that they swam up to their necks, looking at each other and laughing. When they finally climbed out, they discovered that their hair and their dresses were immediately dry again.

"Another one of my surprises," said the Prince, as he took their hands and they walked back.

Chapter 18

When they reached the castle, Mercy greeted them. The Prince asked Mercy to show April Rose her room and asked if Lily would like to join her. She declined, and said that she must go home now, but that she would come and see it another day. Lily and April Rose said goodnight, and Lily went back through the castle to the outer doors.

The Prince kissed April Rose affectionately on the top of her head, and then he went to his princely quarters. Mercy escorted April Rose to another wing of the palace.

This wing had windows which looked out over the Prince's garden, and April Rose was so pleased to see that. Mercy led April to the room which would be hers, and opened the door.

April Rose was delighted at the sight of this room; the walls were decorated with trailing flowers, and the wood furniture pieces had flowers painted on them as well. It was quaint, like the style found in a Victorian home in Europe.

There was a rose-embroidered nightgown and a pair of rose satin slippers by the bed. And on the bed, there was a golden book.

"That is a gift from the prince to you," said Mercy, indicating the book. "It is the most important gift, as it is the book of his promises. You will need to start reading this right away. It is protection for your mind, against the enemy."

"The enemy?" April Rose asked in consternation. "I thought I was safe here."

"Oh, you are," said Mercy in explanation. "This is preparation for when you go to other places."

"I certainly don't want to go to any other place," said April Rose emphatically.

"No, I'm sure you don't, after what you have been exposed to," said Mercy sympathetically. "Now get some rest, for this has been a long day for you."

"Yes, thank you," said April Rose gratefully, and Mercy said good night and departed to her own room.

April Rose hung her dress in the elegant wooden wardrobe and put her shoes on a shelf inside this. There was an ornate vanity with a mirror and a pink marble top. A hairbrush and a hand mirror lay on the top of this vanity, and a glass tray for her ring. She placed her crown by this. She slipped on the nightgown and tried on the slippers. They fit her perfectly and the fabric of the gown was soft.

She found all of her old clothes in a drawer at the bottom of the wardrobe. They had been washed for her and smelled like roses. She searched the pockets and found the keys. The keys were both there---her father's car key and the bronze key which had brought her to this place.

She looked again in the wardrobe where she had hung the dress and saw there were several other dresses in there. There were more underclothes in another drawer. Everything had been taken care of, and she looked around the room gratefully. The Prince was so kind.

She pulled down the white covers on the bed and climbed in, holding her golden book of promises. She read a few of these, and then laid the book carefully on the nightstand and blew out the flame of the lamp. For a few minutes, she relived the day in her thoughts, and then fell asleep. It was a deep sleep, for at last, her soul was at peace; she had found her Prince.

There were more surprises waiting for her in the morning. The lady named Saphire, who she had met when she first came to the Kingdom of Grace, arrived to have breakfast with April Rose. They sat at a table in the wide hallway by the windows that overlooked the Prince's garden. They had lemon and cream cheese muffins, milk and tea for their breakfast, and then they read together in the Prince's book of promises.

Saphire encouraged her to read from this book every morning and every evening, and April Rose promised herself that she would do this, since the Prince wished her to. After all, these were his pledges to her, and to everyone who belonged to him. It would be very ungrateful to neglect such a wonderful gift.

After April dressed, she went down to the Prince's garden, and there he was, waiting for her. She ran to him and hugged him, and he also put his arms around her and held her close. Now she could not bear the thought of living without his love. Again, she thanked him for rescuing her, and for laying down his life to give her this healing, and again she told him that she loved him.

This pleased him so much that radiant light began to come from his face. "Why does your face light up so much?" she asked him and he replied that joy is an energy and it radiates from within. "My joy is your love for me," he said. "It was in anticipation of this joy that I was able to endure what I did."

Her face showed the grief she felt at what he had suffered on her account. "May I---may I see your scars?" she asked timidly, for fear of offending him by her request.

His answer was to unbutton the placket of his tunic and open it enough that she could see the dark area of an ugly scar on his upper torso. He took her hand and gently pressed her fingers into the dark recession on his chest. She felt the damaged uneven skin that would never be smooth again, and her eyes began to fill with tears.

"This is the proof that I love you," he said. "And I am full of joy that you are with me now. I have waited so long for you to trust me."

"I'm so sorry," she said humbly. "I was so wrong to hate you."

He took her hand in response and kissed it. "I forgive everything," he said. "And now you must forgive others who hate you and hurt you because they don't know what love really is."

"I will do my best, although it may be hard," she said. "You will help me with that, won't you?"

"Yes," said the Prince. "I will also give you a trainer. He will be your constant help. You will meet him soon; his name is Sir Guide. He will guide you into discerning truth from lies."

"Is he like you?" she asked the Prince, for she really wanted only the Prince's guidance.

"He is very much like me," said the Prince, smiling.

"We have exactly the same thoughts, and our hearts are the same," the Prince assured her. "Whatever I sense and feel is exactly what Sir Guide will teach you and reveal to you."

"Oh," said April Rose in relief, though she did not fully understand how this could be.

So they walked through the garden for a while, arm in arm, and the Prince shared many secrets with her about her past and about her father and mother's past. She was elated to discover many things she had not known, that revealed the truth about the Prince.

He told her that it was he who named her; that he had given the name to her parents. "You are not just named after a flower," he said, "Although I do love roses, as you can tell. But there is a deeper meaning. I knew there would come a day when you would realize part of you was dead because of the sin-sickness inside you. Just as I came alive again, then my antidote would cause you to rise again from death into a new life."

This new understanding flooded her mind. *April Rose!* She thought to herself---April rose from the dead---and that is what has happened.

"Yes," said the Prince. "Truly, that is what has happened, and it gives me great joy."

And then Lily met them at the gate, for their training would begin.

The Prince had arranged for Lily to participate in the training he would begin for April Rose. "You will both need some different clothing. Let's go back to the palace and you can change into attire more suited for what you will be doing," said the Prince, and he began walking with them up the steps from the garden into the palace.

"What will we be doing?" asked April Rose.

"Horseback riding," said the Prince. "Trust that it will be useful for you."

April Rose had never been on a horse, but she knew her father had been very fond of horses when he was a boy. So she was nervous but excited at the prospect.

Lily had never ridden a horse either, but she was very willing to learn. When they went in, Mercy appeared with riding pants and shirts for the girls. She also had leather boots for them to wear.

The girls changed into these clothes and were very comfortable in them. The pants were a buckskin color and they were soft and supple like doeskin. The shirts were long loose tunics, made of a woven fabric like muslin, with cuffs that buttoned, and an opening that tied with a leather string. The boots were made of soft tan leather, with a black sole and heel.

Sir Guide came into the room where they were waiting, and the Prince introduced him to the girls.

Sir Guide walked with the girls out of the palace and to the stables. Sir Guide was tall and his skin was dark like ebony wood. When he smiled, his eyes twinkled and his teeth were very white next to his dark skin. He wore a loose colorful tunic of red, orange, blue, and gold colors and he wore loose navy pants and brown sandals. His hair was dark and closely shaved. Lily knew him already, and April Rose felt as if she already did.

He began to tell them about the horses they would meet, and about their personalities, and he made them laugh with his descriptions of the horses' particular and peculiar habits.

The first thing they would do was to win their horse's trust; they would go to the stables and spend time with the horses they would be riding.

April Rose would be riding a dark brown Morgan horse named Raziella, which means secrets, and Lily would be riding a Palomino quarter horse with a gold coat and white mane and tail. Lily's horse was named Zahavah, which means gold.

The girls would only be watching and observing the horses today.

"It takes calmness and patience to work with horses," said Sir Guide. "So you can't react quickly or do anything sneaky. It will also require gentle firmness; they need to know you are the leader. Then both you and the horse develop confidence."

"You will need to discover how to interact with your horse in a way that builds trust," Sir Guide told the girls. "Some horses will like to be hugged around the neck or kissed on the nose, and some will prefer a soft stroke on their foreheads or a rub under the jaw," Sir Guide explained. "You can tell if a horse is experiencing anxiety by tail swishing, raising the head or prancing."

So April Rose and Lily sat on the ground by the pasture for a while and watched the two horses, Raziella and Zahavah, as they walked around and interacted with each other.

Sir Guide had brought treats for the girls to give their horses. "Horses do have preferences," he said as he showed the girls the apples and carrots he had brought. "You will have to discover which one they like the best, or if they like both equally."

He went in the corral with the girls as they approached the horses. "You don't want to approach them head-on," he advised the girls. "Approach from the side and don't make eye contact. Then hold out your hand and let the horse sniff you."

The girls both followed his instructions, and after a little while, they gave the horses their treats. The two horses liked both the apples and the carrots and ate all that Sir Guide had brought.

"That will be all for today," said Sir Guide. "But building trust is an important step that cannot be rushed," he reassured the girls.

Then he led April Rose and Lily back to the palace for the next part of their training.

Chapter 19

Lily and April Rose had lunch together by April's room and Lily admired her room very much. "And it is right by the Prince's garden," said April Rose. "I love that I can see it so often."

When they were through with their lunch, they went down to the garden and sat by the water fountain. They were waiting for Sir Guide to come back for their next lesson. They had no idea what it would be, so they played guessing games.

Lily won that game, for she had guessed singing, and that is what Sir Guide had in mind. But he had brought two other students who would participate in this lesson---a younger boy named Amos, and a younger girl named Dulcie.

April Rose began to learn various songs of the Kingdom, and to weave harmonies in and out of the melody. This was something new for her.

Sir Guide also let them choose an instrument to try. Lily chose a mandolin, and April chose a flute that looked like a duduk. Amos wanted to try the darbuka drum, and Dulcie chose a percussion instrument with cymbals like a tambourine.

They laughed at themselves with their awkward

attempts with these instruments, but Sir Guide kept encouraging and instructing and giving them confidence to try.

There were archery lessons, and swimming times in the river, and gardening. They also worked at exercises to strengthen their muscles, and had dancing lessons which were very vigorous. Some days they brought easels into the garden and they painted flowers with water colors. On other days, they helped to bake the scones and tarts that were served on special occasions.

Sometimes Sir Guide brought Lily and April Rose further down the river where the water was much deeper. From here they went canoeing together in a wooden canoe, paddling down the river.

One afternoon, Sir Guide suggested taking a trip to the village so that April Rose could meet Lily's family. And so they did, bringing some tarts they had made, a flower bouquet from the Prince's garden, and two of their best paintings to give to Lily's mother and father.

When they got close enough to Lily's home, her younger brothers and sisters ran to meet the girls, hugging them both, and practically dragged them back to the house. Lily's mother hugged April Rose too, and treated her as family. Lily's father was not home yet; he was farming in the fields.

Lily's siblings promptly tried the tarts but Lily saved some for her father before they ate them all. Lily's mother put the bouquet in a vase and set it in the center of their dining table. She admired their flower paintings and set them on the top of a pie safe until they could frame them and hang them.

"They're very beautiful, Lily and April," said Lily's mother. "I am so proud of you both. April Rose, we are so happy to finally meet you. Lily has spoken so much about you."

April Rose said thank you and she sensed that she was blushing, but no one seemed to notice. This home feels safe, she thought to herself.

Lily showed April Rose all around their house and all the rooms inside; there were three small sleeping areas on one side, a large living area, a kitchen area, and a larger sleeping room for Lily's parents. Behind their house, they had a barn for their farm animals and tools. They also had a chicken coop, and Lily went to look for eggs with April Rose. They found a few brown eggs and brought these to the kitchen, and then they went back and scattered feed for the chickens.

They had a dog that was a family friend and also protected the chickens from predators. He was friendly to April Rose and came for a petting.

"I don't know if he would fight a wolf, but he would definitely let us know if there was trouble," said Lily. "He would kill a snake if he had to."

"Oh, do they have snakes here?" asked April Rose, and she thought of the dancing animals she had seen when she crossed the little bridge. They had seemed so harmless and gentle.

"If they do, they came from the evil kingdom," said Lily. "All the predators are from there. There are no viper pits or broods of snakes here in the Kingdom of Grace."

"Something puzzling happened when I first came here," said April Rose, and she described how she ate one of the pink fruits with peelings similar to a banana. "I didn't know what to do with the peeling, so I laid it on a rock. When I turned around to look back, it was already gone."

Lily smiled. "The little mongoose came out of his hole and took it. They eat those peelings here," Lily explained. "They will even politely take the peeling from your hands if you give it to them."

Lily's siblings showed April Rose their schoolwork; the youngest were learning to read and write and the older ones were learning to do math problems and practical applications of math. "As soon as we are finished, we can go play," the youngest told April Rose.

"What do you play?" April Rose asked her.

"Hide and seek in the barn," she answered. "And we have a big rope swing in the tree."

"Oh, that sounds like fun," said April Rose. She had never had the experience of playing with any siblings, or even any cousins.

"You can play with us," said the littlest girl, whose name was Kerensa.

"Okay," agreed April Rose. "I will."

With that promise, the children sped through their work and finished as soon as possible. Then the youngest, Kerensa, and the next youngest child, Thaddeus, triumphantly took April Rose's hands and pulled her to the barn. Lily followed with her other siblings, Giovanna and Reuben.

Lily and April Rose played hide and seek with the children, and April Rose laughed and ran so much that she was out of breath. Then they took turns in the tree swing.

After that, the children showed April Rose how they jumped from the hay loft into a pile of hay by the barn. April Rose tried it, too, and laughed as she slid down the hay pile.

"Your father won't mind that we scattered some of the hay?" asked April Rose with some concern as she looked at where they had been jumping and sliding.

"Not if we get the pitchfork and rake it back," said Lily. "We had better stop and do that now."

So all of the children, as well as April Rose and Lily, helped to put the hay back where it belonged, and Lily put some hay in the feeding troughs in the barn. "The oxen will be hungry when they come back from the fields," she explained to April Rose.

Then they all went to the well and Lily drew enough water for all of them to wash their hands and faces. There was a washtub and soap by the well for this purpose. Lily inspected the hands and faces of the two younger children, and insisted that they wash again.

"They get in too much of a hurry," said Lily, "and then they put dirt on the towel."

When this was done to Lily's satisfaction, she handed the younger ones the towel that was hanging close by. The younger ones barely dried their hands and faces before they were running to the house. Giovanna and Reuben walked back slowly with Lily and April Rose, trying hard to have a more grown-up conversation with April Rose.

These two were in that in-between stage; too old to run and scream, but still too young to give up playing just yet.

The evening meal was almost ready to be served, and all of the children had a particular role in the preparation. The two youngest cleaned the table and set out all the plates and cups and utensils. Giovanna and Reuben sliced the bread and then brought bowls of food to the table, and Lily's job was to fill each cup from a pitcher.

Lily's father came in, after he had brought the work animals to the barn and given them water. When he walked in, the younger children ran to him and hugged his legs. "What's this?" he asked with a smile. "We have company?"

The younger children yelled, "April Rose!" before anyone else could announce her name.

The father laughed and said "Say that just a little quieter, so I can understand you." As the youngest ones repeated her name more slowly, the father looked at April Rose and smiled. "Welcome, April Rose," he said. "We are very pleased that you have come. We are glad to have you in our home."

"Thank you sir," April Rose answered, and he nodded acknowledgement of her gratitude.

"Well, shall we sit down and eat?" he asked, and then he said, "Oh, but there's one thing I forgot."

Then he went to Lily's mother and kissed her. The two youngest children reacted with comical antics and funny expressions as they pretended to be embarrassed. (And frankly, I'm not sure if the older children actually were!)

"Oh, so you're ashamed that I kissed your lovely mother?" the father said teasingly. Then he smiled and kissed their mother again, and she laughed at the children's silly reactions.

"Now we can sit down to have our supper," the father said with a laughing smile. The father said a blessing over the food, their home, and over each person there. Then the food was passed around the table until everyone had a portion of each dish.

April Rose noticed how this father gave each child a chance to participate in the conversation at the meal, and treated each one with great dignity. He listened and considered carefully what each one said and commented respectfully.

When the meal was over, Lily's mother suggested that Lily escort April Rose back to the palace.

"Giovanna and Reuben are old enough to help with the dishes," she told Lily.

So it was decided, and that was how the day ended. The two girls walked back to the palace, and then said their goodbyes, and Lily went home.

The Prince was waiting in his garden to see April Rose that evening, and they talked. "How did you enjoy Lily's family?" he asked April Rose.

"Oh, it was so much fun," said April Rose. "I enjoyed being with them very much."

The Prince smiled and took her arm and they walked around the garden lit by torches and the moonlight. "I'm very glad," said the Prince. Then he kissed her good night, for he could tell she was extremely tired.

April Rose slept extra well that night, though she dreamed of jumping into piles of hay.

Chapter 20

April Rose and Lily had learned much about their horses; they knew how to groom them and care for them, and how to properly put the bridle and saddle on them. They were with the horses for a while each day, and the horses now affectionately waited for their visits. The girls were both learning to ride, under Sir Guide's tutelage.

And so the days passed so pleasantly---and April Rose realized she was learning to live again. She was learning to love again.

The Prince came often to hear them sing, and he enjoyed it immensely. When he walked with April Rose in the morning---which was her most favorite thing of all---he told her that she was his beautiful rose that bloomed, and the cherished nightingale of his garden.

She loved to hear him say that. One morning she mustered the courage to ask if he would sing with her, and to her surprise, it pleased him greatly that she had asked. So they sang together and then she sang to the Prince---just for him. It was a song of thanksgiving. Her heart was so full of gratitude for his love that she had to express it in a song. She sang of what his love meant to her.

The Prince's face was full of the light of his joy when she sang to him. "You give me so much joy, April Rose, my beautiful daughter," he told her and he gently hugged her. "Thank you for that song---I treasure it very much."

Sometimes at night when they went for a walk together in the garden, April Rose would ask the Prince to sing his lullaby song to her again before she went to bed. And he always did.

One morning when she met with the Prince in his garden, he told her that he was very pleased with all that she was learning, and he hugged her as he often did.

Then he looked her in the eyes and held her gaze as he said something of utmost importance: "April Rose, I think it is time that you and Lily go on a mission of mine."

Her eyes registered shock and she stumbled on her words. "What---what do you mean?"

"I mean," he said, "that I want you to rescue someone else as you have been rescued."

"Does that mean I have to go away from here?" she asked and she began to tremble. "Don't ask me to leave you---I can't. You are my life." Tears began to form in her eyes and roll down her face.

The Prince looked at her compassionately and he replied, "The love I give to you is meant to share. My life in you expands---it does not contract--- when you share it with someone else," he told her. "As for going away, even when you cannot see me, I am with you."

"If you want me to, I will," she said timidly. "But I don't want to."

"At least you are honest with me," he said smiling. "I don't always ask easy things." He paused and looked intently into her eyes. "If I only did that," he continued, "Your trust in me would not grow."

"Where are we going?" she asked him. "And will we be going by ourselves?"

"No, you will not be by yourselves," he answered. "I have someone appointed to go with you. In fact, it will be two people and they will lead the way."

April Rose looked greatly relieved to hear those words, just as the Prince knew she would be. He explained that she and Lily would be applying for work as teachers in a girls' boarding school in an area bordering the evil prince's kingdom. They would be teaching young children to read and write and do basic math. That was another relief for April Rose. She felt confident about teaching young children, but not so much about older ones.

"The problem with this boarding school," said the Prince, "Is that it has been infiltrated by evil and the children are at risk---especially one girl named Elora. She is the one most ready to meet me, and I have heard her tears and longing. Will you go and bring her back to me?"

"Yes," said April Rose. "I will, if you instruct me every step of the way."

"Just as I did for you in the tunnel, I will do for you now," assured the Prince. "I will be with you and I will not forsake you."

"Does Lily already know?" asked April Rose.

"Yes, she does. I have talked it all over with her and her parents, and they have agreed to let her go. Lily said yes also," the Prince replied.

"When I tell Elora about you," April Rose asked rather hesitantly, "What name shall I tell her? Who shall I say sent me? You have not told me your name as the Prince."

The Prince looked at April Rose with such love. "I have been waiting for you to ask me. My name here means Victory. You may tell her that the one who is Victory has sent you."

And so it was settled, and preparations were made.

April Rose and Lily were introduced to the young married couple who would be traveling with them. Their names were Keturah and Aziel, and they were from a country across the sea. They spoke the same language as those in the Kingdom of Grace, but with a particular accent. However, it would not be unusual in the area they would be going into, and would actually serve as an asset.

Keturah and Aziel knew the culture of the city they would be working in, and could easily blend in as migrant workers. They would drive a stagecoach there, pretending to have that sort of vocation, and April Rose and Lily would travel with them as their business customers.

Once there, Keturah and Aziel could continue to assume the role of stagecoach entrepreneurs and possibly they could discover valuable clues while in the process of driving people around the city. It was a port city, well known for diverse trades and a constantly fluctuating population.

Lily and April Rose began to be excited although nervous, and Mercy helped them pack.

They would need clothing appropriate for teachers in that area, as well as traveling clothes. So they each had a small suitcase with the necessary items, and they carefully packed their gold books of promises in a small hidden compartment within each suitcase. The Prince had already warned Lily and April Rose of the hostility in this area towards him and his kingdom.

They would have to remain constantly on guard, especially if anyone from the evil prince's kingdom appeared in that region.

"Above all," said the Prince to April Rose, "Do not lose your key or allow anyone to take it from you, not under any circumstances."

His sternness as he spoke these words was alarming to her, but she knew that he was firmly emphasizing the seriousness of his command.

"Yes, sir," she answered him, and he looked approvingly at her. "You should go to bed early and get some rest," he urged her then. "I will meet you in the garden in the morning."

"May we swim in the river for just a little bit?" April Rose asked because of the soothing nature of the river. She felt this too would be good preparation.

"Yes, you certainly may," said the Prince and the light of his face shone on April Rose.

April Rose said thank you and then she and Lily ran down to the river and waded in. They began to swim as the sun was setting, and as they swam, the sun went down.

They knew that it might be their last relaxing time for a while, so they enjoyed the luxury. Finally they both realized that it was time to end this, and they pushed against the flow of the water and stepped out of the river.

Lily returned home to sleep in her own bed one more time before the trip. April Rose went to her room in the palace.

April Rose woke up before the sun had come up and lay there thinking. She decided to get up and get dressed and go to the garden earlier than she usually did. The prince was already there, waiting for her. "You always know exactly what I will do," she remarked to the Prince in her amazement.

"I'm always aware of you," he told her. He hugged April Rose and they sat together and watched the sun come up. Then they went back into the palace and had breakfast with Saphire and Mercy.

Lily arrived with her family, and many friends from the village and the palace gathered to bid them farewell and to send them on their way with some encouraging words.

Mercy had packed food for the girls and their two companions in a small trunk and when everything was packed and ready, they began to load the stagecoach. Keturah and Aziel loaded the girls' suitcases, and their own, as well as the food and supplies for the horses.

There were many hugs from Lily's family for the girls, and from their friends; and then the Prince hugged each of them.

Last, Sir Guide opened a small bag of something and after he reached in and took some of the contents out, he opened his hand and sprinkled this over the girls and the young couple with them.

It was the golden lacy stuff that hung from the trees; and when he sprinkled it on them, April Rose recognized that it smelled like incense.

"This is my blessing on your mission," said Sir Guide, and then the girls entered the coach.

Chapter 21

April Rose was not prepared for the lurching of the coach as the wheels rolled and bumped over dirt trails. She hoped that she could get used to it and not succumb to nausea. Her friend Lily gave her a concerned look.

At least there was more scenery to look at than that last horrid stagecoach ride in the evil prince's realm. This landscape was nothing like the gray and dreary wilderness of the evil prince's kingdom.

So she focused on observing her surroundings out of the stage coach windows, and tried to keep her mind off of the jolting and swaying of the carriage.

This certainly wasn't the horses' fault; they were a good pair of steady quarter horses who responded well to directions and kept an even consistent pace. And there was a trail here, beaten down by former travelers in wagons and coaches.

With the palace and the village behind them, they were passing through fields on either side of the trail. The crops in these fields around them on both sides, looked something like wheat and it was a golden brown color. Scattered among these fields were green grassy patches here and there.

After a little while, they entered an area with waving green grasses and low rolling hills. This went on for some time, and it felt like a sea of grass. The wind blew the grass in long ripples that reminded April Rose of waves on the sea. She could see mountains far in the distance.

They stopped by a small wood to have their lunch and to let the horses rest for a little while. Aziel went into the woods to see if he could find a small stream. He did, and brought the horses to drink at the stream. Then he returned and Lily, April Rose, and Keturah went in search of the stream. It was nice to leave the cramped quarters of the coach for a few minutes and take a short walk.

The stream was narrow and winding as it went on its way through the wood, and its bed had rocks all along the bottom. Here the water was shallow but swiftly flowing. They could not locate where the stream came from or where it was going. There was no time to explore this any further; they had to return to the coach. They must reach the city of their destination in the shortest possible time.

Just as they came out of the woods, a great dark shadow came over them. April Rose looked up and screamed; there were huge talons descending towards her. A monstrous bird was just over them and it screamed shrilly as it swooped down on them. It almost made her heart stop. Aziel was already running to the coach and he snatched up his bow and arrow, notched it and ran until he was almost underneath the great bird. He took aim and let the arrow fly and it pierced the neck of the bird.

"Back into the woods!" he yelled at the girls, for in a minute the bird was falling. There was a terrible scream from the bird as it fell from the sky and a great crash on the ground not far from where the girls had just been standing.

The horses had been tethered to the back of the stagecoach to graze, and it was a good thing that they were, for they might have bolted at the sight of the bird. They showed evidence of their terror by shaking their heads and pawing at the ground. Aziel went to calm them down by speaking gently and rubbing their heads.

April Rose could not believe what she saw lying there on the ground. "What is this thing?" she asked in dreadful horror. "It is a bird of prey," Lily informed her as she hugged her friend to console her. April Rose was much shaken, but her friend's calmness helped to ease her frightful distress.

As they walked back to the coach, April Rose felt compelled to thank Aziel for his quick reaction and good aim. He was quite matter-of-fact about the incident; he didn't think he had done anything beyond duty. But his next remark caught April Rose by surprise.

"You should have seen your father with a bow! Now that was a fine aim," he said in a tone of great admiration. "Your father could take down one of those wicked creatures from yards away."

April Rose was so startled that she couldn't think for a moment. She just stood there and finally blurted out, "You knew my father?"

Aziel affirmed that he did indeed know her father, though he had only been a boy when Rusty was one of the palace archers. "We boys all looked up to Rusty for his skill with a bow," Aziel told her. "Once there was a flock of those birds that had swarmed the palace walls, and Rusty and the other archers took them all down."

"Did you live at the palace?" April Rose asked next, trying to visualize a timeline in her mind.

"No," Aziel replied. "But I did get to stay there on occasion. We were a merchant family; we traveled and traded goods from across the sea. After my family met the Prince, we pledged our allegiance to him. Several years went by and it was no longer safe for us to remain in our own country, so we came and lived in the village. Sir Guide trained me and others in archery."

Keturah was looking up at the sky, and reminded them all of the passing time. "We must get back on the road," she warned.

Aziel quickly turned and harnessed the horses again to the carriage, while the girls climbed back into the coach. Keturah made sure they had not left anything behind, and then she climbed onto the outside seat of the carriage. Aziel made one last adjustment on the bridles, and climbed up beside Keturah.

They set out again on the road to the distant city of Gruelington.

There were no other mishaps that day, and they were now close to the mountain range they had seen in the distance and through which they must now go. But it was almost night time, and Aziel knew they must look for a place to shelter during the night.

When they came close to the mountain range, they drove alongside it until a canyon was spotted in between the mountains. Here the stagecoach was halted and Aziel climbed down.

He took his bow and quiver, and went into the canyon while the others waited to see what he found. Keturah told the girls that he was looking for a cave. April Rose had not even thought about where they would sleep; but a cave? That was not in her repertoire of experiences!

Well, it would be added, she realized when Aziel came back and told them he had found the perfect place for them to shelter for the night---in a cave. Whether she wanted to or not, April Rose would have to sleep in a cave on this trip. Aziel returned to his driver's seat on the coach, and turned the horses into the canyon.

The walls of the canyon were tall and mysterious, preventing outside vision. They soon noticed that the wind was a frequent visitor to this canyon, as it swayed the stagecoach and made eerie whistling sounds on its way through. It added to the already isolated and lonely feeling of this place.

Now the sun was beginning to go down and it made quite a spectacle on the walls of the canyon, and the sky overhead became orange and pink. April Rose observed that the walls of this canyon almost had a striped effect from the sediment layers which developed over time.

Water had carved this canyon, but when they arrived at the site of the cave, they saw they would not be in danger from flash flooding. There was a steep embankment up to the dark entrance of the cave, and the cave was much higher than the floor of the canyon.

Aziel decided that the stagecoach should be left at a small plateau of the embankment, which was on a lower level, and they could take the horses on up into the cave with them. They disembarked and Aziel led the horses pulling the stagecoach up to this plateau level, and there he disconnected the horses from the coach.

Then Keturah and the girls followed and went up the steep incline to meet up with Aziel. From there, Keturah and Aziel led the horses up the steepest part to the level of the cave. Lily and April Rose followed, being very grateful for the boots which Mercy had provided for this trip. The sturdy heels of these boots kept them from sliding as much.

"Watch out for snakes," Lily advised April Rose, for there were rocks here and there on this naturally terraced slope.

They arrived at the cave shortly before the last bit of daylight disappeared behind the canyon walls, and Keturah lit a lantern and held it aloft so that they could see what to do next.

Aziel lit another lantern and went into the cave. He had a satisfied look when he came out. "It's quite large, and the horses will fit inside," he said.

Holding the lantern high, he led one of the horses inside, and Keturah followed him with the other horse. She had handed her lantern to Lily, so that Lily and April Rose could come after them without being in the dark.

Their shadows looked bizarre and ghostly on the walls of the cave, but they felt safe enough and were all grateful for a place to sleep. Mercy had packed bedrolls in the coach, which they had carried up on their backs, as well as food and the materials to start a fire.

After a thorough examination of the cave for any poisonous creatures revealed none, they laid out their bedrolls, while Aziel began a fire. Supper was a simple meal, with water from the stream they had found in the woods. Afterward, Lily and April Rose read from the gold book of promises by the firelight and thought of the Prince. Those thoughts always reassured them.

Chapter 22

The sunrise was dazzling and resplendent in the canyon. Sunlight came bursting into the entrance of the cave with a brilliance that woke up everyone sleeping on the cave floor. April Rose got up and went to stand in the doorway of the cave to watch the sunlight begin to light up the canyon walls. Lily got up too and came to the entrance, looking out and shielding her eyes with her hand.

The light spread like a slow moving wave over the walls, illuminating the chiseled out shapes that stood like statues in the canyon. The light overtook every shadow in its quest, spreading out until it engulfed every dark shape. It looked like fire as it moved through the tops of the few scattered tall thin evergreen trees that grew on the sides.

Aziel and Keturah came to stand and watch too, as the last of the shadows disappeared. When they turned back into the cave, April Rose knew it was time to pack up and move on.

All four ate a quick breakfast and read together from the gold book of promises. Then bedrolls were quickly dissembled and packed up as well as the provisions of food. Aziel and Keturah led the horses down the steep slope to the plateau, and harnessed them to the stagecoach. They went very slowly down the descent. Aziel and Keturah did not get on the coach, but walked on the sides of the horses, guiding them by the bridles.

Finally they reached the bottom of the canyon and began the trip out of it and through to the other side. A buzzard flew overhead and its shadow passed over them in the sunlight. The bird circled and soared away in another direction. April Rose was thankful it was only a buzzard and not another bird of gigantic proportions.

The ground was at last level enough that they could once again ride on the stagecoach, so April Rose and Lily got in and Aziel and Keturah also resumed their driver's seats.

They came out of the canyon into what looked like prairie, and Aziel knew there would be a water source not far away, as there was more green grass and vegetation growing here.

Soon they saw a creek winding its way through the plain, and Aziel was certain that it would continue on into a small lake. But this creek was enough for their needs. The horses were unharnessed again and taken to drink and April Rose and Lily filled all the canteens with water. They splashed their faces to help remove some of the dust from traveling and from sleeping in a cave.

The stagecoach was equipped with roll-down shades instead of glass for the windows. These were meant to keep out dust, but they also made the coach very stuffy and hot. It seemed best to endure the dust.

Now they must go on, so they entered the hot dusty stagecoach once more, hoping this was the last part of the journey. But as yet, there was no city in sight.

The next part of the trip went through a large wood, and the shade it offered was welcomed.

This forest was not nearly as dark and sinister as the one that April Rose had encountered on that gruesome journey with the malevolent Hanson.

Here, the trees were spread apart and shafts of light came through, so that there was a much friendlier atmosphere. April Rose watched the birds flying overhead and talking to each other in the tops of the trees. Small woodland inhabitants could be seen creeping furtively in the green mossy places below. Yet it seemed to April Rose that here she did not sense stealthy creatures stalking her. The carriage rolled on through the shady greenery at a peaceful pace, stopping only now and then to rest the horses and to get water or for the girls to walk about for a few minutes.

There was another mountain range more to their right in the landscape. Lily surmised that this must be the border between this region and the evil prince's kingdom. One of their stops was by a little mountain stream that came running down from the mountains and went through the wood. Except for insects and the chatter of birds, it was very quiet and they could hear the rushing of the stream.

The horses found enjoyment in this stream and the cool water seemed to refresh their spirits. Lily and April Rose went close to the stream also and washed their faces again. The trees nearby were clustered together overshadowing the stream so it was darker here. Suddenly there was a slight rustle in the bushes across from where they knelt. Lily and April Rose kept very still, listening and watching. They didn't want to panic and run.

They looked at each other and nodded and then slowly stood and began to move away from the stream. April Rose thought she saw a glimpse of a face---a human face---but only for a brief moment and then she doubted herself. That person would have to be extremely short or----that person would have to be a child! Why would a child be out in the woods alone?

She said nothing until she and Lily were back in the coach, and then she told Lily what she thought she saw. Lily had not seen that, so perhaps she was imagining it, April Rose reasoned inwardly. She put that thought aside and concentrated on the rest of the journey and its scenery.

When they emerged from the wood at last, they were again riding through what looked like a prairie with waving grasses, and rolling hills. This seemed to go on forever, and then quite suddenly the trail veered closer to the mountain range, and they were heading into the valley, and there was the city before them.

The sun was beginning to set, and the air was colder now. This city also had a certain dark grim coldness about it; the atmosphere was not inviting or friendly. They were driving into it now, and April Rose looked around at this gloomy town and saw that the buildings were gray and weather beaten. There were no flowers or gardens anywhere.

They arrived at the boarding school, which was equally as dismal. The building was tall, plain, and square with darkened windows and an unpainted porch. This dark structure was as foreboding as the town itself seemed to be. If a city could have an entity, April Rose thought to herself, this one would definitely not be pleasant.

Lily squeezed April's hand; I am sure she was just as dismayed at their destination. April Rose said softly, "Well, the Prince didn't say it would be easy, but he is with us." Lily nodded.

The coach drove to the side of the porch, and Aziel stopped and climbed down. He began taking the girls' luggage off the coach and set it on the porch. Keturah looked at the girls and urged them to be bold and knock on the door.

It took a good bit of resolve to get out of that coach and do this. Lily and April Rose determinedly got out and slowly went to the door. April Rose began to knock briskly and then waited. There was a long pause, which made them even more reluctant, but at last the door opened.

"We are the new teachers, ma'am," Lily told the woman who stood there, looking them over rather disdainfully. The woman was tall with steely gray eyes and a pompous air. Her linen dress was dull gray, and her hair was gray and pulled up into a tight bun, and her expression was grim.

"Come in and fill out your papers," the woman said curtly, and she turned and began to walk away. Lily and April Rose went in and followed the tall austere woman into an office. April Rose filled out the paperwork according to Sir Guide's prior instructions, and Lily did the same on hers, while Aziel and Keturah brought their suitcases into the front room of the house.

It was well that Aziel and Keturah had discussed things before they arrived here, for the woman did not give the girls a chance to say goodbye. She told the girls to get their things and bring them up to their room on the second floor.

"The girls are in the dining room, and I suggest you go there immediately if you want to have any dinner," said the woman in a perfunctory tone.

So Lily and April Rose went up the flight of stairs and the woman followed them up partway and told them how to identify which room would be theirs. They brought their suitcases to this room, but didn't stay long to investigate, as the threat of no meal was too disheartening.

On the way down the stairs, they saw the girl who was likely the maid; she wore a white apron and cap. Their eyes met with this girl for only a second, but there was a kindred recognition. The Prince had not told them very much about Elora; could this be her?

They found the dining room on the ground floor, and all the girls were sitting at a long table, and eating silently. Lily and April Rose found a place to sit at an adjacent table, and the butler brought them each a plate of food. His expression was sullen and dour as he served them and poured their water. The food was tasteless and colorless and absolutely bland. April Rose found it hard to make herself eat it even though she was severely famished.

When the dinner time was up, the woman they had met first, who apparently functioned as the head mistress, came back into the room and stood watching as the girls got up and silently marched out of the room single file.

Then the woman addressed Lily and April Rose again and told them that the bathing room would be available only for half an hour after the girls were in their beds. Thankfully, this room was on the second floor, and the water was piped in, though it was not heated. They did not have any contact with any of their future pupils this night, but the girl dressed as a maid came upstairs after the students had gone to bed.

"I'll bring you a kettle of hot water for your bath," she said in a cordial manner. Lily and April Rose were very grateful. A bath in the big claw-foot bath tubs seemed a luxury after their dusty travel, and Lily and April were glad of it.

The maid came up twice with a kettle of hot water for each of their baths, and brought some mineral salts as well. She introduced herself as Phoebe. April Rose and Lily were grateful for her cordiality and her thoughtfulness, in a very cold atmosphere.

April Rose and Lily would have liked to talk more to her, but they were both extremely tired. It would have to wait until the next opportunity.

Phoebe told them that she had prepared their beds with fresh sheets, and she hoped it would be agreeable. Lily and April Rose thanked her and she gave a little curtsy and excused herself. So far, it seemed that Phoebe was the only amiable person in this place.

There was a slight rustle of whispering voices from the large room where the students slept, as April Rose and Lily walked by this room on the way to their own room.

After that, they heard no more, for they crawled into their beds and promptly fell asleep.

Chapter 23

The next morning when April Rose woke up, she was extremely disappointed to see that there was no window in her room. She felt for a moment as if she was in another prison. Before the feeling of gloom could overtake her, she quickly lit the lamp and took her gold book out of its hiding place, and read the promises of the Prince.

Nothing could change the stability of his promises, or the surety of his intentions. There was no power that could change the efficacy of what he had said. This then was what she must rely on for her peace and joy in the midst of a troubling shifting sort of situation. Yet the uneasiness she felt would most certainly keep her on guard and alert. She must be ever tuned in within herself to hear the voice of the Prince in her mind.

Lily was awake now, and also quickly read from the book of promises. Then they both carefully hid their books in the secret compartments within their suitcases. No one here must know that they were on an assignment for the Prince, for this might jeopardize the mission before it even started.

There was a rap at the door and the head mistress opened it. "Breakfast is at 7:00, and at 8:00 you will meet with the headmaster in his office," she said brusquely and then closed the door.

April Rose and Lily quickly got out of bed and began getting ready. April Rose wondered what she would do without an alarm clock, because there was no such thing here. Without a window, she could not depend on the sun either, to wake her. There was no time right now to figure it out, so she hurried to get dressed.

The students were already in the dining room and hardly looked up when April Rose and Lily arrived. The head mistress frowned because they were one minute late. What was the matter with these girls, April wondered. They looked so dull---as if they were in a stupor.

Breakfast was grits but without any butter or any sugar. There was very weak tea with no sugar or milk, and each girl received only one half of a slice of toast without any butter. They certainly did not believe in luxuries in this place.

April Rose looked at the colorless faces of the girls; they were pasty-white, and their clothes were gray and shapeless. She felt as if she was in a concentration camp, and the head mistress was the warden. She even began to wonder if smiling was outlawed, for she tried smiling at one of the girls and the girl only looked down at her plate.

There was a clock in this room and just now the hour bell rang to show that it was eight o'clock. Lily and April Rose left the table and went into the main hall in search of the headmaster's office. The hallway was dark, and the wood floor and wall paneling was very dark and shiny. They found the headmaster's office and knocked lightly on his door. There was a glass window in the office door, but it was green and very thick with a patterned design. They could not see anything in the room.

Lily and April Rose heard a gruff voice say, "Come in," and they obeyed. When they opened the door, they saw a short bald man sitting behind a large dark wood desk. He looked up at the girls and eyed them rather suspiciously, it seemed to them.

Then he pulled a paper from a desk drawer and with a peremptory gesture he handed it to the girls. "This is your schedule," he said. "Textbooks are in the classroom." He bent down and rifled through another drawer. "And this," he said as he handed them another paper with an attitude of restrained insolence, "is our policies, which you must abide by, or your employment will be swiftly terminated. You are responsible to know them, so I suggest you read it immediately."

He looked them over for a moment, and then tersely commanded: "You may go now."

Lily and April Rose turned to go, and then he spoke again: "Oh…and one more thing….there will be no snooping. You keep your nose out of any business that is not yours." His expression was very snide as he said this. April Rose tried not to show any reaction in her face whatsoever, and she wondered how successful she had been, as she walked out of the office.

Lily and April Rose looked at each other with an expression of dismay and consolation. How much more unpleasant could this environment become? They both hoped they would not find out.

The schedule was rigorous and allowed for no free time. These poor girls really were in a brutal harsh concentration camp of sorts! April Rose resolutely determined in her heart to look for a way to show kindness to these girls.

And so the day began with reading and listening to the girls stumble over words. They read in a dull monotone voice without any expression. April Rose decided that tomorrow's reading lesson would be very different and would involve some games. It was obvious that some of these little girls did not know the basic mechanics of reading very well at all. Perhaps a little fun would help.

Next there was writing, and some of the girls fell asleep over their writing tablets. These children went to bed at a reasonable time; why were they so listless? April Rose looked intently at them while they were writing. She and Lily moved around the room, observing. They both noticed that the girls became tense when they walked close to any of them.

One small girl actually cringed when April Rose came close to her. April Rose could only conclude one thing from that observation: these children must have been abused by former teachers. They were afraid of physical contact.

After writing, there was a math lesson, and this too was perfunctory and without any enthusiasm whatsoever. April Rose decided that this would not continue, either. Math should be an interesting puzzle to solve, or a riddle, not a total drudgery.

There was no recess for these children; they were barely allowed time to go to the toilet room. Lunch was brief, and no talking was allowed; then the children were sent back to the classroom and they were given fifteen minutes to rest at their desks.

After this, all the girls were assigned to chores at the institution. Some were sent to the kitchen to scrub pots and wash dishes; some were assigned to scrub floors, and others were sent to the large laundry room to wash clothes and bedding. They had to work until five o'clock, at which time dinner was served; then they had two hours in which to bathe and prepare for bed. They had to be in bed for eight o'clock with lights out.

What a horrible regimen, April Rose thought to herself. The amount of work time required from these girls outweighed the amount of instruction. And why was there no science or history---or exercise or art? This schedule was totally devoid of such things, and April Rose felt bitterly about the unfairness of the students' situation.

She chafed at the restrictions put upon her as a teacher to these children. April Rose resolved that somehow, she must give these children a taste of joy. She had no idea at present of how this could be accomplished, but she would ask the Prince. She was sure that he could arrange things for this opportunity, though it might seem impossible.

Lily and April Rose also looked for an opportunity to speak with the house maid, Phoebe. None presented itself this afternoon, but Lily and April Rose had decided to venture out and meet up with their friends, the carriage drivers. They agreed to pretend to have a shopping errand and the need to browse the stores in town.

That seemed like a reasonable chore, and they were thankful they had prearranged this meeting with Aziel and Keturah. Phones did not exist, so a regular means of communication would be difficult. Every meeting would have to be prearranged.

So Aziel and Keturah's stagecoach arrived at the boarding school that afternoon, and whisked the girls away before there could be any questioning.

Inside the coach, the girls breathed a sigh of relief. They could speak freely, as there were no other passengers. (This was another thing they had all agreed on) Keturah was seated inside with them, and they had rolled down the window shades for privacy during this meeting.

Lily and April Rose confided to Keturah about the weariness of the girls in the school, and the prison like atmosphere. Keturah was sympathetic and murmured her displeasure at the stringent ways of the school proceedings.

"There is definitely much evil going on in this city behind the scenes," she said in a low voice. "And I suspect that somehow these children are involved in it---but not by choice."

"But what could it be?" asked Lily with horror and consternation in her voice at the disturbing thought of involving innocent children in evil schemes.

"The enemy is crafty and devious," said Keturah. "Either he infiltrates and causes hate and division to allow for his take-over of the authority, or he uses the temptations of the flesh to seduce and weaken until there is so much indulgence that there is no resistance."

"What do you mean by hate and division?" asked April Rose.

"The enemy usually works through some kind of resentment already present," said Keturah.

"Whether it is ill-will between two people groups, jealousy of one group for another, or evil desire to subdue and dominate another group of people, the result is usually the same," she continued. "There will be outbreaks of violence, ruthless attacks, rioting and outrage."

"The town has been strangely quiet and passive," Keturah stated, "So I suspect it is the latter case--- that of indulgence in vices."

"But what shall we do about it?" wondered Lily.

"First we must find out what it is," Keturah replied. "Be very observant and listen carefully, and we will do the same."

"Let's continue to meet once a week and compare what we find out," suggested April Rose, and this day and time were agreed upon.

They could not go back without looking at the town, so Aziel drove the carriage through the business part of the town and they passed by its shops and offices, on its main street.

There was a dry goods store, a millinery shop, (the hat-maker's shop), a bakery, hotel and restaurant, a bank, a hardware store, a doctor's office with an apothecary office next to it, and of course a law office and jail. The girls noted that there was one tailor and seamstress shop, one cobbler's shop, a barber shop, a grocery, a butcher shop, and three saloons. On the outskirts of town, there was the typical blacksmith shop.

The girls decided that the closest thing to a variety store would be the dry goods store, so they went in and explored here for a few minutes, looking for colored paper and things that they could use for creative teaching with games. They purchased a small pack of paper and a pair of scissors, and then headed back to the boarding school.

Chapter 24

They arrived back at the school just in time for supper, which was not a pleasant ordeal. They saw that the girls were served some kind of thin gray gruel that smelled of onions. April Rose managed a few mouthfuls and that was all. She ate the half-slice of bread gratefully.

April Rose and Lily planned their lessons for the next day, using the colored paper to make simple illustrations for learning vowels and letters, and pieces for math games. No one questioned them about their shopping trip or seemed concerned that they had gone anywhere. They were very relieved over this.

They still had found no way to communicate with Phoebe, or with any of the students outside of the classroom. The stern head mistress seemed to always be around with a watchful eye over all of the proceedings with the students.

April Rose and Lily had to wait until after all the students were in bed before they could even use the bathroom facilities for their own needs, but at least they had privacy then.

That night April Rose couldn't sleep well. She

didn't know if it was the bitter taste of onions, or what caused it, but she woke up in the middle of the night. She had a confused sensation because she was disoriented and she could not remember where she was for a few minutes. The room was completely dark except for a little light coming in under the door from the hallway.

Then suddenly she heard a noise---it seemed to be coming from the wall. She got up silently and put her ear to the wall to listen. Something was going on---something that was being kept secret. April Rose realized this must be why there was no window in this wall.

April Rose quietly went to Lily's bed and touched Lily's shoulder. Lily's eyes popped open in great surprise, but April Rose quickly motioned to her to be quiet. April Rose silently indicated that there was something going on in the wall, and she went back to listen. Lily joined her then, putting her ear close to the wall as well. Then they both heard the noises---there was definitely movement.

They didn't dare speak about it, for if they could hear the noises, then perhaps whoever was in that space might be able to hear them as well. Instead, they crept back to bed silently and pulling the bed covers back over themselves, they attempted to go back to sleep.

April Rose's heart was beating faster, and it took a while for it to calm down, but finally she fell asleep.

April Rose and Lily were almost late to breakfast the next morning, but they managed to slip in at the last minute. The students looked glum and just as unresponsive as they had the day before this one. In the reading class, April Rose and Lily did their best to pique the girls' interest and make the reading less dull, but despite their efforts, they did not see even a glimmer of enthusiasm.

In the writing class, some of the children again fell asleep over their tablets.

April Rose and Lily did not have the heart to wake them up, though the others seemed afraid. They are probably afraid of being punished, April Rose thought grimly to herself. She promised herself that she would do her best to win their trust, and she silently asked for the Prince's help.

The math class was just as disappointing to Lily and April Rose; they could not seem to elicit any happy participation from their students. They did not want to insist on this for fear that any possible enjoyment would be hindered by the act of forcing their students to comply.

So their little experiment led only to a more dismal feeling. After lunch, which also did not provide any pleasure at all, they went outside in order to talk and walk around a little.

"We must not give up," said Lily. "Even though the children are so despondent, we must keep trying to help them learn."

April Rose agreed, and they walked around the building to see what was behind the back of the building. There was no garden, or walkway; it was more like a narrow alleyway. They looked up at the building, trying to envision a secret chamber in the wall.

Any understanding of this eluded them.

That afternoon, after they planned the next day's lessons, they decided to explore a little more inside the big institutional house. The wing with the kitchen was their destination, as this would be on the opposite side of the headmaster's office. When the hallway looked clear, the girls headed toward the kitchen and cautiously peeked in.

The head cook had just handed something to Phoebe, and then Phoebe turned to go out of the kitchen. She went out the other way which led to the outdoors. Here was their chance! If they could be quick enough, they might be able to intercept Phoebe and speak privately with her. April and Lily hurried back to the main hall which led to the entrance, and went out the front door. They were so disappointed to see that they had missed their timing—Phoebe was now already walking down the street. Perhaps they could follow at a distance and see where she went.

They decided to try this, and keep some distance between them so Phoebe would not detect that she was being followed. The boarding school was in a neighborhood with some other residences, and it was actually not too far from the main part of town. Phoebe was walking at a brisk pace, so they had to walk fast, but not too fast. They maintained their distance, but kept Phoebe in sight.

April Rose saw a livery stable and carriage house up ahead, and another hotel and boarding house across from them. Phoebe passed all of these up and went on to a partially enclosed local farmer's market stall where she stopped. Apparently the cook had sent Phoebe on an errand to purchase something needed for a meal.

Lily suggested that they take the time to look at the livery stable and carriage house nearby.

Then perhaps they could speak with Phoebe on her way home. So that is what the girls did; they looked in the doors of the livery stable and saw there were many stalls, and then they turned their attention to the carriage house.

The proprietor of this establishment did not seem to be about, and as there was an open breezeway, they walked in and looked around. Suddenly, they heard voices---and one of them sounded very like Phoebe. They did not want to be caught snooping, so they quickly hid behind some wooden crates stacked in a corner.

"Elora will be ready tomorrow at midnight," Phoebe was saying to someone they could not see. "At the dragon's tail."

Lily and April Rose remained very still, listening and hoping there might be more to this strange message, but that was all. Whoever it was with Phoebe left the building, and Phoebe was walking out, going in the direction of the boarding school. She was carrying a bag of produce of some kind.

April Rose and Lily waited until they felt enough time had passed before they slipped out from behind the crates and followed Phoebe. They were hoping to casually catch up with her.

Phoebe was not walking as fast on the way back, which made it possible for them to come alongside her and greet her.

"Phoebe," said April Rose. "I'm so glad we could meet up with you today. We have been hoping to talk with you about the students."

"Oh, hello," said Phoebe. "The cook asked me to pick up some cabbages, so I walked to town. Did you go shopping today?"

"No," said Lily. "We just went for a walk today."

"What did you want to know about the students?" Phoebe asked, and April Rose sensed a kind of wariness in Phoebe's voice.

"Well….is there a girl named Elora?" April Rose wasn't sure if she should ask this yet, but how else would they ever find out? Phoebe looked very disturbed, and then she said emphatically, "There was once, but she is not here anymore. Please do not bring up that name. It will cause too much pain and grief for everyone."

"Oh, I'm sorry," said April Rose. "Then she was a student who died?"

"I can't tell you anything more," said Phoebe. "Please do not bring up that name." Phoebe then started to walk away from them at a faster pace.

"Wait…" implored April Rose. "Could you tell me why the children are so tired?"

Phoebe shook her head no, and increased the distance between them and her. "Well, that was ruined," April Rose thought to herself, and silently called out to the Prince for His help.

Chapter 25

After that fiasco, April Rose was not at all sure about what to do next. She was discouraged, but the next morning, as she read in the gold book of promises, she felt as if she heard the Prince tell her to be patient and to depend upon him and not her own ingenuity.

Later that day, the thought came to April Rose that perhaps she and Lily could secretly investigate the students' room while the students were doing their chores elsewhere. Right after lunch, April Rose mentioned this to Lily when they had a private moment together. The same thought had come to Lily, so they agreed that this seemed to be the answer for their next step.

They made their plans; one would keep watch for anyone coming up the stairs, while the other one searched the room for any hidden clues.

Lily stood guard at the hallway upstairs while April Rose went into the students' sleeping quarters. She stood there and surveyed the room for a long moment. There was only one window on one wall of this long room. Two rows of small beds filled the room, and underneath each bed there was a box for each girl's clothing and personal articles. There was a small lamp table, but no other furniture and no other decorations, except for a large drab oil painting on one wall.

April Rose went up to this painting to examine it further. She could see that the painting itself was not at all remarkable in any way; it was a very dark and drab landscape that did not appear to have any semblance of a clue. April Rose touched the frame of the painting and it did not shift; apparently it was anchored to the wall at all four corners.

This was strange, she thought, and she began to pull at the edge of the painting. She was shocked when the wall behind the painting opened as she pulled at the frame; it was a door! And behind this door was an opening; there was a hidden tunnel within the wall.

Just now, Lily was frantically signaling to April Rose; April Rose quickly closed the door with the painting and slipped out of the room and into the hallway. She and Lily managed to get into their own room before the advancing footsteps reached the threshold of the upstairs hallway. They waited breathlessly, pretending to be occupied with items in their room, while the footsteps resounded in the students' room.

After what seemed an exorbitant amount of time, the footsteps retreated and went down the stairs again. Lily and April Rose remained in their room out of extra caution, and used the time to plan the next day's lessons.

When that was accomplished, they dared to go down the stairs and go for a walk outside.

They walked quickly down the road so that they could talk privately, but they also watched the gray skies as they did so. The girls did not want to get caught in a downpour if these gray skies indicated that a thunderstorm was coming.

"What did you find?" Lily finally was able to ask April Rose.

"Behind a painting, there is a door to a tunnel in the wall," April Rose answered. "This is the same wall of the house in which we heard the movement at night."

"Where do you think it leads? And why?" wondered Lily to her companion.

"The tunnel must lead to stairs somewhere," said April Rose, thinking hard about this mystery. "But then where?"

"It must be that some kind of illicit, subversive, and clandestine activity is taking place during the night, and the children are forced to do it," mused Lily. "No wonder they are so tired in the morning."

April Rose thought of history lessons she had learned in the past; why were secret tunnels made and how were they used? In the days of castles, secret exits were made for the royalty to escape during a siege. Their enemies also made use of tunnels to dig under the castle and undermine its foundations so that a wall would collapse and they would gain entrance.

In other time periods, tunnels were made to help escape persecution or detection. They were used to smuggle illegal substances---or people---in or out of a country. One thing was very puzzling to both April Rose and Lily: it did not seem likely that Phoebe would be involved in anything harmful to the students. If they were any judge of character, they did not think it possible for Phoebe to be a part of something evil. Yet they knew that Phoebe was keeping secrets from them.

The Prince had sent them specifically to rescue a girl named Elora---so she must exist, even though Phoebe appeared to indicate she did not.

"Wait a minute---" said April Rose. "Phoebe didn't say that Elora did not exist---she said she wasn't here anymore. She never said that Elora died."

"That message was so strange---Elora will be ready tomorrow at midnight---what could that mean?" Lily questioned.

"And the meeting place will be this 'dragon's tail,'" was April Rose's comment. "If only we knew where that was."

They did not find out the location of this dragon's tail, and the next morning there was a girl missing from their classes. It was a girl named Branwen, and she seemed to disappear overnight. Yet her disappearance was not even discussed, and there seemed to be no reaction.

Apparently, this meeting had taken place, but it was not about Elora after all.

Finally April Rose asked the headmistress about the missing girl, but all she heard was a terse reply that the girl's parents came to take her home. Everyone else was afraid to say anything, or else they were just too tired and numb to care.

It would be a few more days before their planned meeting with Aziel and Keturah, and it was hard to wait, but they had no choice in the matter. They continued to look for help from the Prince each morning and evening as they read his promises and this sustained them.

April Rose and Lily continued to try and awaken an interest in learning in these young weary souls who sat in their classroom day after day. Once, it seemed to them that they discerned a tiny bit of inspiration, and this spark was their one and only consolation. They refused to give up; to accept defeat would be a travesty and a mockery of their intentions. They must try to ignite that spark.

They knew deep within that the Prince would not be pleased with any hopelessness, because his kingdom was built upon hope that came from his character. To deny hope would be to deny the Prince. So they struggled through the classes.

The day finally came for their meeting with Aziel and Keturah, and they waited outside on the porch for the coach to arrive. Anxiety began to creep up on them, as the minutes ticked by and the coach did not come. Finally they had relief as they saw the familiar shape in the distance.

Keturah was inside waiting for them, and she was very apologetic about the delay. "We have made a significant discovery," she told April Rose and Lily excitedly. "Some of the local stagecoaches are involved in smuggling from the Evil Prince's realm into this area."

"What are they smuggling?" Lily asked.

"Opium," Keturah told her. "This is a favorite device of the evil prince, for the more addiction there is, the less resistance, and the more control he will have over a populace."

"What are they doing with it once it is smuggled in?" April Rose asked. "Surely they are not selling it out in the open."

"No," agreed Keturah. "They are not---but how they are dispersing it is still an unsolved riddle."

Then Lily and April Rose told Keturah about the tunnel they had found.

Keturah thought about this news and then she said, "There surely must be some connection, but I don't know how yet."

"We also do not understand how Phoebe is involved with all of this," said Lily. She and April Rose told Keturah about the mysterious message they had heard Phoebe give to someone in the carriage house.

"It's unfortunate that you did not see who she told this message to---that would explain a lot," said Keturah. "Maybe you should keep following her whenever she leaves the house."

April Rose and Lily agreed to do this, and they all decided that they should begin meeting twice a week instead of just once a week, to compare all their findings.

So they parted company until their next meeting.

Chapter 26

Lily and April Rose continued with their efforts to improve their pupils' skills in reading, writing, and deciphering, all the while looking for opportunities to follow Phoebe.

These were rare; most of the time, Phoebe was downstairs and she lived in the wing on the side of the kitchen area. Phoebe was kept very busy with various housekeeping duties such as laundry and errands for the cook, as well as assisting with the routine management of the girls in their chores.

April Rose and Lily began to briefly observe the girls at their chores in the afternoon, as sometimes Phoebe was with them and overseeing their work. April Rose and Lily did not want to attract attention to this endeavor, so they didn't stay long in one place. They tried to take in as many details as possible in that short observation.

They noted that Phoebe did seem to have some limited rapport with the girls, although if Phoebe said anything, she was very discreet and guarded in her mannerisms. April Rose thought she had detected an element of trust between Phoebe and the girls. If she leaned close to give directions, the girls did not cringe or shy away from Phoebe.

Their students no longer reacted to April Rose and Lily in fear, either, when they went by their pupils' individual desks to check their writing or their mathematical equations. This was a great relief and compensation for not displaying an attitude of discouragement around the students. April Rose was grateful for the Prince's insistence on having patience and endurance.

Now they would need it even more, in their pursuit of clues, to solve this mystery of the tunnel.

The missing student Branwen never returned to the boarding school, and there was never any mention of her again. She simply vanished without any explanation. April Rose and Lily wondered if this is what had happened to Elora.

They heard the noises again in the wall at night, but they had no idea of how to intercept what was going on without being caught. The only recourse was to continue dogging Phoebe's movements. This day they caught sight of Phoebe walking to town, so keeping an appropriate distance between them and her, they followed Phoebe. If she turned, they ducked out of sight, hoping they were fast enough to avoid being seen.

It turned out to be a disappointing venture; Phoebe went only to the farmer's market to purchase some vegetables, and then she turned to begin walking back to the boarding school. On an impulse, April Rose and Lily went to the farmer's market and bought some fruit for the girls. The proprietor of the market looked at them curiously, and asked if they were going to eat all the fruit themselves.

"Oh, no, ma'am," April Rose answered politely. "We bought it for our students."

"Oh," said the woman knowingly. "You have heart. That is rare in this town."

"Thank you," said Lily. "Well, we must be getting back."

"Take care," said the woman. "Be on your guard."

They left the market booth and quickly tried to catch up with Phoebe, but she eluded them again. However, just as they walked in the door of the boarding school, they saw Phoebe heading to the kitchen, and they followed her. Phoebe handed her bundle over to the cook and then she went out of the kitchen to the servant's quarters. April Rose and Lily followed her out to the hallway and then to Phoebe's room---but she had just closed her door. The girls were dismayed, but they turned and went upstairs to put the fruit in their room.

That night after supper, April and Lily decided to do something daring. The students had gone to their room to prepare for their bedtime routine, but the head mistress had not yet come upstairs to enforce her rules. April Rose and Lily slipped into the girls' room and Lily whispered, "We have some fruit for you. If you eat it quickly, you will not get caught."

The girls' eyes grew large with shock and wonder, but they quickly gathered around April Rose and Lily and eagerly took the fruit. They devoured it swiftly and their pleasure was evident, though they were nervous and frightened at the same time.

Lily and April Rose heard the heavy steps of the "warden" as they called the head mistress, and they quickly removed any leftover evidence of the forbidden food and retreated to their own room. It was all they could do to keep from giggling aloud because their joy was so great over giving to their students in this way. How they wished they had more money to spend.

Something else unusual happened that night as April Rose was sleeping; she had a dream. In her dream, she saw the Prince was standing near her and oh how she longed to see him in real life---but he was close to her in her dream. He had a word of instruction for her, and she listened carefully.

"Phoebe is on my side, though she does not know me yet," the Prince told April Rose. "Give her any help that she needs, for she has been a generous benefactor of many children."

"But she doesn't even trust us!" said April Rose in her dream. "How could I help her?"

"You will see in time to come," said the Prince. "Remember to keep your key with you always."

Then she woke up, and it was time to get up. She and Lily read in their gold books and refreshed their hearts with hope in the promises. The Prince was always as good as his promises, and there was no unfaithfulness in him or his words.

April Rose put the key in her pocket, and carefully hid the gold book in her suitcase.

After breakfast, April Rose and Lily began their classes and their young students displayed a tiny bit more enthusiasm for the learning process. April Rose and Lily were grateful for even the smallest bit of improvement.

After lunch, they retreated to their room---but it looked disturbed. Someone had been in here.

Their things had been rifled through, for their two suitcases were not where they had left them. With rapidly beating hearts and panicky thoughts, they opened their suitcases and checked the secret compartments within them.

They both exhaled a big breath in relief, for the gold books were still there.

April Rose was thankful for the dream, and that she had heeded the warning and slipped the key into her pocket. She did not fathom how anyone would know anything about this key, but whoever came to look among their things, did not find what they were looking for. Nothing had been taken.

Now April Rose had the time and the privacy to tell Lily about the dream she had last night. They were both relieved that Phoebe was not cooperating with the evil prince and his plans. At last they could trust her, and hopefully she would begin to trust them. As yet, they had no idea how to win her trust, but the Prince had a plan and they would have to follow his voice.

This afternoon, Aziel and Keturah would be coming for their meeting and April Rose and Lily looked forward to this very much. They were waiting on the porch when the carriage arrived.

The Prince had been working behind the scenes already, and he had a great surprise ready for his daughters April Rose and Lily when they stepped into the waiting carriage. Phoebe was sitting with Keturah inside the carriage; the window blinds were down so that no one could see this. April Rose was speechless with shock to see Phoebe.

"Well, sit down," said Keturah, smiling.

"You can stop following me now," said Phoebe, and she was smiling too.

April Rose and Lily were still too dumbfounded to smile yet; their mouths were open in an "oh" shape and they were frozen in motion, but they finally managed to sit down.

"How?" began Lily, but she was so bewildered that she couldn't finish her sentence.

Keturah graciously explained that she and Aziel met one of the stage coach drivers who was actively resisting the evil prince's gain in power, and he had introduced them to Phoebe. So now they knew that they were all on the same side, though Phoebe and her friend had not met the Prince of Grace. They simply knew of him, but they were not acquainted with him.

April Rose told of her dream the night before and what the Prince had told her about Phoebe. "So he was already preparing us for this meeting---but I was still shocked to see you in here," exclaimed April Rose.

Now it was Phoebe's turn to be shocked. She had not known that the Prince of Grace was so keenly aware of her activities on behalf of the children.

"Yes, he sent us here," Lily emphasized, "But he told us we would be helping Elora."

"Then I am sure you will be," said Phoebe. "I will have a lot to explain to you about her."

"So you knew we were following you?" asked April Rose, as she and Lily sat together in the coach with Phoebe and Keturah.

"Yes," said Phoebe. "I knew."

And then she could not help herself; she laughed merrily. "I'm glad I can finally laugh again about something," she said with a kindly look at the girls.

Chapter 27

April Rose and Lily were rather embarrassed, but they both realized that Phoebe wasn't trying to shame them or ridicule their efforts.

"I am sure that I have had much more practice than you, at going undetected in my secretive activities," Phoebe reassured them.

"Tell us about Elora," urged Lily, for this had been such a puzzling aspect of this situation.

"First, let me tell you more about the boarding school," said Phoebe. "The girls who live there are basically like orphans—their parents were bribed into giving their children over to this boarding school. They were sold to this enterprise."

"So these children are more like slaves," continued Phoebe. "At night, they are sent through a network of underground tunnels to deliver opium to many different people all across the city."

"Like little rats, these children scurry through the dark underground at night," Phoebe said. "After I found out about it, I couldn't just ignore this. So we found a way to intercept the girls and help them escape from such a life."

"So Elora is one who escaped?" asked Lily.

"Yes," answered Phoebe. "She was the first girl to escape, and her name is the code name for the project. That is why I did not want you to bring up her name."

"I understand," said April Rose. "But where are the girls now? And how did you explain their sudden disappearance?"

"I cannot tell you where they are," said Phoebe soberly. "It is better that you do not know too much. As for the explanation, there is a legend that we made use of---the legend of a serpent that lives in the underground tunnels. People believe that the girls were killed by this serpent."

Lily's face grimaced at the thought of such a tale.

"Of course," explained Phoebe, "We can only rescue one girl at a time every so often, so we have to wait and choose the night….and the girl….and this breaks my heart every time. I would like to get them all out at once, but then our plan would fail."

April Rose was sad to think of such a dilemma, too. "If there is anything we can do to help, please let us assist you," she implored of Phoebe. "That is why we are here."

Then Lily remembered something troubling: "Someone searched in our room today."

"Whoever it was did not take anything," said April Rose.

"It wasn't me, or the cook," said Phoebe. "She is on our side. But I can't vouch for the butler or the head mistress, because they are the ones who send the girls into the tunnels."

"No wonder those girls are so tired," said Lily with great compassion in her voice.

"Yes," said Phoebe. "They live wretched lives here in this place. Since your prince is so aware, I am wondering….if perhaps he might know of a way we could get them all out…..but then how would we ever get to ask him?"

"I can ask him," asserted April Rose. "He hears me whenever I call to him."

"I hope one day I will get to meet him," Phoebe said wistfully.

"You will," affirmed April Rose. "He hears your heart cry."

"I think that if I could not see him, I would begin to think he was only a person of my imagination," said Phoebe.

"He sees us more clearly than we could ever imagine," said Lily. "He has the ability to see straight into our hearts and to constantly know what we are thinking."

Phoebe laughed at that, but not scornfully. "So I could never hide from him," she said.

"No, we never can," agreed April Rose.

"Well, then, please ask him for a plan," Phoebe asked very seriously.

"I will," said April Rose. "But I must warn you that he does not always tell us the particulars all at once. He insists that we trust him enough to take one step at a time."

"Very well," said Phoebe. "I have no other options; no one else has any sort of plan."

Their visit was over that day; but to avoid any arousal of suspicions concerning their friendship, Phoebe was let out of the carriage at an ample distance from the boarding school and she walked back the rest of the way.

April Rose and Lily continued to ride with Keturah until sufficient time had passed to make it appear that they had not been with Phoebe.

They were all pleased to finally confide in Phoebe.

Aziel and Keturah now knew which of the drivers belonged to the smuggling ring and which did not. Since they were new to the area, those involved in the opium traffic were trying to entice Aziel and Keturah into the business. They had not made it clear where their allegiances were placed, so they were not in danger yet. However, they both felt the threat would be coming. In that case, they would not be able to come to the boarding school to see April Rose and Lily. They would have to designate a secret meeting place, and they had begun to search for this.

When April Rose and Lily returned to the boarding school, they sensed great tension immediately.

The head mistress met them at the door and told them coldly that the head master wanted to see them immediately. April Rose and Lily turned to go down the hall to his office.

The hallway was dark and sinister, and there was an evil feeling that tried to shake their confidence. They refused to give in to that feeling, and Lily knocked bravely on the door.

"Come in," said the headmaster in his gravelly gruff tone. He had no welcoming warmth at all, in his voice.

The girls opened his door and went in.

"Sit down," he said to them tersely. "I have reason to believe that you are not getting more progress from the students because you are too soft on them. These girls are lazy, slow and stubborn. We have a reputation to keep, and I do not want that ruined. If these girls fall asleep and they do not do better in their schoolwork, you are to punish them."

"What sort of punishment?" asked Lily quietly.

The headmaster drew out a flat stick from behind his desk and handed it to Lily. "Beat them," he said cruelly. "And I want to see the evidence that you are, or you will be terminated."

"You're dismissed," the headmaster said rudely.

The girls stood up and tried not to let their facial expressions reveal any of their horror. They turned quickly and went out, closing the door behind them. They could say nothing about this here, so they went up the stairs to their room. They would have a little time before the evening meal to talk and discuss this situation.

Their hearts were grieved. "I don't think I can do that!" said Lily in great distress.

"What shall we do?" moaned April Rose.

They managed to get through the evening meal without crying or betraying their emotions. Their hearts felt numb, and they went through the motions of eating and getting ready for bed. When they were sure it was safe, they took their gold books out of the hiding places and read the Prince's promises by candlelight.

It seemed to Lily that everything she was reading conveyed the thought of confiding. "I think the Prince is trying to tell me something," she said.

"I think he is convincing me that we must confide in the girls what the headmaster said to us."

"If you believe so, then I am with you in that decision," said April Rose sincerely. She had come to trust in Lily's obedience to the Prince since their initial encounter.

So it was decided; they carefully hid their gold books and blew out the candle. Now they should be able to have enough peace to sleep, and be prepared for the next day and its challenges.

The Prince was guiding them, and this was their comfort. April Rose was longing for his love in this cold-hearted place.

Chapter 28

April Rose and Lily woke up very early and they both knew it was because they would need extra strength today. They did not delay to read in their gold books and listen intently with their hearts to the Prince. He confirmed that they were to confide in the young girls they were teaching.

Breakfast was over now, and it was time for them to proceed to the classroom. Lily carried the hated stick in a bundle of other things so it would not be visible. She and April Rose hoped their faces did not reveal the shame they felt over such an ugly assignment.

They followed their usual classroom proceedings, but before they began their lessons, April Rose nervously began her speech. Lily stood beside her to give April Rose confidence as she spoke.

"Children," she said. "I have a very grievous sad announcement. Miss Lily and I may not be able to teach you any longer. The headmaster thinks we have not been stern enough, and he insists that we must punish you children with beatings. He also demands that there must be evidence of this. If we do not follow through with these instructions, we will no longer be able to teach here."

Then April Rose could not go on with her speech, because she was crying. Finally, she regained control of her emotions, enough to say the rest: "I don't think we can bear to beat any of you for not trying harder or for falling asleep."

Lily found a handkerchief for April Rose, and April took it gratefully and wiped her eyes and nose. Lily looked at the children tenderly and she voiced the same feeling—that she could not do this to any of the children.

Some of the children then began to cry silently, but several of the older girls leaned over to each other and whispered something in secret.

Then one of these girls in this little group stood up. "Miss Rose and Miss Lily, we don't want you to leave. We will do the beating and leave the marks on each other so that they will not dismiss you. Please let us do that so you can stay and teach us," she pleaded valiantly.

Then it was even harder for April Rose and Lily not to cry, for they were so amazed at being loved and appreciated like that by these girls. April and Lily did something they had never done before; they went to each girl and hugged her.

They had their reading lesson, and then their writing. It was during their math class that the girls administered punishment to each other, leaving a visible mark on several of the girls. They knew the headmistress would check for this in the evening, and they were prepared.

April Rose and Lily turned away and cringed to hear the blows, but they knew it was an act of love and bravery. The students began to plan ahead on who would carry it out and on whom, so that none would be overly hurt or feel the pain worse than any other.

This cheered April Rose and Lily; they felt that somehow the character of the Prince was being revealed to these children through their lessons, and influencing them.

They wished that they could tell Phoebe about this evidence, but it would not be wise to speak of this in the house. That afternoon, Keturah and Aziel came by the boarding schoolhouse in the carriage, as they had arranged. April Rose and Lily were thankful for the chance to speak freely.

Keturah was inside the carriage, and her face was very serious. She said, "This is the last time we will come by the boarding school, because we have reason to feel that now it might become dangerous to you and to us, but we have found a place to meet. We must let Phoebe know also."

So they drove to the new meeting place, but did not stop. They only identified it as the old grist mill which was now deserted. It was built close by the stream that came through the woods, and it was down the road from the livery stable and carriage house. There was a hill behind it, and a wooded area on the hill, which they thought would provide sufficient hiding places.

They agreed to meet there in the afternoon in three days' time. April Rose had an idea; she had remembered that the cook usually sent Phoebe on an errand to the farmer's market every other day. She would most likely be going on the next day, so April Rose and Lily made plans to go to the farmer's market for their own errand.

This time they did not have enough funds to buy fruit for their students, so they bought something for Phoebe at the farmer's market. Then they walked around and looked awhile at the horses in the livery stable and looked inside the carriage house. When they came out again, there was Phoebe at the farmer's market.

They went up to her and greeted her and asked if she had time enough to show them the mill, since they had never seen one before. At first, Phoebe seemed to hesitate, and then she agreed. So they turned and began to walk in the direction of the mill. Phoebe was pleasantly surprised at their little gift of fruit, and she ate it immediately while they walked.

The mill was up on a hill; it was a gristmill which had a water wheel on the side. The building was the typical box shaped three story wood frame building and it was a weathered gray. It looked abandoned, and April Rose and Lily wondered why it was no longer in use. Phoebe told them that the wheat farming in their area had declined due to a drought some years ago, and the farmers had switched to a different crop.

They climbed up the hill and looked at the trough which would have allowed water to flow over the wheel. They went to the building and discovered that the old doors were not locked and they could go in. The ground floor had large bins to collect the flour and the second floor held the millstones to grind the wheat. The top floor was bare; this is where the farmers would have brought the dusty sacks of wheat to be ground.

Phoebe finally asked why April Rose and Lily wanted to see the mill, and they told her that Aziel and Keturah had picked the mill for a meeting place. The first meeting would be in two days, at this time, and they decided to meet in the woods, just behind the mill.

April Rose and Lily also told Phoebe about the headmaster's rule concerning beatings. They told Phoebe how the children determined to do it to themselves in order to spare April Rose and Lily this grievous task, and to retain them as their teachers. Phoebe had tears in her eyes as she listened, and April Rose and Lily were both glad to see her compassion and understanding.

"So did your Prince give you any directions about rescuing all the children at once?" Phoebe was anxious to know.

"No, not yet," answered April and Lily voiced the same thing.

Phoebe looked disappointed at that, but then she said, "Maybe before our next meeting, he will tell you something. I think we should go back before it looks suspicious on our part for staying away too long. You go first this time, and I will follow after."

April and Lily agreed and began briskly walking back to the school.

"We must ask the Prince more earnestly for his answer to this dilemma," said April Rose quietly on the way back.

"Yes," said Lily. "But we will have to trust his timing in everything, even if he does not answer us right away, or as soon as we would like."

"You're right," said April. "I was beginning to feel anxious about it."

"And we know so little about the rescues that are going on even now, that we could not possibly figure out anything on our own," Lily mused.

"We will have to wait. Sometimes that is the hardest part," said April with a sigh of resignation.

They walked in the house, went up the stairs and opened the door to their room, and gasped.

Their suitcases were on the floor completely opened and all of their belongings were strewn around them.

April Rose felt her pocket---yes, the key was in it. She had not forgotten, thankfully. Quickly, they closed the door and searched in the secret hidden compartments for the gold books. They were still there. Both girls took a deep breath after that wild moment of fright.

As they gathered their things and repacked them in their suitcases, they were looking for some kind of clue as to who this could be that was searching in their room.

April Rose wondered if she caught a faint whiff of

tobacco; and if so, who used it? If there really was the smell of tobacco, it seemed the only likely suspects would be the headmaster himself or the surly butler.

They could not determine why or what this person could be looking for, and that was a great mystery. They asked the Prince for a clue that night before they went to sleep.

Surely this could not be a small matter, and the unknown reason was very troubling.

Chapter 29

That night, April Rose dreamed again of the Prince. He was standing there in their room talking to her and he said: "The evil prince is looking for your key, April Rose. He knows you have one since you were able to escape his prison. This key represents the reverent awe you have for me, and it is the key to great treasure. It opens the door into my presence."

When she woke up in the morning, April Rose remembered his words and told them to Lily. Lily's eyes grew wide with wonder when April told her all about that key. "You must keep this on you at all times," she said. "Even when you are sleeping."

Lily made a lanyard out of a piece of leather she had found in the carriage house. This was for April to wear the key at night. April marveled at Lily's creativity in making this, and was greatly relieved to have it. So during the day, the key would remain in her pocket, and at night she would sleep with the key on the lanyard around her neck.

"Well, it isn't the evil prince himself that is doing the searching," said Lily, "If we are correct about the tobacco smell, it must be that the butler or the headmaster is working for the evil prince."

Then to April's horror, she realized something. "That might mean that they know who we are," she said in whispers to Lily. "But why would they let us continue, if they know?"

Lily now had a horrifying thought. "Could it be that we are the bait?" she whispered.

This was a sobering thought, and the girls quickly got out their gold books to comfort themselves with the Prince's good words. They carefully hid them again and prepared to go down for breakfast and their classes.

Their tired little pupils faithfully did their duty of leaving marks from the whipping stick, which they continued to execute at the end of the school day, so as not to spoil their classes. They were really trying to learn despite their terrible lack of sleep and proper nutrition. April Rose's heart ached with the desire to deliver them all from this horrid cruel lifestyle. She knew that Lily felt just the same.

There was only one more day before the meeting with Phoebe and their friends, and April Rose silently implored the Prince for his plan to release all of the children.

Suddenly, that afternoon April had a flashback in her memory of the journey here. She remembered how she and Lily had gone to the stream, and there was a rustling in the bushes. She thought at the time that she had seen a face peeking out at her---the face of a child. She had dismissed this thought as too irrational to be believed.

Now, she was not so sure. Phoebe had not disclosed where the missing children were kept; could it be a hideout in the woods? When they had privacy, she shared these thoughts with Lily and they pondered over the possibility.

That night the Prince answered April Rose. She had another vivid dream, and in this one, she was in the woods, and she saw a child coming up out of the ground through a trap door covered with foliage. "Yes," said the Prince. "You were right, my April Rose. You did see a child that day and they have a hiding place in the woods. You must bring all the children to the woods. I will tell you the next step after that. Be careful and cautious and listen for my voice."

Now April Rose was ready and prepared for the meeting that afternoon. She and Lily walked to the mill and went up the hill to the woods behind it. Phoebe was there waiting for them, and in just a few minutes Aziel and Keturah had arrived in their carriage and parked it in the woods. They came to the mill on an obscure road that led them directly to these woods behind the mill.

When they had gathered together out of sight of any road, April Rose told them all about her most recent dream and what the Prince had said to her. Phoebe was shocked that the Prince had revealed where the children were, but she quickly realized that it was more proof of his reality. This made it easier for her to trust his plan and his help.

"Well, now that you know about their hiding place, I will tell you more about our enterprise," declared Phoebe. "We have arrangements with some of the stagecoach drivers to bring the escaped children from the tunnels to the woods. We have secret arrangements with the farmer's market and some of the farmers. They are supplying food for the children, and the stagecoach drivers deliver it to them. I just didn't know how much longer we would be able to keep doing this."

"How many children are there now?" asked Lily.

"There are six," said Phoebe. "Including Elora and Branwen, and four girls that you never met. Elora has been the leader, and she helps the other girls who escape."

"What about the serpent legend? Are the girls scared in the tunnels?" asked April Rose.

"No," answered Phoebe. "We have prepared them for that---they know it is not true. We had to tell them so that they would not panic when they are underground."

"How many girls are in the school?" asked Keturah.

"We have eighteen girls," responded Lily.

"That means we will need at least three carriages to bring them to the woods," mused Aziel.

"And we will need four carriages to bring them from the woods to their new home," said Keturah. "I'm sure that they are small enough that we can fit six in one carriage."

"I have another question, Phoebe," said April Rose. "What is the dragon's tail?"

Phoebe looked startled. "How did you know about that?" she asked incredulously.

"Lily and I followed you and we hid in the carriage house," replied April Rose. "We heard you talking to someone about the dragon's tail and Elora."

"Oh, so that is how you knew about Elora," said Phoebe with a sigh of relief.

"No, that is not how we first knew about her," Lily reminded her. "The Prince specifically mentioned her. He said he had heard her cries. He told us he was sending us to help her."

"I wonder if he meant her or the whole endeavor," remarked Phoebe. "If he heard her cries, then he surely must have heard the others. They have all cried to be free of slavery."

"But what about the dragon's tail---what did you mean by that?" implored April Rose.

"That is a section of the tunnels that ends in a sort of point---it becomes very small and narrow like the end of a dragon's tail," explained Phoebe to the others. "Only a small person can squeeze through there. But this is the way out that we have used for the girls' escape. This end of the "tail" curves upward and comes to the surface inside a cave on the side of a hill. In the cave, there is a hidden trap door to get out."

"How does Elora help the other girls to escape?" April Rose wondered.

"We go in a carriage to the woods and bring Elora back to the trap door in the cave," said Phoebe. "She enters the tunnels there and meets up with the girl who is escaping, and guides her the rest of the way to the dragon's tail."

"After we get all the children to the woods, then what?" asked Lily.

"Do you mean how can we bring them to the Kingdom of Grace?" asked Keturah.

'Yes, I suppose I am asking that," answered Lily.

"A ship," said Aziel emphatically.

"Does the Prince have a ship?" inquired April Rose.

"Not that I know of," said Aziel with a smile. "But never underestimate the Prince. Just when you think you have figured out what he will do, he does the unexpected. He is full of surprises."

"The Prince told me in the dream to wait for his instructions after we get the girls to the woods," April Rose reminded the others. "We'll have to wait and see what his plan will be."

"That is really all we can do," said Keturah. "We certainly don't have a ship or any way to transport them that far. I don't think we can ask the other stagecoach drivers to go that far."

Phoebe was thinking about another dilemma. "How could we put the headmistress and butler to sleep while we get all the children into the tunnel?" she asked the others.

Lily thought of something. "Do you have a medicinal herb garden?" she asked Phoebe.

"No," Phoebe replied. "But the cook may---or she may know who does."

"We'll need valerian," said Lily. "And how will we get it into their food?"

"The cook can arrange for that," said Phoebe. "The headmistress and waiter eat by themselves in the kitchen after everyone is served. The cook has to give them special portions, so it will work out perfectly. Now, we have a plan---so let's get back to work."

This meeting ended with much satisfaction, and April Rose and Lily were very grateful for the instructions from the Prince, and to finally have answers from Phoebe.

Chapter 30

So the plans were made, and the friends parted ways and went back to their jobs. They were all tremendously relieved but also full of tension. On the way back to the school, Lily and April Rose recited some promises from the gold book softly to themselves to ease the anxiety. These promises of the Prince brought such peace to their hearts in the midst of the unknown.

Two days went by while they waited for Phoebe to find the herb they would need as an anesthetic and sleep inducer. April Rose and Lily were very diligent with the girls' lessons, as they knew these were some of the last ones they would ever do for them. They wanted to give them the very best that they could while they had this opportunity.

On the second day, April Rose and Lily noticed that the girls were a little more energetic than usual; they seemed to possess a more hopeful attitude. April reasoned that Phoebe had begun to speak with them about the plan as they were doing their chores.

That night, April Rose slept uneasily; this troubled her for she knew she would need her strength for the ordeal ahead of them. Finally, she seemed to hear the Prince's voice in her dreams, and he was singing his lullaby song for her. She slept well after that, and woke more refreshed than she thought she would.

The girls continued to provide the evidence of beatings for their punishment. April Rose still winced as they hit one another. She would be so glad when this was over for them---and for herself. She had managed somehow to survive on the meager tasteless food, but the evil attitude of this place was wearing on her. Her longing to go back to the palace and walk with the Prince in his garden was growing more intense.

She knew it would be worth it all when they had delivered these children to the Prince for his good safekeeping and nurturing, and that was the factor that gave her endurance.

They were meeting at the mill this afternoon to make the final plans.

Lily and April Rose walked up the hill to the woods behind the mill, and Phoebe was already there with Keturah and Aziel. Their faces showed signs of strain, and April Rose wondered what had happened.

Aziel explained what they had been discussing with Phoebe. "There have been threats against us.

They suspect we are spies. They have insisted that we join the opium smugglers in the next shipment to prove we are not working against them."

Phoebe looked worried. "I'm concerned it might be a trap," she said seriously.

"Can we do the escape before this next opium shipment?" Lily wondered.

"The shipment is coming in three days," said Keturah. "I don't know if there is time."

"If we can have everyone informed in two days, we would be able to," said Phoebe.

"What about the valerian? Did you find a source?" asked April Rose.

"Yes, we did, and it is being prepared," answered Phoebe. "The cook knows just what to do, and she is ready. I will pick it up and bring it to her early tomorrow afternoon."

"What do the girls think of the rescue plan?" Lily wondered. "We thought you must have told them because they were more spirited than usual."

"I did tell them," said Phoebe. "I told them it would be in four or five days. It is wonderful to see some hope come into their eyes. But I warned them that they must pretend to be just as dreary as they usually are. Of course, in your classes it is not as necessary unless the headmistress comes in."

"What will we do about food while we wait in the woods?" April Rose inquired. "And the legend of the serpent won't help if all the girls are missing."

"I thought of that," said Phoebe. "We need to bring extra food to the hiding place in the woods now to be prepared. One of the drivers will deliver this supply tomorrow night. But I know that we will not be able to stay very long in the woods. You are right about the legend; it will not help us if all the girls are gone. They will search for us with dogs. What does your Prince say? He is our only hope."

"He said nothing yet," replied April Rose. "But I trust him."

"Are you sure of that?" asked Phoebe with grave concern.

"Yes, I am," answered April Rose. "I would trust him with my life."

"Well, I am glad you are certain," said Phoebe. "We will be in danger. If he does not rescue us, our lives will be forfeit."

Aziel, Keturah, and Lily also expressed their utter, undying faith and trust in the Prince, so Phoebe was convinced enough to make a decision.

"I think we had better plan on doing the escape two days from now," she said. "That way we can avoid the possible trap for Aziel and Keturah. The extra food supply will be there tomorrow night and I will also obtain the valerian tomorrow."

"So the escape will be the next night?" asked Lily.

Phoebe confirmed this, and then Keturah and Aziel discussed plans with her about getting this message to the other drivers who would also be assisting in the rescue.

"We will need extra lanterns," said Phoebe to Aziel. "Can you obtain those?"

"Yes, we can," he agreed. "Does Elora know all the plans?"

"Not all of the plans, but during that last opium delivery made by the girls, she met them in the tunnels and the girls explained as much as they could to her," said Phoebe. "Tomorrow night when the extra food is delivered, the driver will explain more in detail to her."

Phoebe looked at Lily and April Rose. "Are you ready for this?" she asked soberly. "You too will have to escape through the tunnels, and so will I."

"Will we fit through the dragon's tail?" asked Lily with some concern.

"That remains to be seen," answered Phoebe. "If not, we will have to assume the risk of coming out of the tunnels at one of the delivery stations."

"And leave the girls by themselves to get out?" asked April Rose.

"Elora will be their guide," Phoebe assured them. "She knows her way through all the tunnels. As long as the stagecoach is there to pick them up, all will be well, even if we should have to escape another way. Either way, you will have to leave with nothing but the clothes you are wearing."

This thought had not yet occurred to April Rose and Lily; but after thinking about this for a moment, they realized that everything they had brought could be replaced---except the key. They could hide the gold books in their clothing and leave everything else behind.

"If we have to come out a different way, how will the stagecoach driver know where to pick us up?" April Rose wanted to know.

"We will have to choose an alternate exit---I think we need to decide now, so that at least Aziel and Keturah will know the location," said Phoebe.

"There are twelve delivery stations reached from underground," Phoebe told them. "There is one leading to the mayor's mansion, one leads to the sheriff's office, one leads to the home of the bank owner, another to the proprietor of the hotel, and the rest lead to the homes of the most elite and important officials of the city."

April Rose and Lily were surprised to hear this. "So all the government leaders of this city are involved in this crime?"

"Of course," said Keturah. "That's how the evil prince works. He gets the leaders addicted."

"Do you know the home of the tax collector?" Phoebe asked Aziel. "It is the one closest to the Dragon's Tail."

"Yes," affirmed Aziel. "It's the corner of Mulberry and Ash, if I'm not mistaken."

"That is correct," Phoebe confirmed. "We will come out there if we cannot fit through the smaller tunnel of the Dragon's Tail."

So it was settled; the five friends parted company and began their preparations.

Chapter 31

The next day felt like a very long day. April Rose and Lily read the promises of the Prince in their gold books, and hid them carefully away. Then they went through the usual routine, but it felt rather like they were sleepwalking and simply going through the motions.

Their young students put on their dreary looks and hid their excitement well. They performed their duty with the beatings as usual, and they droned through their lessons in the typical dull stupor they usually exhibited. April Rose and Lily were proud of the girls' discipline in concealing the secret plan.

April Rose and Lily spent the afternoon preparing for their final lessons with the girls, on what would become their last day at the school. They worked diligently though they were somewhat distracted by an inner alertness to everything around them. They were completely trusting in the Prince to give them success with their rescue endeavor, but they knew they must be careful.

April Rose and Lily could almost read each other's minds this day, which was helpful, because they did not dare to discuss anything out loud while in the school building.

Phoebe was able to communicate more discreetly with the students while they were doing chores, and so she made sure that all the girls knew what was planned.

Later that afternoon, Phoebe went on an errand for the cook, and also came back with the valerian concoction which would induce a sound sleep for the headmistress and the butler. This potent ingredient was carefully hidden away in a secret cabinet known only to the cook and Phoebe. For extra measure, the extract also contained a bit of juice from the midnight flower---not enough to poison, but certainly adding to the anesthetic properties of the mixture.

Phoebe was concerned for the cook's welfare in the aftermath after their escape, but the cook was quite cheerful instead of fearful. She had thought of a magnificent fabricated story of attempted theft and planned to make things look ransacked--- especially near the money vault.

The timing of all this was excellent because the headmaster was away on business. The cook would claim that the thief used hypnosis and ether gas and made them all unconscious. She was sure that she could feign delirium resulting from the after effects of the ether.

Phoebe was greatly relieved to hear of this idea.

So everything was falling into place; while out on her errand, Phoebe had also secretly met with the coach driver who would deliver the extra supplies to the woods, and she had confirmed to him that these supplies were ready and available for him to receive this night. In addition, he would give Elora further instructions.

The only thing that perturbed Phoebe now was the silence of the Prince. He had not yet revealed the next step to April Rose and Lily. It was a difficult thing for Phoebe to execute this plan with a great part of it still unknown. She took her responsibility to these girls very seriously.

The day finally ended, but there was still no word from the Prince. April Rose and Lily read in their gold books, and his words reminded them that the prince had promised he would take care of them, and they did not need to be afraid of any kind of abandonment.

They went to sleep thinking on these things.

The morning of the eventful day, April Rose and Lily woke up happily and reported to each other that they both were given a dream of the Prince. He had told them the same thing: He said that he would be with them and he would guide them step by step. They were comforted just in seeing his visage and form in the dream, and to hear his compassionate and compelling voice.

Breakfast was the usual nauseating bowl of gray porridge and a half slice of bread with very weak tea. Afterward, they went immediately to their classroom and prepared to teach their students, taking care to follow all the usual procedures required for any ordinary day.

Their students did the same and acted as if this was only another wearisome day in their bleak lives. April Rose and Lily performed well as their teachers, and taught lessons with their typical perseverance and persuasion. Finally, class was dismissed, and the girls went to lunch and then afterward to their work assignments.

April Rose and Lily prepared lessons as if they would be teaching on the next day, just in case the watchful eyes of the headmistress happened to be on them. They spent all afternoon doing this, as they needed the diversion to keep their minds from wandering into any fearful thoughts. Sometimes April Rose had to quell a sensation of panic that tried to come up in her stomach.

The food at the supper meal certainly did not aid a nervous inner feeling. It was barely digestible, but April Rose and Lily did their best to fill their uneasy stomachs with something.

Their young students did the same, and then were excused to go upstairs and begin the routine of preparing for bedtime. Phoebe had instructed the girls to put on their nightgowns, but as soon as the headmistress and butler were asleep, they would again put on their regular clothing and shoes.

April Rose and Lily would change to pants and shirts instead of long dresses. Phoebe agreed that this was wisdom, and she also had obtained a pair of pants and a shirt. If they found themselves in a situation in which they would have to run, it would be much easier if they were wearing pants instead of dresses. April Rose felt more confident about wearing pants for another reason; her key would be more secure in a tight pants pocket.

Downstairs, the cook had prepared meals for the headmistress and the butler, and laid this out for them in the small dining room reserved only for the staff. She had thoroughly laced it with the valerian mixture, using spices to cover up any trace of the smell or taste. The particular meal she had made happened to be the butler's favorite dish, and it was well-liked by the headmistress as well. The cook was certain that they would both eat all of their portions that she gave to them.

After the cook had served the meal, and the headmistress and butler were seated, the cook busied herself in the kitchen washing the cooking pots and utensils. Every now and then, she would stop and listen for the cessation of sound from the dining area. After a while, she noted that no more sounds were coming from the room where the headmistress and butler were eating. The cook tiptoed into that room and saw that both the headmistress and butler were slumped over the table with their heads in their now empty plates. The plan was working.

Phoebe came from her room just then, and saw the delightful sight; she had a gleeful smile on her face as she hugged the cook. "Anything of mine that is left in my room is yours now," she told the cook with a somber voice and serious expression. "I have to leave it all behind."

The cook had tears in her eyes, and dabbed at them with the corner of her apron. "Take care and be safe," she told Phoebe, and then she hugged Phoebe once more.

Phoebe moved quickly toward the stairs, and she climbed them softly and swiftly. At the head of the stairs, she turned toward April Rose's and Lily's room and rapped gently on their door. Lily slid off of her bed and cautiously opened the door. She was relieved and elated to see Phoebe's face was peeking around the door. Lily and April Rose were

dressed and ready. "It's time," said Phoebe. "The headmistress and the butler are fully asleep in the dining room. As we can never be totally sure how long they will sleep, we need to get moving. I'll tell the girls to get dressed in their regular clothing."

There was no need; as eager and watchful as the girls had become, they had heard Phoebe coming up the stairs, and one girl had peeked out to see who it was. When she told the others that it was Phoebe, they immediately began changing into their daytime clothing.

April Rose and Lily withdrew the gold books from the hiding places in their suitcases, and tucked them inside their clothing. Lily asked about the key, and April Rose pulled it from her pants pocket just to see it once more, and then pushed it down deep into the pocket. She put the lanyard into her other pocket, thinking that perhaps she might have a need for it later.

They looked carefully around the room one more time, blew out the light, and left the room. Then they walked across the short hallway and joined Phoebe and the girls in their room.

Everyone gathered around Phoebe as she gave directions. There were only six lanterns to pass around, for this was all that Phoebe could procure and smuggle upstairs without detection. The

were already hidden in the tunnel, but now must be taken out and lit. She pulled at the painting on the wall which opened to the tunnel, and began handing out the lights to the oldest of the girls. "You must stay together in groups of three or four," she said, and immediately the girls quickly and quietly assembled themselves. Phoebe reserved one light for herself and April Rose and Lily.

Phoebe lit a long sulphur match stick in the flame of the lamp in the room, and proceeded to light each lantern. She also wore a small leather pouch fastened to her waist and reassured them all that if the lanterns went out, she had flint and steel and a tinder box in this pouch. After all the lanterns were lit, she made sure that the flame was completely extinguished on the sulphur stick and then tucked it into the pouch. Now they were ready.

"Elora will meet you in the tunnels," said Phoebe. "You must stay together. Elora will guide you all to the Dragon's Tail, and the coach drivers will be there to bring you to the hideout in the woods. April Rose, Lily and I will be right behind you. We may not be able to go out the same way, but we will meet up at the woods. Be brave and strong. I love you all," she said.

Chapter 32

Phoebe began helping the girls one by one, into the tunnel, keeping the groups of three or four together. Each girl with a lantern went in as the leader of that group of girls. When they were all in, Phoebe turned and looked at April Rose and Lily.

"Now it is our turn," she said. "Please hold the lantern for me while I get in." She handed the lantern to April Rose, who waited until Phoebe was ready to take the lantern from her.

"Whoever is last, please pull the door closed again," Phoebe instructed.

April Rose looked at Lily for reassurance, and Lily squeezed her hand. April Rose then took a big determined breath, and climbed up into the tunnel. Lily came after her and pulled the door with the painting as a camouflage, closed behind her. They were in the tunnel, and it was dark.

Just ahead, they could see the light of Phoebe's lantern, and further ahead they could see a string of bobbing lanterns, as the girls crouched and went slowly through the tunnel. The ceiling of the tunnel here was so low that April Rose and Lily practically had to crawl during this part. They were both hoping it was not this way throughout the entire tunnel passage.

Thankfully, this branch of the tunnel was very short, as it led soon to narrow stairs going down. This part was particularly frightening to April Rose, because the descent was so steep, and it seemed to go on forever. They had reached the ground level, and the stairs continued to go down before them. She felt as if they were going several stories underground. Here, the air was musty and damp. April Rose stepped carefully, as she did not want to fall down these stairs, knocking the others down like a stack of dominos. It was tedious and a very tense descent.

April Rose exhaled her tension when they finally reached the end of the stairs. "Are you okay?" whispered Lily to her friend. "Yes, thank you!" April whispered back gratefully.

The tunnel floor leveled out after the stairs ended, and they were in what looked like a room, with several tunnels branching off from it. All the girls were crowded into this room; they had stopped to wait for each other and for Phoebe. Now the girls looked expectantly to Phoebe. April Rose noticed a girl she had not seen before; this must be Elora, she thought to herself. She looked carefully at Elora, though trying not to overtly stare at the girl.

Elora looked to be about ten years old, at the most, and she was dressed in boys' clothing. Her hair and face were definitely feminine, though, so she could not very well pretend to be a boy. April Rose presumed that the clothing was probably more suitable for the rugged life this girl must be living at present. Her hair was black and braided, and her skin was a beautiful dark caramel brown. Elora had huge dark eyes with very long dark eyelashes; she looked at April Rose, and when their eyes met, April thought of the eyes of a fawn.

There was something about this girl that piqued April's interest; she felt as though she had seen her before---or knew her somehow. Was this the child she had seen in the woods?

Phoebe was explaining now to Elora what she, April Rose, and Lily would have to do if they saw they could not fit through the opening of the tunnel at the Dragon's Tail. She explained that the three would instead go to the station which opened to the tax collector's home. Elora listened carefully and she nodded in understanding. Then Elora motioned to the girls and she led the way into the tunnel which would take them to the Dragon's Tail.

After all the girls had entered this tunnel, Phoebe went in and April Rose and Lily followed. It was extremely dark. There was no light at all except that which came from the lanterns. They walked in single file, and the ceiling was low, but not so much as the first segment of their passage had been. A taller person would have had to bend over, but they only had to crouch down a little, bending their knees somewhat. The children did not have to bend over at all.

April Rose had not been in small dark places such as this, except for that one horrible time when she was escaping from the evil prince. She had a suffocating feeling inside, and she had to make herself focus on the light ahead and take slow deep breaths so she did not feel so overwhelmed. Suddenly she heard the voice of the Prince in her mind and felt a warm sensation in her heart. "I am with you," said the Prince, "Don't be afraid."

"I miss you so much," she told the Prince with her thoughts. "I know. I miss you, too," he replied. "It will all be worth everything, when you come back to the castle. We will rejoice together."

"Thank you," she said to him in her mind and she smiled. His kindness to her felt like an embrace. Oh, she couldn't wait to be back with him again! But something good would come from this ordeal, and it would bring happiness to many, she was sure. If it brought happiness to others, then it truly would delight the Prince, and she would be glad.

Lily touched her shoulder just then and whispered: "Did he speak to you too?" she asked, and April Rose whispered back, "Yes, he did!"

They were greatly encouraged and it didn't seem quite as dark as before.

The tunnel they were in had many twists and turns and winding curves. Elora confidently led the way through all these, holding a lantern up to see her way. Elora must possess a very good sense of direction, April Rose thought to herself.

April Rose had even more compassion for her students after seeing what it was like in these tunnels. There seemed to be no end; it felt as if they had been walking in this darkness forever. No wonder these girls were so weary. Every other night or at least several times a week they had been sent into the tunnels to deliver the opium.

These girls only had a full night's sleep for half of their week, which meant only half of their young lives, for the duration of the time they had been sold into this slavery. Their plight was only slightly compensated by a little bit of education, which they could barely retain due to their weariness.

Still, April Rose hoped that the girls had absorbed something from their teaching. She looked forward to seeing these girls have a good education once they were free. Yes, that would be worth this entire ordeal, she thought to herself. She hoped for a good home for each girl.

April Rose and Lily plodded on through the vast darkness and through the narrow space with that hope in mind. The children probably did not even dare to hope for that, but they trusted Phoebe.

Phoebe trusted April Rose and Lily, and they in turn, trusted the Prince.

A lot depended on trust, April Rose thought to herself. She remembered how she had not trusted the prince at all when she came to the Kingdom of Grace. Now her life and the lives of others depended on that trust in the Prince. So much had changed. She wondered what her father would think if he could see her now! She missed him very much at that moment.

Then she remembered his story, and how the Prince had rescued him, and then he and his friends rescued her mother. April Rose realized her life had always depended on this trust in the Prince. She herself was the product of his rescues, in more ways than one.

She would have no existence if the Prince had not rescued her father and her mother when they were children. There really was not much existence at all without the Prince. His love WAS the reason for existence; without it, living was not really life. She would never want to live without it again. He could heal broken hearts, she reasoned. He could heal her father's broken heart, too, and April felt just then that she would be part of that healing.

April Rose realized with a jolt that the little caravan through the tunnels had stopped. The light from the lanterns remained still, as all the children had stopped. A message was passed down the line from child to child until it reached Phoebe, and then she told April Rose and Lily: "We are about to enter the Dragon's Tail."

The caravan started moving again; April Rose saw the lights swaying and bobbing up ahead as the children began walking in this new direction. From here, the Dragon's Tail looked no different than the other tunnel segment, but of course they could not see details in the dark.

She had no concept of how long this tunnel was, or when it would curve upward. They faced the unknown since this exit might be too small for her and Lily and Phoebe. She hoped Phoebe knew the way to the station at the tax collector's house, because Elora would no longer be with them. She and the other children would soon be on their way to the hideout in the woods.

There was another long time of plodding through darkness, and then at last the caravan stopped. They had come to the very end of the Dragon's Tail. April Rose could not tell if the tunnel had become narrower yet, since she was at the end of the caravan with Lily.

Suddenly, there was a faint shaft of light, and it was not from the lantern. This was moonlight; Elora had opened the tunnel door which led up into the cave. Elora crawled out first into the cave and checked to be sure that it was safe. The coach driver was there waiting, and two more were hidden in the woods surrounding the cave.

Elora came back in, and began sending the first group of girls to get in the waiting carriage. When this carriage was full, the driver flicked the reins and the horses began moving. The next carriage came close to the cave and waited, and Elora sent out the next group.

April Rose was impressed with Elora's leadership skills, and her dedication to helping her fellow students. She would look forward to becoming better acquainted with Elora.

Elora waited for the third carriage and sent out the last few girls to get in this one. She spoke quietly to the driver about the narrow opening and the problem that existed with this, and asked him to wait. Elora then came back inside the tunnel to see what would happen.

Phoebe climbed up into the opening which was the tail end of this tunnel they had dubbed "The Dragon's Tail." It did indeed curve up, and the opening was child-sized. Phoebe could not get through the space. Elora told the driver about the alternate plan, and she went back into the tunnel to speak with Phoebe.

"Do you know the way, or should I come with you?" asked Elora in a concerned voice.

"I believe I can find it," said Phoebe. "I know the landmarks. You go on to the woods---the girls will need your support."

Elora looked relieved, and then she climbed out and entered the carriage, which immediately set out in the direction of the woods, some distance away from the city.

Chapter 33

Phoebe closed the trapdoor which had opened to the cave, and they were buried in darkness once more. They had but one lantern left with them; all the others had been sent with the girls. The girls would need these lights in the underground room hidden in the woods.

It was so deadly quiet that Phoebe, April Rose, and Lily could almost hear their own heartbeats. The heavy silence felt oppressive to them, in the dark musty underground tunnel.

Phoebe turned to go back the way they had come, holding the lantern up high at intervals to reveal any landmarks which would indicate where they should turn next. April Rose and Lily followed right behind Phoebe, literally walking in her shadow.

Suddenly, Phoebe stopped abruptly and turned to face April Rose and Lily. "I have been feeling the strangest sensation," she said in an awed tone of voice. "There are only three of us, but it feels as if there are four---as if there is someone else who is with us."

April Rose and Lily looked at each other and smiled with joy. "There ARE four of us," Lily answered. "The Prince is with us, though you cannot see him."

Phoebe's face looked puzzled. "Is he only a spirit?" she asked her friends. "No," replied April Rose. "He does have a body, but he is able to be many places at the same time, in spirit."

Phoebe still looked perplexed. "I don't understand this Prince of yours, but if he can hear me, I'm glad he is with us," she said. "I will be grateful for his help to get out of this tunnel."

They continued walking through the Dragon's Tail tunnel, slightly bent over, until it ended in an intersection with other tunnels leading to various places. Phoebe stood there, holding up the lantern to reveal any symbols to indicate the right tunnel. Finally, Phoebe saw what she was looking for; it was a crude etching that represented a coin.

"This is it," Phoebe said. "This tunnel will take us to the tax collector's home."

"When we get there, will we have to come out in his home?" wondered Lily. April Rose was glad Lily had asked, because she too had concerns about this.

"We will come out into a secret room," explained Phoebe. "All of these big mansions have secret rooms built into them. I confess that I do not know how we will get out after that. I hope your Prince will show us; and with determination, I am sure we will find the way out."

That was not very reassuring news, but April Rose could not fault Phoebe for her lack of information. She still did not know how the Prince planned to evacuate all the children from the woods hideout, either. There were unknowns, but there was no turning back now.

They pressed on through the dark tunnel toward an uncertain dilemma, trusting in their hope, and hoping in their trust.

They had to stop for a moment, and put a new candle in the lantern, lighting it from the old candle which had by now melted down into a stub. After Phoebe was sure that the new one was thoroughly lit and would not flicker and go out, she put the stub on the tunnel floor and ground out the wick with her boot.

Then the trio proceeded to go on through the tunnel in its winding course through the dark underground. The curves were almost always unpredictable, and April Rose remarked that this tunnel felt as though it was patterned after the movements of an earthworm. Lily agreed and they both laughed at the absurdity.

Phoebe however cautioned more silence, as she sensed that it would not be much longer until they were in the tax collector's house. April Rose had heard of secret rooms built into old mansions by eccentric owners, but she had never imagined that she would be invading a house through one of those hidden passageways.

Suddenly she had a disturbing thought that had not occurred to her before. "Phoebe," she urgently whispered, "What if the door from the tunnel to the house can only be unlocked from inside?"

"I understand your concern," Phoebe whispered back. "The girls were instructed to wait until the door was opened to deliver the opium, and they did, but some of the older girls thought that they saw how the doors could be opened from the outside. Elora has tested their idea on the tax collector's door and found that it worked."

"Smart girls!" whispered Lily.

"Elora is very brave," remarked April Rose in a low voice. "How did she dare to open it, not knowing if someone would be in the secret room?"

"She just listened, and took the chance," explained Phoebe. "I think that her hearing has been much heightened by all the time she has spent in these tunnels---she relies on her hearing more. As a precaution, she disguised herself in all black and wore a black hood. We had this outfit made for her—this is what she usually wears in the tunnels so that she is less visible."

"What is the secret to opening the door?" Lily whispered to Phoebe.

"To the right of the door at the base, there is a disguised hole," said Phoebe in a whisper. "Inside this little alcove, the girls found a round tool. As there is a round indention on the door, the girls reasoned that this must be a kind of key. Elora tried it out and it worked---it must be magnetic. She turned it around in the indention and heard a series of clicks, and then the door could be easily opened from the outside."

After this reassurance, the girls continued on through the silent darkness of the tunnel, guided by the lantern. The tunnel floor seemed to be gradually and steadily inclining upwards, which was another indication that they were not far from the tax collector's home.

The secret room was most likely in the basement of the official's home, so April Rose surmised that they had been traveling at a level two stories deep underground—possibly three, since the tunnel floor slope was being raised only to the level of the house's basement.

They continued to trudge upwards for a while, and then there was a sharp turn in the tunnel, and after the turn, there it was. They found themselves at the door of the tax collector's house. The three remained perfectly silent, involuntarily holding their breath, so that they could listen for any sounds coming from the secret room.

None were detected, so Phoebe moved the stone piece which covered and disguised the tiny alcove near their feet, and she tediously removed the circular magnetic device. It almost looked like a chess piece; it was white, with a round base, and had a knob on top that one could hold to turn it in the indented space.

Phoebe paused and looked at the faces of her friends as if to ask if they were ready. April Rose and Lily gave a slight nod of agreement, and then Phoebe put the round piece into the indention on the door. She turned it slightly, then listened, and turned it some more. This time, they all heard the slight click-click-click in the overwhelming silence of the tunnel.

Phoebe gently pushed at the door, and it began to open. She held it ajar, and then she handed the magnetic key to Lily, and pointed towards the alcove. Lily understood by this gesture that she needed to put the key back into its hidden place, and she did so, and carefully replaced the cover in front of the hole.

Then Phoebe pushed at the door some more, and it slowly opened wider. The room was dark, but Phoebe held up the lantern and they looked around the room. The walls were a dark red brick, and along one wall there were tall walnut stained wooden cabinets. The door that they came in through was disguised on this side by red bricks so that when closed, it blended completely into the brick wall. The closed door was now undetectable. On one side of the room, there was a glass and wood curio cabinet with unusual and grotesque artifacts.

So the man didn't only collect taxes, April Rose thought wryly to herself. She forced herself to look away from these macabre items, and stared very intently at the tall wood cabinets. Judging from the way these were recessed into the wall, one of these was most likely a door. Phoebe was already searching and feeling the grooves of the cabinets. Lily and April Rose joined her and each of them explored a section of this wall of cabinets.

Lily discovered a seam which ran down the wall alongside the cabinet, and she pushed at this one section. The door was heavy and thick, and it took all three of them to push it open.

On the other side, it was a heavy bookcase. There was probably some sort of lever behind the books to open the door from this side, April Rose guessed. There would have to be some sort of mechanism since the door was so heavy. She was relieved that they only had to push against it from the outside. Now they were inside the mansion, and this was apparently a gentlemen's room with a billiard table, a poker table, and a bar for serving drinks. They moved around slowly and quietly, looking for the exit from this room, and listening for any movement above them.

In one corner, there was an oval door with carvings on it, and a brass handle. When Lily pulled this door open, they saw a narrow winding flight of stairs going upward. They hesitated, wondering if this was the only exit, and then April Rose saw a tall wardrobe with mirror insets on its double doors. She opened these doors out of curiosity, only to find that there was no back to this wardrobe. It was an entrance to the next room.

The room they went into now, was obviously the opium room. There were many velvet covered chairs and small tables, and there was a peculiar smoky smell. The wallpaper was of velvet with a paisley pattern, and the central light here was a hanging chandelier. Opulence was the theme of the room and there were mirrors hung on every wall and above the marble framed fireplace. There was only one full-length mirror, and when Lily pushed on it, it opened into an elegant wash room, with a marble basin on a stand, and a marble commode. There didn't seem to be any exit from this room, so they turned to go back up the narrow stairs.

Since the owner of the house was considerably wealthy, the stairs were covered in a flowered carpet, and this would help muffle the sound of their feet. So they began to climb the narrow staircase, stepping as softly as they could and listening for any other sounds.

Phoebe held the lantern aloft, as they quietly went up the narrow winding stairs, not knowing at all what they would find on the next floor above.

Chapter 34

The staircase ended at a narrow door, which they discovered was another concealed door. After they went through and carefully closed it, the narrow door was indistinguishable from the wall covering around it.

They found themselves underneath a grand, massive staircase with a curved ornately carved bannister and a balustrade of carved pillars. The wide staircase was on one side of a very spacious hall with extremely high ceilings, enormous gold chandeliers, and very tall paintings in elegant gilded frames hanging on the walls. On either side of the large hall, there were huge rooms meant for entertainment, open on one side to this foyer.

To their right, there was a dining room with a very long buffet table in its center, and many velvet covered chairs along the walls. On their left, there was a ballroom with intricate murals on the walls, huge arched windows, and two grand pianos facing each other.

And in between these two large rooms, there was the front door. Their eyes were drawn to the door, but they concluded that these tremendously large double doors would be exceptionally heavy and hard to open. Silently, Phoebe pointed to another exit out of this hallway, which was along the back wall on their right.

As Phoebe had suspected, this exit led into a large kitchen, beyond which was a pantry room. Before they reached the pantry room, there was a door leading out of the kitchen into a hallway with many doors leading to other rooms. At the end of this hallway, they at last saw what they were looking for: a door which led outside.

They came to this door and saw with dismay that it could only be opened with a key. Just at that very moment, they heard a noise coming from above them. It had to be either someone on the stairs, or someone in the bedrooms above.

Phoebe, April Rose, and Lily in panic glanced at one another and then desperately looked around for the key, hoping to find it hanging on a hook somewhere. April Rose began to feel despair, until suddenly she heard the voice of the Prince in her mind. "Use your key, April Rose," the voice said. "It will open any door."

Quickly she removed it from her pocket, and slid the pronged end into the keyhole. Phoebe and Lily stared wide-eyed as April Rose turned the key, and the door was unlocked. She carefully put the key back into her pocket, and beckoned to her friends. Phoebe cautiously opened the door.

Silently they slipped through the door, coming out into a paved courtyard with a high wooden fence around it. They saw the gate and headed towards it, almost tiptoeing so their shoes made no sound on the stones of the paving. The gate had a latch which they slid to unlatch, and they each passed through the opening. Just as they did so, a dog barked in the distance, and they saw a light instantly appear in an upper window.

Phoebe frantically blew out the candle in their one lantern, to avoid detection in the dark. They waited breathlessly before making any other movement, in case the dog was let loose.

Then April Rose saw the dim shadowy outline of the stagecoach parked in a small wood on the grounds of the mansion, and she headed towards it. The clouds shifted and the brief moonlight that shone through was just enough in that moment to give confirmation to the girls, that the coach did indeed belong to Aziel and Keturah.

Phoebe and Lily followed behind April Rose, avoiding the rocks that might crunch under their feet. April Rose was close to the coach when she had a strong feeling that something was not right;

an uncanny suspicion and dread came over her, and she stopped.

"It's a trap," the Prince's voice spoke urgently into her mind. "Run!"

Just at that moment, a face leered out at her from the open window of the coach. This was the face of someone she had hoped to never see again; it was the face of Hanson.

"Run!" April Rose whispered hoarsely to her two friends, and they all began to run wildly away from the mansion and towards a wood further away in the distance.

The two men seated on the driver's bench of the carriage jumped down and began pursuing the girls. Hanson was focusing all his cruel energy on catching April Rose, and he pursued her with an angry vengeance. She ran hard and fast and she caught up with her friends, but the men were now gaining ground quickly and would soon be upon them. April Rose heard Hanson's heavy breathing just behind her, and his cold slimy hand was close as he reached out to grab her.

Without warning, a man appeared out of nowhere and stood between the girls and their pursuers. He was dressed in a silver helmet with a faceguard, silver breastplate, and silver gauntlets. In his hand was a long gleaming silver sword which he deftly brandished in a threatening gesture towards the three men in pursuit of the girls.

Their pursuers took one look at that gleaming sword and stopped abruptly in horror. There was no mistaking the look of terror on their faces at the sight of this warrior in silver armor.

"Go back to your evil master!" the man in armor said with such authority, that the three pursuant men immediately slunk away, then turned and fled into the darkness.

"Go and untie your friends," said the man in armor. "They are in the stagecoach."

That was all he said to them, but his authority was so great, that they did not dare to ask him any questions or delay doing as he said. The three girls began walking back to the coach, hidden in the shadows of the grove of trees. They looked back once, but no one was there. The man in the silver armor had vanished.

Arriving at the coach, they discovered that Aziel and Keturah had been gagged and tied up and lay on the floor inside the coach. The three girls quickly freed them, and Aziel and Keturah sat up gratefully, though they still looked somewhat dazed from their shocking capture. "Do you think you can drive?" asked Phoebe quietly, with much concern in her voice.

"Yes," said Aziel. "We are ready to complete this mission." And with that speech of determination, he climbed out of the coach and helped Keturah to stand and get out of the coach as well. Then they both climbed up to their perch on the driver's seat.

All this time, the horses had stood still and quiet, patiently waiting for their real master's command. The three girls entered the coach and then Aziel flicked the reins and the coach slowly began to move as the horses pulled it out of the shelter of the trees.

When they were far enough away from any of the houses, Phoebe broke the silence in the coach by asking, "Was that the Prince?"

"I have never seen him dressed as a warrior until this night," said April Rose. "But, yes, that person was undoubtedly the Prince."

"Did you see the look on their faces?" remarked Lily, and she almost giggled.

"Yes," said April Rose, "I did, but I don't think I can laugh about it just yet. I was frightened almost out of my mind. The man who got out of the coach was the man who captured me when I first came to the Kingdom of Grace," April Rose confided to her friends in the safety of the coach.

"What happened?" asked Phoebe.

"I didn't trust the Prince at that time," said April Rose sadly. "I was running away from him, and this man Hanson tricked me, and took me to the evil prince. I was locked in a dungeon, and the worst part was that they poisoned me and I lost the ability to speak after that."

"What did you do?" Phoebe asked, wondering how April Rose had escaped.

"I did the only sensible thing. I called out to the Prince with my mind, and he came and rescued me," said April Rose. "I had found this key back home, and I didn't know what it could do, but that is how I came here in the first place. This key opened a door into the Kingdom of Grace. When I was in the dungeon, the prince made my chains fall off my hands. Then he told me to use the key on the door of the dungeon, and it opened."

"And how did you get away?" was Phoebe's next question.

"The Prince was waiting for me outside the castle. He has a beautiful white horse, and we rode back together to his home," answered April Rose.

"Then he restored my voice when he healed me with his antidote." April Rose told them.

"What do you mean by that?" Phoebe asked in a very puzzled voice. "What antidote?"

"There is a disease inside of us that we are born with, and it makes us impure," replied April Rose. "The only one who has the cure is the Prince."

"I have never heard of this," Phoebe informed her friends. "Are you sure this is true?"

"I am more positive of this than anything else in my life," said April Rose, "although it did take a long time for me to believe."

"What about you, Lily?" Phoebe wanted to know. "Was it hard for you to believe?"

"Mine is a different story," Lily explained. "I knew the Prince since I was very little, and it is much easier to believe when you are a child."

"I am looking forward to speaking with your Prince," said Phoebe with longing in her voice. "I have so many questions."

The girls could not talk any further about this, as they were nearing the woods. Aziel stopped the coach, and Keturah came inside the coach so that

Phoebe could sit by Aziel and direct him to the hideout deep in the woods.

Aziel had many questions about the hideout; who had made it and how? Surely the children could not have devised such a thing or dug such a deep hole themselves. "No," explained Phoebe. "It had already been dug, but we don't know by whom or why. Only a few know about it, and we acquired their help to improve on the construction."

"The walls are dirt with many rows of stones packed in to strengthen them, and the roof is made of slender timber logs laid over the top of the hole," Phoebe related. "It wasn't waterproof enough, although the roof slopes back to allow for drainage. So we hauled planks of wood sealed with tar and laid these over the timbers," continued Phoebe. "Then there was the problem of heating it without catching it on fire; so we brought a small potbelly stove with a chimney and vented it up through a hole in the roof. Last, we used the existing foliage growing around it and caused it to grow over the roof, creating a natural camouflage. Then little by little, we covered the dirt floor with scrap pieces of wood that we salvaged."

"You have done well," remarked Aziel with admiration in his voice. "The Prince notices kindness like yours; it will not go unrewarded."

"I don't need a reward," Phoebe replied. "It will be enough to see that the girls are safe."

"This Prince rewards us with things that cannot tarnish or fade or diminish with age," said Aziel. "His rewards are not ever token things. He always knows what will delight us the most."

They traveled in silence for a little while, and then Aziel began to wonder about the conditions of the closest harbor, and whether it was isolated.

"What is the nearest harbor like?" Aziel asked Phoebe. "Will it be crowded, and difficult to get the children on board a ship without detection?"

"Oh, no," answered Phoebe. "We will not have to be concerned at all about that. This harbor has been abandoned for some time, as the city chose to make a port closer to its area of commerce."

"So this harbor is not visible to the other one?" asked Aziel.

"No, thankfully it is not," said Phoebe. "The miles of distance, and the extreme curve of the coastline prevent vision of any activity between the harbors. Do you know the prince's plan of rescue?"

"Not yet," said Aziel. "I am just thinking about the possibilities, and considering them. But whatever he does will be the best possible solution."

Chapter 35

The carriage left the outskirts of the town, and headed back in the direction they had come from, on their first day of arrival in this place. However, Phoebe guided Aziel to depart from the main road at a certain point, and to take a less traveled road leading to the woods.

Aziel had regained the sharp focus of his eyes, and he spotted the narrow road which went directly into the woods. He turned into this road, though they had to go very slowly now, as it was quite a squeeze to get the stagecoach through the trees here.

Finally, Phoebe directed Aziel to stop the carriage; the trees would become even denser after this point, and they would not be able to get through. Aziel and Phoebe climbed down from the driver's bench, and Aziel helped the girls and his wife, out of the carriage. They would all have to hike from here to the hideout. The carriage was well hidden; in fact, it took a few minutes before they saw the other three carriages dispersed here and there among the trees.

Phoebe relit her lantern, and they began the trek deeper into the forest. It was still night time, and the trees stood tall and silent like sentries, and their bark looked almost black. The light from the moon reached the forest floor here and there, and turned the foliage a blue green color. The copious fern which spread and covered much of the forest floor reminded April Rose of a soft feathery sort of blanket. There was the occasional spark from the light of a firefly, the whispering sound of the wind through the leaves, and an unseen owl hooting in a mournful way.

Phoebe led the way and the light from the lantern was bobbing just ahead of her as she held it aloft to see her way. When a cloud drifted in front of the moon now and then, they were plunged into deep darkness. Then the lantern light seemed to shrink in size; it looked so very small and feeble within the space of such a huge canopy of black hanging over them. They could see no stars on this cloudy night, so they were grateful to have the moonlight, however sporadic it might be.

Sometimes a pair of eyes gleamed in the lantern light, and something could be heard scurrying away. They came to a narrow, but swiftly flowing brook, and took time to get a drink from its clear water running over a bed of small stones. After they drank from the brook, they crossed it and continued in the direction in which Phoebe was leading the little group of travelers.

There seemed to be no evidence at all of anyone living in this wood, and April Rose marveled at the seclusion of this place. It was like another world, especially at night.

And suddenly they were there; Phoebe knocked on the forest floor and they heard the sound of her knuckles rapping on wood. Then a foliage covered trapdoor opened and out stepped Elora to meet them, followed by the rest of those who were in the hideout. They were all there; the twenty-four rescued slave girls, and the other coach drivers.

Of course, they had all been concerned about the delay in the arrival of Phoebe, April Rose, and Lily. Everyone was dismayed to learn of the attack on Aziel and Keturah, and how these fiendish men had chased after April Rose, Lily, and Phoebe. The students who knew April Rose and Lily as their teachers threw their arms around them, and embraced their teachers. Elora and the other girls who had been hidden for a while, hugged Phoebe.

Phoebe suggested that they all go down into the hideout and have something to eat. Then they should pack up the food that was left. "I think we will all be leaving this place tonight," Phoebe said. "We have seen the Prince."

So one of the men held up the trap door, and the group carefully climbed down the steps into this underground shelter, one at a time. The hidden space was quite large, though the roof was low, and roomy enough to be comfortable even for thirty people or so. Instead of chairs, there were blankets, and rough shelves for supplies leaned against the earth and stone walls.

April Rose looked around this secret room; it did remind her of a storm shelter she had seen when she was little, although this one was larger.

Everyone sat on the blankets and lanterns were hung on some large metal hooks protruding from the timber in the roof. Elora and the older girls passed out biscuits and cheese and fruit to each person. There was a wooden bucket for water with a dipper, but there were not many wooden cups, so these were shared and passed along. Not very sanitary, April Rose thought to herself, but in this place of refuge, one could not remain bothered by such considerations.

Suddenly, Elora stood up and said, "Someone is coming. I feel the vibrations in the earth." And she was right; soon they all heard the sound and felt the vibrations of hoof beats.

No one spoke after that; they remained as still as possible. They listened intensely as the sound of the hoof beats became louder and more distinct. The sounds grew closer and closer and the eyes of the children showed increasing alarm.

Then it sounded as if the hoof beats were almost on top of them, and after that, there was complete silence for what seemed to be an unbearably long moment. They hardly dared to breathe as they waited in the underground room, glancing at the horror visible in each other's faces, until a sudden knock on the trap door broke the silence.

"You are safe now," said a kind voice with great authority. "You can come out now."

One of the drivers lifted the trap door and looked out and what he saw amazed him. There was a man in a silver helmet and breastplate standing nearby and he was accompanied by six other men dressed in similar fashion. Every one of these men had a silver sword girded to their sides.

"Who are you, sir?" asked the driver in a shaky awed voice.

"I am the Prince of Grace," the armored man in front of the others answered him. "I have a ship waiting in the harbor to take the children back to my kingdom. I will need your assistance to deliver them to the ship."

"Yes, sir, your majesty sir," replied the driver, stumbling over his words in his wonder at this personage standing before him. Then he excitedly addressed the group waiting below.

"The Prince of Grace has come," he declared with great joy. "He has a ship waiting in the harbor to take all the children safely away from here!"

"Quickly, children, let us pack up the food so we do not waste it," instructed Phoebe, and all the children complied. "I understand the stagecoaches will bring you to the ship."

After all the food and supplies had been gathered into four bundles, these were given to the coach drivers to bring with them on the journey to the harbor. The oldest of the children held the lanterns for the others.

The Prince and his men stood further back as the trapdoor was held open for the little procession of people to emerge from the secret hideout. As they came out, the children were in awe at the sight of the men in their armor.

When everyone was out of the hiding place, and the trap door was concealed again, the Prince held up his sword to point the direction back to the stage coaches and then he led the way. The band of people began to follow him, and two of his men stayed behind to be the rear guard for the group of people on their way to a new life.

When the procession reached the place where the stagecoaches had been left, the Prince waited while each driver got his coach ready, and six of the children were seated safely in each of the four carriages. The Prince gave a short whistle and ten beautiful horses, each equipped with saddles and bridles, emerged from a short distance away in the shadowy woods.

April Rose and Lily were overjoyed when they recognized that two of these horses were their very own steeds. The Prince raised his face shield and smiled at the girls. He was pleased to see their joy. "You will be riding back with my men and I," he said graciously to April Rose and Lily. "And I also have a horse for you, Phoebe. I would like you to accompany us as well, and I assure you that your horse is gentle and well trained."

"Thank you, sir," said Phoebe humbly and she gave a little bow. "May I ask if you mean just until we arrive at the ship, or did you mean for the entire journey?"

"I would enjoy your company for the entire journey, Phoebe," replied the Prince. "The girls will be safe on my ship with my staff assisting them."

"Then I would be honored, sir," replied Phoebe, and she bowed again. It was more than honor that she actually felt; she felt loved and cherished.

So April Rose and Lily mounted their horses and Phoebe mounted the horse designated for her, and they waited for directions.

The Prince led the procession with the girls on their horses following behind him, and next the stagecoaches lined up behind the girls, with the Prince's men following behind the coaches.

It was almost day when they arrived at the harbor; most of the children had fallen asleep on the way, leaning on each other inside the coaches. They woke up when the swaying motion of the coaches stopped and they sat up and looked out of the windows in anticipation.

The coaches and horses were standing on the wooden dock, and the boarding ramp was being lowered onto the dock. These girls stared ahead transfixed; they had never seen a ship before, and this one was a beauty. It was a Caravel ship with a square sail on the mainmast, and foremast, and a lateen sail on the mizzen.

A very tall dark-skinned man was standing regally on the deck of this ship, waiting for its passengers. April Rose recognized him immediately, and had to suppress a squeal of joy at seeing Sir Guide.

The Prince turned around and addressed April Rose with a smile. "Yes," he said, "Sir Guide will accompany the children on the ship for the journey home. And there's one other person you will be delighted to see."

At that statement, Saphire joined Sir Guide on the deck of the ship. April Rose was elated; she knew that her students would not feel awkward or at all uncomfortable since Saphire was there.

Then the children were helped out of the coaches and received onto the ship by Sir Guide and by Saphire. April Rose observed the faces of the students and was relieved to see that they were not frightened. She would have liked to be in two places at once; her desire to be with the Prince was great, but she also had been concerned about the children's comfort.

Next, the Prince addressed the coach drivers who had brought the children to the harbor. He had something very special to tell these men.

Chapter 36

"Aziel and Keturah are already in my service," said the Prince, "And I sent them here to help in the rescue of the children who were enslaved. I would also like to extend the invitation to the rest of you coach drivers to come with us."

"Sir," explained one of the men, "We would be delighted to come with you, but what about our families?"

"The ship will sail, but if you choose to come with us, I and my men will wait for you to go and get your families," said the Prince. "You will have to persuade them to leave all your belongings, and I will replace everything that you need."

"I will go, sir," one of the drivers immediately answered, and he turned his carriage around to return to the town. The two other drivers also turned around to go back to their town. Both of these drivers affirmed that they would rejoin the Prince with their families.

While they waited, the Prince gave April Rose, Lily, and Phoebe permission to board the ship and speak to the children one more time before the ship departed from the harbor. They were elated to do so, and quickly dismounted and ran to the ship. They walked up the ramp onto the deck.

April Rose gave Sir Guide and Saphire each a big hug, and then hurried to the children. The children were ecstatic at the thought of sailing on a ship, and excitedly showed their teachers and friend the bunkbeds they would sleep in on the lower deck.

Just then, the sun began to rise, spreading pink and orange glowing light over the water and then turning it to gold. The little girls all clapped their hands in joy and squealed with delight at such a beautiful display of color. Their entire world had been wrapped in gray up until now.

"I think I want to wear a dress made out of that," said one small girl. "You mean the colors?" asked April Rose, and the little girl nodded solemnly with her eyes fixed on the sunrise. "I think that can be arranged," April Rose assured the little girl, smiling down at her. That little girl took April Rose's hand in hers and looked up at her with those big solemn eyes and said, "Thank you." After that little girl's poignant speech, April Rose began to have tears come to her eyes, but she smiled.

There were many other moments like that for April Rose and Lily before they disembarked from the ship and returned to their horses. This time, April Rose had to use her sleeve to wipe her eyes, but she didn't care. She had no handkerchief in her pocket, but the key was still safely in there, and that was far more important.

The ship set sail, and the children stood on the deck and waved goodbye to April Rose, Lily, and Phoebe as it moved away from the dock. Sir Guide held up the smallest child who was too short to see over the side of the ship. April Rose and Lily and Phoebe waved and waved until the ship was too far away and they couldn't see the faces of the little girls anymore.

"I think you have made an impression," said the Prince to April Rose and Lily, and he smiled.

"They made an impression on me," said April Rose, smiling through her tears.

They sat there on their horses and waited a while longer, and then at last, two carriages returned with family members sitting in them. Phoebe was overjoyed to see the face of the cook in one of those carriages. The cook had been fired from her job after her "evidence" was discovered, and the headmaster believed that the school was almost robbed. She had gone to a relative's house, who happened to be one of the coach drivers.

"Where is the third carriage?" asked the Prince of the other drivers who had returned.

They both looked down sadly, and shook their heads. "His family wouldn't come," said one of these men. The Prince looked sad for a moment, and then he said, "Not all will follow me---but you have made the wiser choice."

And so they set out for the Kingdom of Grace, with the Prince and his men leading the way, and April Rose, Lily, and Phoebe among them, and the stagecoaches following behind them.

Their journey took them along the seashore as they had left the woods with the hideout behind them when they came to the harbor. This was a desolate area; there was no sea commerce along this route. April Rose enjoyed the solitude and quiet as they rode by the sea with its lapping waves and rolling motion and its endless horizon.

There were seagulls gliding overhead and the wind rustled clumps of seagrass along the shore. April Rose watched as the frothy waves rushed in and painted the sand, and then slid back to allow another wave to pour its foamy layer over the cool sand. The rhythmic sound had a soothing effect as the sequence of waves tumbled in over and over each other.

The dark blue streaks of the sky near the horizon gradually faded to lighter shades, as the rising sun lit up white clouds above the blue. April Rose watched in fascination and wonder at the continual rushing forward and pulling backward of the waves and their foamy white edges, spreading out thinly over the sand.

"Who set this in motion?" April Rose asked the Prince as they rode by this scene. She had slipped into an open space next to him, in order to ask.

He lifted his face shield and turned to look at April Rose. "My lovely daughter," he said to her with a laughing smile, "Why do you ask?"

"It was you!" April Rose said joyously. "Of course it was you!"

She had the sudden urge to bolt forward and race her horse into that golden streak of sunrise lying on the water, but she knew she could not waste her horse's energy. They had a long way ahead of them. She wanted to walk in bare feet on the wet sand and stand in the wind. But it could not be today; so she would enjoy it with her eyes.

"I know your longing," said the Prince lovingly. "That is why I made the sand and sea. When you look at the waves endlessly coming and going, know that my love for you will never end. The full depth of the ocean has never been probed, and so is my love for you. It is so deep that it can never be fully comprehended---only enjoyed."

Phoebe was listening to all of this conversation in wonder. Lily was just absorbing all of the ocean sights and smells; she looked lost in the imagery of it all, and rode by this on her horse dreamily.

They came to a place where the cliffs began, and the caravan stopped here for a brief rest. There were places where they could sit on the rocks of the cliff, and Lily discovered that canteens and provisions had been packed in their saddle bags. April Rose, Lily, and Phoebe ate some sweet honey bread for their breakfast, fed and watered their horses, and then walked over to greet Aziel and Keturah. Phoebe ran on to give the cook, whose name was Joanna, a big grateful hug.

Then it was time to return to the trail. They would be leaving the sea behind them here, and would begin crossing a great prairie until they came to the canyons.

April Rose began to be aware that she had not slept all night; her head would sink down and then jerk up as she resisted falling asleep. She and her friends fell back in the line as they were moving slower than before.

The Prince looked back at the three girls and he held up his hand to stop the procession. He turned his horse around and trotted over to the girls. "You must ride in the carriage for a while," he told them.

"I know that you did not sleep at all last night. We will lead your horses."

Aziel and Keturah's carriage was empty, and the three girls were very grateful to curl up on its seats and sleep for a while. They were so tired that even the swaying and jolting over uneven ground did not wake them. They slept through half of the ride over the prairie.

When they awakened, it was past noon, but they were stopping for a brief rest close to a small grove of trees. There was a creek nearby, and the horses drank and grazed for a short time, while everyone ate their lunch and walked around a bit.

April Rose and Lily saw two birds of prey circling in the sky at a distance, and felt a shudder of horror. The sentries had also seen them, and they were prepared and ready for any attack, but the two monstrous birds never came closer.

"They probably wouldn't dare," said Lily. "They see the Prince and his armed men."

Everyone mounted up as the carriages were prepared again, and the caravan set out once more. The girls felt more rested and had decided to ride their horses again. Phoebe had not done much riding before, but she had been around the horses quite often while meeting with the drivers to arrange the individual rescues they had carried out, as well as deliveries.

They rode through the tall grasses of the prairie with the afternoon sun at their backs. The wind rippled the grass in furrows and blew through their hair, which kept them cool. They knew that the Prince intended to reach the canyon by nightfall and camp there.

They had almost reached the edge of the canyon as the afternoon shadows became darker. Here, the Prince sent two of his men on ahead to scout out the caves on the upper ledges, while the rest of the caravan waited in the shade of a few trees, not far from the rock walls of the canyon. When the two men returned, they had good news. They had found a large cave.

It would be large enough for the entire group and their horses. There was also a lower level where the stagecoaches could be left safely; even if there was a flash flood, it would not reach them. So the procession set out for this location and they found it was not too far away.

The way to the cave was not particularly hard to climb, either, and there was a large flat area right outside of the cave. While they still had daylight, preparations were made to build a campfire on this flat space that was rather like a small plateau.

Joanna and some of the women gathered the food supplies that had been brought from the hideout, and improvised a means to make a meal from what they had with them.

The sun began to set, sending golden orange rays over the rust colored mountains and creating dark shadows in the crevices. As the sun went down, the wind was cool, and the carved rock walls became very dark. Here on this small plateau, the fire was warm and red and crackling with little sparks. They sat close to each other around this fire, and it truly felt like a family. The Prince began to sing a blessing and his voice carried through the canyon. Then the food was served, and water was shared, and everyone was satisfied.

Even the terrifying scream of a mountain cougar somewhere in the distance could not disturb the peace that they felt while on this cliff plateau, because the Prince was with them.

Those who knew the Prince already reveled in this peace they felt in his presence, and those who were just introduced to him, were caught up in the reverie of something they had never felt before.

Chapter 37

When the meal was finished, blankets were brought from the coaches up to the cave. These had been gathered from the hideout along with the food, and it was a helpful decision. All those who had no bedroll were supplied with a warm blanket. Three areas were designated in the cave: a place for the horses, a sleeping area for the women, and a sleeping area for the men.

A few lanterns were lit and placed in several high strategic places within the cave, so that no one would stumble in the darkness. The Prince also insisted that all the drivers must get extra rest after their exertion during the night, for many of them had lost much sleep. His own men also had gone without sleep. So he sent everyone into the cave except for April Rose, Lily, and Phoebe.

"I won't keep you up much longer, either," the Prince told the girls. "But I have not been able to have any talks with you alone, so I am reserving this time for you. Phoebe, I want to explain my intentions to you. I have adopted April Rose and Lily as my daughters although they still have their own family as well. I would like very much to have you as my daughter also, and extend my care to you in the same way I have done for them."

"I am extremely honored, sir," said Phoebe. "As I have no family at all, it would be wonderful to have one. But I have no idea of the requirements to be part of your family."

"I am sure that April Rose and Lily have told you of my antidote," said the Prince. "I have only one requirement that I must ask of you. I ask that you would surrender your life to me and allow me to administer my antidote to you. The alternative is a dismal one; you would not be able to remain with me without this change within you."

"So it is true about the disease?" asked Phoebe.

"Yes, it is true. The disease would destroy you eternally without my antidote," replied the Prince. "I obtained the antidote through my sacrifice---I was killed by my enemy, but this death fulfilled the covenant which would provide an antidote through my blood."

"How is it that you are alive, if you died?" Phoebe asked the Prince. "I don't understand."

"I truly died," said the Prince, "but the covenant also required a resurrection to ratify it. My father gave my life back to me after all conditions for the covenant had been accomplished."

"How would this antidote change me?" Phoebe

sincerely and soberly questioned.

"April Rose, would you like to explain that for Phoebe?" asked the Prince.

"I was a miserable person before the antidote changed me," replied April Rose. "I was so full of bitterness and grudges and I couldn't really love my own father. I am still me, but yet not who I was before. It is like I was a prisoner, and I didn't even know it---and yet I blamed other people for my unhappiness. Now I am free to be who I am really supposed to be."

"At present, we need to sleep, and you will have some time to think about all this, Phoebe," said the Prince kindly. The Prince had removed his armor, and now he hugged each of the girls and sent them into the cave. Then he banked the fire for the night, and also went inside.

The next morning, the Prince was standing outside the cave, looking over the canyon and watching the sun rise over the rock walls. Phoebe came out of the cave and joined him to see the view. The rising sun spread its light over the cliff walls in golden-orange splendor. The light was glorious, but Phoebe saw a light more beautiful in the face of the Prince that she stood by.

"Good morning, Phoebe," said the Prince, and he

smiled at her with love in his eyes.

"Good morning, sir," replied Phoebe. "What shall I call you, sir?" she then asked him.

"My name is Victory," he answered her. "May I call you by your name?" she asked.

"Yes, you may," he replied. "I do not want to remain distant to you, Phoebe."

"Victory, I did not know if I could trust you, but now I have seen your deliverance with my own eyes," Phoebe told him earnestly. "I see now why April Rose and Lily trust in you."

"When you surrender your life to me," said the Prince, "You will see even greater things. I will always take care of you, for the rest of your life and forever. I will not ever leave you."

"What about Elora? What will become of her?" asked Phoebe with concern in her voice.

"Elora is a very brave girl," said the Prince. "She has exceptional abilities, and I will ensure that she has ample opportunity to develop those gifts. I have claimed her as my own. When she knows me, she will be comforted."

"Thank you sir," said Phoebe gratefully. "I am so glad she will be under your protection."

"I tell you the truth," said the Prince emphatically, "If you had not left when you did, Elora would not have survived. The evil prince and his fiends were already planning her capture."

Phoebe's face registered shock and dismay at this revelation, but the Prince gently took her hand and reassured her. "I have watched over both of you for some time," he told her. "And in my kingdom, you will find everything you need. I am the one who fulfills the desires of the heart."

The others were beginning to stir, and wake up, and the Prince began to stoke the coals so that a small flame rekindled. The ladies in the group warmed the bread over this fire and drizzled honey over the slices. This and some fruit made a very nourishing breakfast. After that, the group began to pack up the supplies and blankets, fed and watered the horses, and prepared to leave their camping place in the canyon. The fire was put out and smothered with the sandy dirt so prevalent in the canyon. The carriages were loaded once more, and the horses were harnessed to them.

Aboard the ship, the young girls were waking up in their bunkroom below deck, and went up to the top deck in great excitement. Everything about their sailing excursion was fascinating to them. They watched everything that the ship's crew did, and at times, they were almost in harm's way due to their curiosity and eagerness to understand all of the workings of the ship.

Saphire had to caution them to be careful when the crew was moving around quickly. Just now she brought them down to the galley to get some breakfast. There was no proper dining room with enough tables for the children, as only the ship captain's office had a table, but there were plenty of barrels and crates in a storage room so the children gladly sat on these.

While they ate, Saphire told the children stories about the Prince and his kingdom, and read some of his promises to them. She described what the kingdom looked like, and amazed the children with these illustrations. Some things they could not readily grasp because they had never seen such wonders in their limited experience, but their anticipation was growing.

Saphire requested an audience with Elora alone, so while the others were with Sir Guide, she and Elora had a chance to talk privately.

"I wanted to speak with you alone before we arrive at our destination," Saphire told Elora. "I wanted to reveal the truth so that you will not be so shocked when hearing things about yourself, that you didn't know before now."

"About me?" questioned Elora.

"Yes," said Saphire. "Your real name is not Elora. Your birth name, given to you by your parents, is Yadira. When they perished, you were adopted by someone who did not really care for you, who sent you to the boarding school for evil purposes."

"How do you know this?" asked Elora.

"The Prince has been watching over you," replied Saphire. "He has been protecting you."

"If that is so, why did he leave me there so long?" Elora asked, looking perplexed.

Saphire indicated all of the other children who were within their view, and she replied, "These children would not have survived, if you had not been there. You are a very brave girl, and the Prince is so proud of you."

Tears started to appear in Elora's eyes, and began trickling down her face. Saphire held Elora in her arms and comforted her in the manner that a true mother would do for her child.

Finally Elora raised her head, and said, "So I'm Yadira?"

"Yes," affirmed Saphire, "And many of your people live in the Prince's kingdom. They are extremely talented scouts in the wilderness, and highly skilled at archery and horsemanship."

"I have a people?" Elora asked in wonderment.

"Yes, you do," answered Saphire. "They are well known as people of the book, for they are very faithful to the Prince and his promises."

So Elora became Yadira; she told all the girls the story that Saphire had told her. The girls were very happy for her, although it did take them a while to remember to call her by Yadira.

In fact, it took some time for Yadira herself to get used to the change in names, and to remember that she was no longer called by Elora.

I am sure that it would be a very shocking thing to discover that your identity is not what you thought it was. Yet, in Yadira's case, the unpleasant life was behind her, and the new identity revealed to her would become a great source of joy.

Chapter 38

It seemed to the travelers that the rest of their
journey would surely proceed without any kind of
trouble, but that happy circumstance was not their
experience.

As the procession of horses, riders, and coaches
left the canyon and came out into another open
prairie, a band of thieves came swiftly out of the
adjacent woods on horseback and accosted them,
surrounding the coaches and cutting them off from
the rest of the group. These villains attempted to
yank open the doors of the carriages and steal
whatever they could from the terrified passengers.
They looked like wild ruffians and they had long
knives in their hands.

The Prince and his men immediately turned and
rode hard with swords unsheathed, ready to battle.
The thieves tried to flee back into the woods, but
the Prince's men blocked their way, and they had
no alternative but to fight or surrender. The Prince
and his men herded the thieves away from the
coaches, and a fierce battle took place there in the
prairie grasses.

This battle was ended quickly, as the thieves were
no match for the Prince and his men. The Prince

had his men take the thieves' weapons and their horses. The Prince sent the thieves away on foot, with their hands tied behind them. "Tell your master to keep his thugs on his own land," said the Prince to the disgruntled men walking away.

While the extra horses were tethered to the backs of the stagecoaches, the Prince made sure that everyone was unharmed and no longer unsettled by the attack, and the caravan started out once more. Thereafter, two of the Prince's men flanked the stagecoaches and two rode at the rear of the coaches, while the other two stayed in front with the Prince and the three girls.

In midafternoon, they saw the gleaming white turrets of the Prince's castle in the distance, and rejoiced at the sight. Phoebe was in awe of what she saw ahead, and felt as if she must surely be dreaming. As they drew closer and closer, the girls became more and more excited, but they were still not prepared for the exuberance of the welcome waiting for them.

There were trumpets blowing and drums sounding to announce their arrival, flags were waving and banners were hung on the castle walls. There were people cheering and children shouting and running, and a great deal of commotion going on. It was a confusion of color and sound everywhere.

Most of all, there were smiles and clapping as the returning travelers approached the castle.

When they reached the colored stone walkway, the Prince's groomsmen came to receive the horses and bring them to the stables. The Prince's coach drivers also took over bringing the coaches to the carriage house, after all the passengers and drivers had alighted from the coaches. The crowd followed along on either side as the group now walked on the stone walkway and up the brick steps which led to the corridor before the entrance of the castle.

April Rose noticed that Phoebe looked nervous, and she took Phoebe's hand in hers with a gentle squeeze. Lily did the same on the other side of Phoebe. The new families showed no fear or apprehension upon their arrival, but only smiles.

These were the families of the two coach drivers who had chosen to follow the Prince. And at this moment, they were extremely grateful for the invitation from the Prince himself.

The Prince and his men led the procession forward and they stopped to salute the rest of the royal guard who stood at attention. They raised their swords together in salute. Then they went up through the corridor and inside the great doors, followed by all who had returned with them.

There was a moment's hesitation for some, when they saw the inscription over the door, but they had come to trust in the Prince enough to enter. They had received his favor, so surely there would be a place for them, they reasoned.

And of course there was. Once the Prince had explained his complete offer with the antidote and all its benefits, there was not one refusal. This evening, every guest had opportunity for a warm bath, fresh clothing, and to stay in one of the many guest rooms in the palace. There were delectable pastries and lemonade provided for them in their rooms, for the main course meal would not be served until the children arrived.

The captain of their sailing ship was none other than Roger's friend Nate, who used to take Roger and Sundae sailing in a small craft when they were in the Kingdom of Grace. Now Nate was commissioned to sail the Prince's large sailing vessel. The port where this ship now docked was some distance from the palace, so carriages had been sent to transport the children from the ship to the palace, along with Sir Guide and Saphire.

The children's eyes were wide with wonder at the sight of the white gleaming castle with its round walls and turrets. They were speechless for a long while, and stared at nothing but the castle as they came nearer and nearer to it. When they arrived at the colorful stone walkway, the Prince's attendants opened the doors of the carriages and escorted the children up the walkway and the steps and through the corridor to the main door of the castle.

Mercy greeted them and brought the children, accompanied by Saphire, to a small dining room where they were served pastries and lemonade. Next, they were shown the rooms where they would be staying, and then they were escorted to the bathing rooms and each child received a fresh outfit of clothing and shoes. Several young ladies assisted the younger girls with their bath and in getting dressed. When all this was done, and the girls were ready, everyone went to the royal dining room to dine with the Prince.

The girls were nervous and giggled, not so much because they were afraid, but because they were now in a place where they felt safe to laugh. Sir Guide and Saphire sat near the girls and relished the way the children enjoyed their surroundings. April Rose, Lily, and Phoebe also sat near the children and watched the little girls' expressions with great satisfaction.

The Prince and his men were no longer wearing their armor, so the children and the others got their first look at the face of the Prince. He stood and welcomed everyone to his palace, and then Sir Guide said the blessing over the meal, and the servers began to bring out platters of food. The children could hardly believe the good things that they saw on their plates.

"It's so pretty!" many of them exclaimed, and then they began to taste it. Their faces showed their surprise at the many new and different tastes of this food. This delighted the Prince immensely, and he could not stop smiling as he observed their blissful reactions.

So that wondrous day ended with so much joy, that these children and the newcomers could not imagine any more happiness than this. They did not realize that the best was yet to come. For now, they were satisfied and content simply to sleep in these beautiful rooms.

Lily's family came to take her home, and they met Phoebe and greeted April Rose as if she was family also. Then April Rose and Phoebe walked back to their rooms. Phoebe was ecstatic over the nightgown she found on her bed, and the way the sheets smelled like roses. At last, the two girls bid each other good night, and went promptly to sleep.

Phoebe's room was next to April Rose's and she came to April's room the next morning. "What will happen next?" she said eagerly, and April Rose explained the ceremony of the Prince, and the meaning of his scepter to administer the antidote. The girls had breakfast by the window overlooking the garden, and Phoebe expressed amazement at such a beautiful place. Just then Mercy came to meet the girls, and said that the Prince would like to speak with them in the garden.

When they arrived, the Prince told Phoebe to feel free to walk all around the garden, for he needed to speak with April Rose privately for a moment, and then he would speak with Phoebe. Phoebe could hardly wait to explore that beautiful garden, and she wandered all around its curving paved walkways, and meandered through its archways, watching all the colorful birds and the delicate butterflies which inhabited this luscious garden.

April Rose, in the meantime, was thankful to be alone with her Prince for a moment, and to sit by him and gaze at his face. "I am sure that I am the happiest girl in the universe at this moment," she told him. "I have no desire but to be with you."

The Prince put his arm around her shoulders and pulled her close to him. "My April Rose," he said. "You are a delight to me." Then he took her hand and they walked around the garden together. "Wherever you go, I will be with you," he told her. "I will never leave your side." She looked up at him, somewhat dismayed. "Are you sending me away again? I've just come home to you," she said plaintively. "Your stay here will soon be ending," the Prince answered gently. "But my love for you will never end."

April Rose put her arms around him then and hugged him tightly. She laid her head on his chest and could feel his steady heartbeat. He put his arms around her, too and held her for a little while. Then he softly said, "I must speak with Phoebe." He took April's hand and they walked together to where Phoebe sat watching the hummingbirds feed on some lilies. "I've never seen such tiny birds," she said with awe. The Prince sat down by her and April sat on Phoebe's other side. "Those are called hummingbirds," he said.

"Phoebe, I have so much to show you," the Prince said. "But I need to know your decision."

"Yes," said Phoebe. "Yes, I want whatever is your desire to give me. And I will do whatever you need me to do."

The Prince's joy began to spill out as light coming from his face. "This very afternoon, we will settle the matter," he told Phoebe. "And for now I must leave both of you, and speak to the children and the other families who have come."

He walked away, leaving the girls in a sense of awe. "It's almost like he leaves a fragrance after he walks away," Phoebe expressed, with great admiration in her eyes.

"What does it smell like to you?" asked April Rose curiously. "Umm….," said Phoebe as she paused to reflect on the question. "I think I would have to say that it smells like this garden."

"I thought so!" said April Rose. "I have thought he smelled like roses and the ocean---not the nasty fishy smell, but the smell of clean sand and blue sparkling waves."

That afternoon, Phoebe pledged her life and her love to the Prince, and received the antidote. Then she was able to watch as each of the little girls, beginning with Yadira, also was adopted into the Prince's family and was cleansed of the fateful sin disease, with the Prince's antidote.

Their little faces gleamed with light as they eagerly touched the Prince's scepter and the antidote removed the effects of the malady. They still may not have comprehended the full significance of what took place, but they knew it was good. They had been around evil, and knew the difference.

The sense of safety and belonging that came with the Prince's rescue gave them reason to trust.

Next, the two stagecoach drivers and their entire families received the antidote and became part of the Prince's family. There was great rejoicing from all the people who came to witness this.

Last, the Prince called Lily, April Rose, Aziel, and Keturah to come forward. He commended their bravery and expressed his gratitude for all their sacrifice to rescue the children. He presented to each of them a golden circlet crown which he himself placed on their heads.

And all the people celebrating this day with them gave them a tremendous applause. April Rose felt as if she was in a dream as he placed the golden crown on her red wavy hair. She wished her father could have seen this moment. She looked out into the crowd and saw that her father's friend Cedric was cheering for her very enthusiastically, and that made her smile and cry at the same time.

And now, the Prince invited everyone to a banquet on the lawn of the Palace, to celebrate this victory.

Chapter 39

The palace grounds were lit with white lanterns all around, and there were many white covered tables scattered all across the palace lawn, with one long table on a raised dais.

This is where the Prince would sit with the guests of honor for that night. All of the new members of his family were seated here, as well as the four who had gone on his mission.

The Prince stood and hushed the crowd, and then he sang his love song to his children. There were tears in Phoebe's eyes, and in Yadira's. The new children were utterly mesmerized.

Then Sir Guide blessed the meal, and the food was served. During this meal, Cedric, along with his family, came to greet April Rose. Cedric's wife reminded him of the dinner invitation he had made to April. Channah, Cedric's wife, took the initiative to make the plans for the meal at their home.

"April Rose, I think we should have you come tomorrow at noon," she said. "Would that be alright with you?" April Rose did not want to lose the opportunity, so she agreed, especially since she did not know how much longer she would be in the

Kingdom of Grace. That thought made her sad for a few minutes, but then she saw the Prince was standing and inviting all the children to see his river. She couldn't miss that moment! "Come on," she urged Lily and Phoebe. "Let's go see the Prince's river!" They all quickly got up and went with the Prince, as he led them back through the palace to the other side where the river was.

The Prince laughed to see the girls run down to the water and begin splashing, after he told them they could go in wearing their dresses. April Rose, Lily, and Phoebe pulled off their shoes and ran to join the children. The fun these three were having encouraged the fearful ones to come into the water, and soon even they were shouting and splashing too. There was more laughter that night than April Rose had heard in a very long time.

When it was time to get out, the children were absolutely shocked that their dresses and hair were immediately dry again. Phoebe, too, was amazed by this unusual phenomenon. She kept exclaiming over and over that this was miraculous. The Prince just laughed at their surprise. "Another one of your secrets," April Rose said to the Prince, laughing. "He is full of surprises," she told Phoebe. "Get used to the unexpected."

Lily agreed, and remarked that this was true.

The Prince just smiled and took the hands of the youngest children to walk them back to the palace, and the rest of the little girls crowded around him and walked as closely as possible. After all the children were ready for bed, the Prince gathered them around him and read to them out of a gold storybook with pictures, about the Kingdom of Grace. Then he sang to them and hugged each child goodnight. Mercy and Saphire walked with the girls to their rooms, and tucked each of them in bed, as a mother or grandmother would do. Mercy and Saphire had rooms across the hall from the girls, so that the children would not be afraid in such a large building as this was.

Phoebe and April Rose sat at the little table by the window overlooking the garden and talked a while about the joys of that day. Then they said good night, and each went to her room.

April Rose woke up early, got dressed, and went to the stables. She spent some time talking to her horse and petting her in the stall, and then she saddled her and brought her out to the pasture. "It may be the last time I see you," she said softly to her horse, and patted her.

The sunrise was just peeking out over the horizon line, and the gray sky was beginning to turn to blue. April Rose pressed with her knees and the horse began to trot and then went into a canter which later moved into a gallop. The sky seemed like a blue bowl over them and it felt as if the pasture was endless under the sky. The wind blew her hair back as the horse ran through the now golden field under the early morning light.

Finally, they turned back to the stable, and April Rose slowed her mare's pace, and gently reined her in. She dismounted and led her horse into the stables, unsaddled the horse and brushed her well. Then she hugged her horse from the side, with her arms around the horse's neck, and kissed her goodbye. April Rose left the stable, trying not to cry.

Phoebe was sitting by the window when April got back, and they had breakfast together there. April read in her gold book and Phoebe read in her book that she had just received. After this, they went down to the garden and walked around. April Rose knew that she was going to have to explain to Phoebe where she was going and why. That was a difficult conversation, but April Rose got through it without bursting into tears. It was Phoebe who cried this time.

The Prince joined them in the garden for a little while. He knew that April Rose had told Phoebe the whole story. He comforted them both, and confirmed to April Rose that this would be her last day in the Kingdom of Grace; he would be sending her back in the morning.

The Prince suggested that April Rose and Phoebe visit with Lily and her family at her home for the rest of the morning, and then he knew that April Rose was having lunch with Cedric's family. "You can walk back together this afternoon, and be sure to invite Lily to come," he told them.

Phoebe enjoyed seeing the village and meeting Lily's family, immensely. She would be sharing the midday meal with them, while April Rose went to Cedric's house. April Rose was smiling as she walked to Cedric's house not far away from Lily's. She knew that Phoebe had not seen family life very much, and she could tell already that Phoebe was attracted to this.

Cedric and Channah welcomed April Rose gladly, and their children, who had seemed so shy before, eagerly pulled her by the hand to show her special things at their house. Cedric, of course, wanted to know more about his old friend, and April Rose told him that her father was staying with Roger at the moment, and helping out at the boys' ranch.

Cedric's eyes were shining to think of this---he was exhilarated that Roger had a ranch, and had invited Rusty to help. "I need you to give Roger a message from me," he said. "I think he will want to know about some of his old friends from here. Please tell him that his friend Abel married Kamaris, and that Deonsel married Abel's sister Rhoda. Can you remember all this?" April asked for some paper and a writing tool and wrote this down. "Oh, one more thing," Cedric remembered just then, "Tell him that the gypsy musicians finally had children." April Rose made a note of that information too, on the piece of paper. She folded this and carefully put it into her pocket. April Rose said goodbye to her father's friend and Cedric told April Rose that if she was his daughter, he would be extremely proud. Channah agreed.

April Rose left then and went to Lily's house, and the three of them walked back together to the Palace. When they arrived, the Prince asked what April would like to do that afternoon. (Although, of course, he already knew what she would say) She smiled and said, "I would like to go back to the shepherd's cottage where I first met you, and see it one more time."

"It is granted," said the Prince, "And I'm sure that Phoebe and Lily would not mind going, too." They didn't, so the three set out together on the path to the cottage, laughing and talking happily on the way. When they arrived at that memorable stone cottage, the Prince stepped out dressed as the

Shepherd. April ran to him, and hugged him. "Oh, Ro'eh, how I love you," she said, and he held her close in his embrace.

They walked around and looked at all the things that had made such special memories---even the herb garden. Her crutch was still there, leaning against the wall, and she picked it up and looked at it, smiling. "Ro'eh, you are so good to me." She set the crutch down with a sigh, and said, "I hope no one is as foolish as I was, to run away from you." The Shepherd Prince smiled at April Rose and said, "You were not the first to do that, and probably will not be the last."

It was time then to walk back to the Palace, and so they did.

April Rose took her last luxurious bath in the large marble bathtub at the Palace, and put on the filmy white dress she had worn for the ceremony when she was adopted by the Prince. She put on her gold crown, knowing it would be the last time she would wear it.

She finally found out why the painting of the birds in the hallway leading to the throne room, had seemed so familiar to her. She went back to that hallway with all the twinkling lights in the ceiling and looked closely at those paintings. Mercy had told her that it was her father who had painted those birds. April had recognized his painting style. Sir Guide came up beside her just then and said very proudly, "Rusty was my finest student in painting."

"And I want you to know," Sir Guide continued and his eyes twinkled, "that I am extremely proud of his daughter, too. She is brave and beautiful and very skilled. You will do well on all of your missions for the Prince."

"He is sending me on another mission? I thought I was leaving," she answered with a confused look on her face.

"Your mission is back at your home," Sir Guide said smiling, "And it will be your greatest yet."

"Oh…" she replied, and hugged him, not knowing what else to say. He hugged her back, and had such a radiant smile on his face. "Let's go to the banquet," he said then, and taking her hand, they walked outside the castle to the lawn, where again it was set up for a meal.

Everyone from the village was there; this was the culmination of April Rose's visit to the Kingdom of Grace, and it would be a great celebration. The Prince sang to April Rose, and then the musicians of the Kingdom gave a short concert, and the young ladies of the Kingdom performed a ballet type dance on a platform set up for this purpose.

The young men would not be outdone, and some of them performed a Celtic type dance, which made April Rose miss her father. She had seen him dance like this before.

Last, there was a fantastic fireworks display, with all the spectacular designs they could imagine and create. Phoebe and Lily and all the children sat by April Rose and enjoyed this with her. Phoebe had never seen anything like this before, and neither had the children.

A short while later, April Rose saw a young woman that looked remarkably like Yadira. "Who is that?" she asked Saphire. "That is Adah," replied Saphire. "She is one of the people of the book, and they are usually guides for anyone who has to travel through the wilderness. It was Adah who guided Roger and his friend Abel through the wilderness on their rescue mission."

"She looks so much like Elora---I mean, Yadira," April Rose exclaimed.

"That is because Yadira is one of the people of the book," Saphire explained. "Adah and her husband are here to meet Yadira, and to adopt Yadira into their family. They can train her in the ways of their people."

Then April Rose saw Yadira standing near Adah and her husband, and Yadira looked so happy. April Rose was so glad that she had seen this before she left. "And Phoebe," April Rose asked Saphire privately. "Where will she stay?"

"The Prince would like her to stay with him at the palace, until she is married," said Saphire. "That is what he did for your mother, because she was an orphan. When Pearl was very little, she lived with me and I took care of her. I loved your mother."

There were tears in April's eyes as she thought of her mother, and she hugged Saphire.

April Rose, Lily, Phoebe, Aziel, and Keturah spent the very last part of that evening sitting by the water fountain in the Prince's garden, reminiscing about all their adventures.

That night, April Rose dreamed about her father; he was sitting on a bed and holding a framed photo of April Rose in his hands. He looked so sad, and then April Rose knew that it was truly time to go home.

Chapter 40

April Rose got up early the next morning, before it was almost light and went to the garden, and the Prince was there. "I dreamed about my father last night. I know it's time to go home," she told him with tears in her eyes. "I don't want to leave you, or my friends here, but I know my dad needs me."

The Prince took April Rose in his arms. "Yes, he does need you, along with a few other people," he told her. She hated to leave the safety of his arms, but she knew she must. "Go and get ready," the Prince told her. "When it is time for you to leave, I will escort you and we will talk some more before I send you back."

Reluctantly she walked away and went up the steps into the castle. Phoebe, Lily, Saphire and Mercy were waiting for her. The way they were acting, it felt as if it was a surprise birthday party, instead of a going away party. They took her by the hand and led her down the hall.

"All the children want to eat breakfast with you," Phoebe told her. When they got to the little dining room, all the children yelled her name, and waved little flags they had made, as if she was a great celebrity. April Rose was astonished and a little embarrassed, but very happy that the children did this for her. Then a special breakfast was served, and everyone ate and enjoyed the meal. There were no tears at this point, and April was glad.

When the meal was over, all the children hugged April Rose, and Yadira waited shyly to talk to her after all the girls left with Saphire and Mercy. "That day I saw you in the woods by the stream, I knew you were coming to help us," she said very seriously to April Rose.

"So it *was* you!" April Rose exclaimed. "All this time, I have been wondering about that. I'm glad you came to tell me before I left with that mystery unsolved."

Yadira hugged April Rose tightly and said, "Thank you for all that you did for us." Then she let go and turned to walk down the hall and catch up with the other girls. She stopped once and turned to wave goodbye, and then hurried down the hall.

Lily and Phoebe walked with April Rose back to her room. They waited outside for her while she changed back into her old jeans and t-shirt. She put her key in one pocket, along with the note from Cedric's house, and then put her father's car keys in her other pocket. "I surely can't forget those," she thought to herself. She hung up her dress in the closet and looked around her room for the last time. Her gold circlet crown was on the dresser and she looked sadly at it. She still had on her ring from the Prince, but she did not know if she could take it home.

Then she walked out and joined her friends. The Prince was waiting for her in the main entrance hallway, and he took her arm to escort her out the arched doors of the entrance. Two doormen held the door for her and the Prince, and it made her feel like real royalty. She could not believe what she was seeing when she stepped beyond the threshold of the door.

Everyone from the village had lined up on either side of the corridor and walkways to bid April Rose goodbye. They were all waving at her. She could hardly see, because of the tears in her eyes. The Prince looked fondly at her, and said with a wry teasing smile, "Do you need a handkerchief? I know you don't like to use your sleeve."

That made her laugh, and she admitted that yes, she did need a handkerchief, and the Prince gave her one with her name embroidered on it and a tiny rose in the corner.

"Oh, it's beautiful!" she said. "Can I bring it home?" The Prince nodded his permission, and April Rose caught her tears with this beautiful handkerchief she would treasure forever.

Phoebe and Lily followed right behind them, all the way down to the colorful walkway, and everyone on either side was still smiling and waving at her. April Rose was beaming, though her eyes were still leaking tears.

The Prince stopped here, and told everyone that the rest of the way, he would be escorting April Rose privately. He thanked everyone for their love and celebration of this time. April Rose gave Lily and Phoebe each, one last hug. Then he and April Rose began walking away from the castle. April Rose turned and waved one more time at Lily and Phoebe who still stood watching on the walkway. All of the other people also remained where they were until April Rose and the Prince had passed through the border of the evergreen trees.

They came to the musical brook and the forest creatures came and danced for April Rose. She clapped for them, and they gave an appreciative little bow before scampering away. April Rose wanted that walk to last as long as possible, but much too soon, they were back at the first garden where she had come into the Kingdom of Grace.

"Let's sit a while," said the Prince, and he cordially indicated the white chairs in this garden. So they sat and she just looked at him intently, hoping to memorize his facial features.

"I have some things to tell you," he said. "The bronze key will disappear when you go back to your world, for it only represents what you now have in your heart. Just as you had to protect that key from the enemy who would try to steal it, you must protect your faith. Even in your world, the enemy will try to steal your faith from you."

The Prince went on to say, "Your faith is the key to great treasures of wisdom found only in me and my kingdom. The enemy cannot use that key, but he will try to prevent you from finding those treasures, by stealing your faith."

"How do I prevent this enemy from stealing it---if it isn't an actual key?" April Rose asked in a puzzled voice. "How could he steal my faith?"

"Some of his most common methods are doubt and discouragement," replied the Prince. "You must read my promises every day and fill your mind with them. You will find a book of my promises in your world, too."

"What about this ring?" April asked, and she indicated the one that the Prince had given her.

"Will it disappear also?" she asked. "Yes," said the Prince. "It will. Not because I don't want you to have it, but because there will be something that will take its place."

"No one can take your place!" April Rose said vehemently. "I will never let that happen."

The Prince smiled lovingly at her, and said, "No, nothing and no one will take my place."

"What will I do when I can't see you!" she cried. "That is the worst part of leaving."

"You must listen for my voice," the Prince told her. "I will never leave your side---never. I will speak to you from my promises, and I will speak into your mind. You must pay close attention at all times." Then he stood, and she did also, knowing this time was ending.

"I will," she promised him. "Would you sing for me one more time before I go?"

And he did; he sang the lullaby song that he first sang to her as the Shepherd. "Now I must ask you something," the Prince said. "I want to hear you sing to me when you go back into your world. I will be listening and I will rejoice to hear your voice. Will you sing for me?"

In reply, she threw her arms around him and hugged him tightly. "Yes, oh, yes," she said. "I will be your songbird always."

She let go, and he took her hand and led her to the Door, which suddenly appeared in the garden.

She hesitated, and wanted to linger a little longer, but the Prince said, "I love you April Rose. Please share my love with your father and many people you will meet."

"I love you," she said, and she saw the light begin to radiate from his face. He let go of her hand and she turned toward the door, but could not make her feet move. Suddenly, a strong wind came rushing by her and it pushed her through the door.

She stumbled out into the darkness of the garden shed, but when she looked back where the door had been, now there was only the back wall of the shed. She felt her pocket, and the bronze key was no longer there. Quickly she felt inside to see if the handkerchief was there, and the small piece of parchment paper with the names Cedric had given her. She sighed with relief; they were both there.

She stepped out of the garden shed into the bright sunshine of the early morning. It was exactly the same time as when she had left this place. When she walked by the stone angel on her way out of the prayer garden, she stopped to look at the face of the angel once more. Again, the angel always had that smile that seemed to indicate she knew secrets. Well, now April Rose did, too.

She unlocked her father's car, got in and drove immediately to Cornelia's house. Cornelia was so glad to see April Rose, and she looked at April's face with a knowing look. "You've been with the Prince!" she said with joy in her voice.

"How did you guess?" April Rose asked. "When you spend time with him, your countenance changes," replied Cornelia. "I can just tell by the way your face looks."

"I am so excited for you!" Cornelia said, and she practically danced in her kitchen, and April Rose felt her joy. "Now, you must go to your dad without delay," Cornelia insisted. "He needs to see this."

"That is exactly what I want to do. I want to drive to that boys' ranch today," April declared.

"Well, that is going to be a very long drive," warned Cornelia. "Let me see if I can arrange a stopping place for you to sleep, and then you can continue your journey tomorrow morning."

Cornelia had a friend who owned a bed and breakfast place in a town that would be about halfway to the boys' ranch, and Cornelia said she would be happy to pay the bill for April Rose to stay there tonight.

So it was settled. April went back to her house to get her suitcase, and then she began the journey to the boys' ranch. She couldn't help but sing most of the way down there, and she had a very strong feeling that the Prince was listening.

Cornelia's friends were gracious and kind, and the bed and breakfast place was so quaint. They had breakfast ready for her very early, so she could get back on the road quickly. Cornelia had told them that April Rose was going to meet her father.

So now here she was driving down the highway; and she could hardly wait to see her dad.

April Rose was so amazed when she thought of all the changes that had happened while she was in the Kingdom of Grace, and yet absolutely no time had passed at all in her own world.

Another one of the Prince's surprises, April Rose thought to herself and smiled.

Chapter 41

The sun was bright when April Rose drove up onto the grounds of the boys' ranch. She wasn't quite sure what to do first, but she parked the car and got out and looked around.

Then she saw the pasture and someone was riding a horse out there---and it sure looked like her dad. The horse and rider turned and came closer and she saw it was him---it *was* her father. "Wow!" she thought to herself. "I never dreamed he could ride like that."

Rusty could not believe what he was seeing---he saw a girl standing not far from the ranch house, and it looked like she could be his daughter. Then he saw his car parked there on the grounds, and he knew it really was April Rose!

He rode the horse to a stopping place, and slid off the saddle, quickly tying the reins to the post. He started walking very rapidly to the gate of the pasture, and his heart was beating fast. Just as he went out of the gate and began the long walk toward the house, April Rose started running.

"Daddy!" she yelled as she ran toward him. Her red hair was flying back behind her in the wind.

It was a glorious sight that day for him---to see his red-haired daughter come running through the grass as fast as she could, to meet up with him, yelling at the top of her lungs, "Daddy!"

Maddox heard the noise, and he stepped outside, followed by Jolene, the cook, and they witnessed this sight. "I think this is a miracle," said Jolene to Maddox, and he smiled at that happy thought. He only wished that Roger and Cammie could have seen this.

When April Rose caught up with her dad, he picked her up and swung her around as if she was a little girl. "Daddy," she said, laughing and crying at the same time, "I have missed you so much, I just had to come and see you."

"Oh, April," he said. "I am so happy you came," and he hugged her again. "I don't know what to say----I'm so surprised! I feel as if I just became alive again."

"That's how I feel too, Daddy---because I did," said April Rose. "I died, and then I became alive again." She put her arm around her dad, and he put his arm around her, too.

"What do you mean?" he asked in a worried way, and looked at her face intently. "Did something happen to you?"

"Yes," she said and grinned. "Something drastic happened to me and it was very good. I went to the Kingdom of Grace, and I received the Prince's antidote."

He looked so shocked, and then his face broke into a grin. He started laughing and laughing and couldn't stop for a while, then he hugged April Rose again and held her close.

"I can't wait to hear what happened," he said. "But I had better take care of that horse first. Come with me and see the horses." April Rose was elated to see her father so happy.

They walked together to lead the horse back to the stables, and he took the saddle off and put it away, and then he led the horse back outside and let her run free in the pasture. There was a shady place under some trees, and his horse trotted off to meet the other horses there.

"How long will you be able to stay?" asked Rusty. "What about your classes?"

"If it's okay with you and Roger, I'd like to stay at least a week," said April Rose. "I will need to make some major decisions before I can go back to the university. And I just want to be with you."

At that, Rusty hugged his daughter again tightly.

"I'm so glad to have you here, and I'm sure that it will be alright with Roger and Cammie," answered her father. "They are still not back yet from their honeymoon, so I'm extra glad that you can stay longer so they can meet you."

All of the ranch staff was so excited to meet April Rose, and quickly made arrangements for her to stay. A guest room close to her father's room was prepared for her, and everyone made her feel welcome. The boys all treated April Rose as if she was a princess, and they really worked on their manners, which made Rusty smile. April Rose insisted on helping out wherever she could, and she used some of the new skills she had learned while in the Kingdom of Grace.

Rusty was so pleased to see how April Rose could ride, and they spent much time together taking care of the horses, and at least once a day, they went for a long ride together. This gave April time to tell her dad more of the details of her visit to the Kingdom of Grace.

April Rose also helped her dad with the archery classes, and he was very surprised at her skill. "Well, I'm your daughter," she teased. "I'd better have some archery skills!"

"What makes you say that?" he asked, and she told him how many people in the Kingdom of

Grace remembered and admired his archery skills. Rusty smiled and looked grateful.

The week passed quickly, and April Rose was sad to see it coming to an end. She decided to stay one more day, so she could visit with Roger and Cammie a little longer, as they were not back yet. Rusty was still concerned about April's classes that she was missing, but she finally told him what she was thinking of doing.

"I'm going to move back home, Daddy," she said, "That is, if it is okay with you. I'm going to transfer to the local college and I am going to change my major to elementary education and a minor in social work with families."

Rusty could not say anything for a moment; he just smiled and smiled. "I will be happy to have you back home, April," he said, "and I think that is a wonderful choice."

Roger and Cammie came back, and were delighted at the surprise of having April Rose at the ranch. They admired her skill with the horses and her developing archery skill. "I think we need to have both of them come and help out at the ranch whenever they would like to," Cammie said, and Roger agreed. They had a private meeting with Rusty and April Rose, and invited them both to come back and stay with them at least once a year, if they would like.

"Yes, we would!" said Rusty and April Rose together, and laughed. Then April Rose took the folded parchment paper out of her pocket, and read what Cedric had told her to tell Roger.

Roger's eyes looked misty, and he looked as if he was far away in thought for a moment. "That note brings back so many memories," he said wistfully. "Thank you for delivering this message. I'm so glad to hear about my old friends."

"And thank you for waiting until we got back," said Cammie. "We are so delighted that we were able to spend some time with you, April."

Rusty decided that he would go back with April Rose and help her move back home, and Roger and Cammie understood his choice. Rusty and April would be able to make the drive in one day, since they could take turns driving.

Cammie got up early and made her famous biscuits for breakfast, and fixed a package for Rusty and April to take with them. "You two had better come back soon," Cammie told them as Rusty and April Rose waved goodbye to Roger and Cammie. "If you keep making those biscuits, you know I will be coming back for sure!" said Rusty, laughing.

The drive home gave Rusty and April even more time to talk about all the strange and wonderful things that had happened to her in the Kingdom of Grace. She told him all about the key she found in the grass by the angel, and the door in the garden shed---that wasn't there anymore. "The key is gone too," she said. "It was only a symbol of faith."

"I think I understand that, now," said April Rose thoughtfully. "Faith is the key that unlocks the door to the Kingdom of Grace---but it's a gift. He gave me the key---he gave me faith."

"I do still have one physical thing that he gave me," she said and she pulled the handkerchief out of her pocket. "I have this---it has my name embroidered on it, and a rose," she described to him since he was driving and couldn't look at it.

"I still have the birdcage your mother gave me," he said smiling. "I am glad you met Cedric. He is part of the story behind that birdcage."

"I remembered that story when I met him," said April Rose. "I met his wife, and his children, too. They have big dark eyes with very long eyelashes, and they are so cute."

"Daddy, will you teach me how to play the flute?" she asked suddenly. "That was another thing that people there told me about you, and I didn't even know. I didn't know you could ride horses like you do, or that you were such a good archer."

"I *did* know you could paint, and I saw the birds you painted on the mural in the hallway," she said proudly. "I kept thinking there was something familiar about those birds—it was your style. We all had lessons with Sir Guide in painting, but maybe you could help me practice. I have so much more to learn."

"I would be happy to paint with you," said her father. He could hardly believe what he was now hearing her say. She had never had this interest before now, and certainly not to do this with him. He was overjoyed at the thought of doing things together.

"I haven't played the flute in a long, long time," said Rusty. "I used to play it for your mother when we were children."

"Well, I would like to hear you play," said April Rose. "And I would like to learn. I had some lessons with Sir Guide, and I played a duduk a little bit, and I liked the melancholy sound."

"Oh, and one more thing," said April Rose. "We saw the young men do those Celtic dances, and I have seen you dance like they did, and I want to learn that, too."

"And one more thing," said April Rose. "We need to make a garden---with some herbs, too."

Rusty grinned. "We have a lot of things to do together!"

"Yes," said April. "That's another reason that I'm moving back home."

April Rose looked up dreamily and said, "It's so crazy that I had to go to another world to discover what an amazing dad I have. The love of the Prince made my heart come alive."

"I see that," said her father. "And I am so amazed. I will be forever grateful for his love."

Chapter 42

When they arrived at their home, even the atmosphere felt different to April Rose. She was seeing all the old familiar things with new eyes, and it was refreshing to her. The colors seemed brighter, and the house did not seem dull and stale and old anymore.

April Rose followed her inclination without delay, and did the necessary steps to transfer from one college to the other. She and her father went to retrieve her things from the dormitory.

April Rose explained to her roommate as simply as she could; April told her that she had a very big change of heart, and her goals had changed. She confided to Deidra that she had met the one who laid down his life to rescue us, and that her life would never be the same.

April Rose's roommate said very little after that; this faith concept was beyond the scope of her understanding, for Deidra lived in a world ruled only by sensual desire and its gratification, and self-focused feelings. Anything besides this was not in her sphere of comprehension. She was quick to dismiss anything that did not fit into the realm of sensual indulgence.

April Rose began attending the classes at the local college, and everywhere she went, she felt the presence of the Prince with her. She spoke to him often and remembered to sing to him, and she read in the book of promises that her father gave to her, upon their return home.

Rusty showed April Rose the treasure box that he and Pearl used for special things; he showed her the letters from Audrey and Roger that he kept in this box. April washed her handkerchief, and when it was dry, she folded it carefully and put it in this special box, along with the piece of parchment paper that Cedric had given her. She had written on that paper with a quill pen, and the ink was dark and black. April hoped it would not fade with time, and that she could see the words always.

April Rose emailed a letter of thanks to Roger for all his hospitality, and remembered to tell him that she had seen Adah, who was now married and was adopting one of the orphans who had been rescued during April's visit to the Kingdom of Grace. She also told him of Nate, who was now the captain of the large sailing vessel the Prince would employ at times.

In reply, Roger sent a message by phone to April Rose, and thanked her for the good news! He also promised to keep in touch, and looked forward to having them at the ranch again.

Rusty kept his promise to April Rose, and he began to teach her how to play the flute, and to help April with her painting skills.

Despite the requirements of her college classes, she made time to work in the garden with him, and began to learn the type of Celtic dancing that Rusty could do so well. The archery and the horsemanship would have to wait until their next trip to the boys' ranch, but they already had made arrangements to go back together.

One day when there was a long break between classes, April Rose noticed a small chapel on the campus grounds, and decided to investigate this. She opened the wood door, and looked in. Only one other person was sitting there in one of the pews. He turned around to see who else was coming in, and he smiled at her.

April Rose recognized him as someone who had attended her high school when she did.

Since he was friendly, she decided to go in and tell him hello, although she had not known him very well when they were in high school. When she approached him, he looked at her and smiled again. She sat down on the same pew that he was sitting in, and couldn't help but stare. "You look like someone who has been with the Prince," she said in an awed voice.

His smile increased, and he said, "If you mean the Prince of Peace, yes, I have met him."

"Oh," she said, "I have recently met him and now I can't live without him."

They proceeded to become reacquainted, for neither of them could remember each other's name. He told her his name was Gage. He invited her to go that night for a small concert at an open-air restaurant on the campus. "I will be singing there," he told her. "I sing about the Prince and invite other people to know him."

After that first night, Gage found out that April Rose could sing, and she began to sing with him at these concerts. Rusty would go and listen to them sing together and felt even more healed of the grief that used to tear at his heart so severely.

Eventually, April Rose and Gage convinced Rusty to play his flute along with the accompaniment.

In the days that followed, Gage became so much a part of their lives that it felt perfectly natural for April and Rusty when a year later, Gage slipped a ring on April Rose's finger and pledged his love to her for the rest of his life.

"So this is what the Prince meant!" April Rose thought to herself as she looked at the underneath of the ring. There was an inscription and it said, "To my April Rose from Gage."

And so they were married in Cornelia's prayer garden and Roger, Cammie, and Sundae all came to the wedding. Audrey grieved that she could not be there, for her mission had taken her out of the country. She and her husband and their children were living in another country, and were helping to rescue children there who had been orphaned, and were endangered.

Audrey sent a beautiful wedding gift: a pair of satin and lace pillowcases that she had made for them, a flowered porcelain tea kettle, and a set of fine china teacups with a design of delicate roses on them. April Rose admired the gift very much.

Gage and April Rose moved into a house of their own, but it was not very far from April's childhood home, and they still spent much time with Rusty. The boys' ranch was still part of April's life, and now included Gage, and he was just as enamored with the ranch as she was.

Several years later, a little girl arrived. She had straight black hair like her grandmother Pearl, and big round eyes like her daddy's. April Rose and

Gage named her Viola Pearl, after both of her grandmothers.

Viola Pearl was the delight of her grandfather Rusty, who pushed her in the swings at the park, took her to the zoo to see the monkeys, and took her for rides in a wagon around the neighborhood, just as he used to do for April Rose when she was a little girl.

He told her stories of the Prince who loved them, and he sang the songs of the Prince to her when he kissed her goodnight.

Rusty taught her many things, but most of all he taught her that faith in the Prince is like a key that opens the door to a very great treasure—the kind that never rusts or rots or fades away---the kind that lasts forever. It's the treasure of his love.

My husband and I worked with children for over thirty years at our local church and the school that was operated by our church. For many years, we shared the Gospel with children and their families through summer theater productions.

We did children's church and chapel and helped with many other ministries at our church, which involved children and youth.

It has been our privilege to watch many of those children grow up into adulthood.

One such person is Lindy Simmons. I was amazed to see her unusual talent with photography. She has the rare gift of turning portraits into a work of art, and I appreciate that gift very much.

I asked her to do my portrait photos for this book and my next ones, and I hope to give her portrait photography some notoriety.

If you would like to see more of her portraits, see lindysimmonsphotography on Instagram.